CORGI SF COLLECTOR'S LIBRARY

BAREFOOT IN THE HEAD

His name was Colin Charteris – and that
was the only positive thing about him . . .

In the nightmare, hurdy-gurdy world
of an epoch gone mad, he began to
search for . . . something . . . something
he was not even sure he would recognise
when he found it . . .

When they told him he was a hero,
he believed them, and found himself
leading a cause he did not understand
and could not hope to win, a cause that
was doomed in the disintegrating
world about him . . .

Brian Aldiss

Barefoot in the Head

CORGI BOOKS
A DIVISION OF TRANSWORLD PUBLISHERS LTD

BAREFOOT IN THE HEAD
A CORGI BOOK 0 552 09653 9

Originally published in Great Britain by
Faber & Faber Ltd.

PRINTING HISTORY
Faber & Faber edition published 1969
Corgi edition published 1971
Corgi edition reissued 1974

Corgi Books are published by Transworld Publishers Ltd
Cavendish House, 57-59 Uxbridge Road,
Ealing, London, W.5.
Made and printed in Great Britain by
Hunt Barnard Printing Ltd., Aylesbury, Bucks.

ACKNOWLEDGEMENTS

THIS novel, shorn of some of its pop songs and poems, has been appearing – differently fashioned – in chunks in NEW WORLDS over two years, thanks to the encouragement of its editor, Michael Moorcock; although the original chunk, "Just Passing Through", appeared in IMPULSE for February 1967, edited by Harry Harrison. To both of these gentlemen and to the Procul Harum of "Whiter Shade of Pale", not to mention the shade of P. D. Ouspenski (1878–1947) – my grateful acknowledgements.

> *"Tell the Vietnamese they've got to draw in their horns and stop aggression or we're going to bomb them back into the Stone Age."*

> General Curtis Lemay

BOOK ONE

Northwards

JUST PASSING THROUGH

THE city was open to the nomad.

Colin Charteris climbed out of his Banshee into the northern square, to stand for a moment stretching. Sinews and bones flexed and dainty. The machine beside him creaked and snapped like a landed fish, metal cooling after its long haul across the turn-pikes of Europe. Behind them the old cathedral, motionless though not recumbent.

Around them, the square fell away. Low people moved in a lower alley.

Charteris grabbed an old stiff jacket from the back seat and flung it round his shoulders, thinking how driver-bodies FTL towards disaster in a sparky modern way. He jacketed his eyes.

He was a hero at nineteen, had covered the twenty-two hundred kilometres from Catanzaro down on the Ionian Sea to Metz, department of Moselle, France, in thirty hours, sustaining on the way no more than a metre-long scar along the front off-side wing. A duelling scratch, kiss of life and death.

The sun faded pale and low over St-Étienne into the fly-specks of even turn. He needed a bed, company, speech. Maybe even revelation. He felt nothing. All his animating images were of the past, yesterday's bread.

Outside Milano, one of the great freak-out areas of all time where the triple autostrada made of the Lombardy plain a geometrical diagram, his red car had flashed within inches of a multiple crash. They were all multiple crashes these days.

The image continued to multiply itself over and over in his mind, contusing sense, confusing past with future: a wheel still madly spinning, crushed barriers, gauged and gaudied metal, fanged things, snapped head-bone, sunlight worn like thick make-up over the impossibly abandoned catagasms of death. Stretching in the square, he saw it still happen, fantastic speeds suddenly swallowed by car and human frame with that sneering sloth of the super-quick, where anything too fast for retina-register could spend forever spreading through the labyrinths of consciousness.

They still died and cavorted, those cavortees, in the bone-box in Metz cathedral square, infection spreading, life stuttering. But by another now, they would, the bodies would, the bits would all be neatly packaged in hospital mortuary, a mass embroidering the plain-burning candles in an overnight crypt, the autostrada gleaming in perfect action again, the rescue squads lolling at their wheels in the Rastplatz reading paperbacks. Charteris's primitive clicker-shutter mechanisms were busy still rerunning the blossoming moment of impact.

Pretending, he forced his gaze over the cathedral. It was several centuries old but built of a coarse yellow stone that made it – prematurely flood-lit in the early evening – look like a Victorian copy of an earlier model. Europe was stuffed with these old edifices and more lay in the strata below, biding their time, soundless, windowless.

The ground fell steeply at the other end of the square. Steps led down to a narrow street all wall on one side and on the other all prim little drab narrow French worn façades of hutches closing all their shutters against the general statement of the cathedral.

Across one of the houses a sign read, 'Hôtel des Invalides'.
' "Krankenhaus",' Charteris said.

He dragged a grip out of the boot of the Banshee and made towards the shabby hotel, walking like a warrior across desert, a pilot over a runway after mission ninety-nine, a cowboy down silent Main Street. He played it up, grunting every other stride. He was nineteen.

The other cars in the square were a scratch bunch, all with French neutral numberplates. Removing his gaze from his own landscapes, Charteris saw that this part of the square functioned as a used car lot. Some of the cars had been in collisions. Prices in francs were painted on each windscreen. The cars stood apart in their corral, nobody watching them, no longer itinerant.

This city seemed closed to the nomad. The Hôtel des Invalides had a brass handle to its door. Charteris dragged it down and stepped into the hall beyond, in unmitigated shadow. A bell buzzed and burned insatiably until he closed the door behind him.

As he walked forward, eyes adjusting, the hall took on

existence – and another existence patterned with patterned tiles where other people jurassickly thickened the air and a shadowed saint stood upstairs in dim – and dusty detail. A pot plant languished here beside an enormous piece of furniture, a rectangular and malignant growth of mahogany, or it could be an over-elaborate doorway into a separate part of the establishment. On the walls, enormous pictures of blue-clad soldiers being blown up among scattering sandbags.

A small dense coffin-shaped figure emerged at the end of the passage, black in the black evening light. He drew near and saw it was a woman with permed hair, not old, not young, smiling at him.

'Haben Sie ein Zimmer? Ein Personn, eine Nacht?'

'Ja, monsieur. Mit eine Dusche oder ohne?'

'Ohne.'

'Zimmer Nummer Zwanzig, monsieur. Ist gut.'

German. The lingua franca of Europe.

The madame gestured, called for a girl who came hurrying, lithe and dark-haired, carrying the grand key to Room Twenty. Madame gestured again, disappeared. The girl led Charteris up three flights of stairs, first flight marble, second and third flights wooden, the third being uncarpeted. Each landing was adorned as the hall had been, with large pictures of Frenchmen dying or killing Germans; the period was the first world war.

'So this is where it all began,' he said to the back of the girl, ascending.

She paused and looked down at him uninterested. 'Je ne comprends pas, M'sieur.'

That's not a French accent, any more than Madame's was Kraut, he told himself.

No windows had been opened on these landings for a long while. The air was tarnished with all the bottled lives that had suffered here, pale daughters, spluttering grandfathers with backache. Constriction, miserliness, conservation, inhibition, northern Europe, due for any any change, good Christians all rejoice. Red limbs leaped again as if for joy within the bucketting autostrada cars. Leaping death always to be preferred to desiccating life – if there were only those two alternatives.

His own quicksilver life proved there were decks full of alternatives.

But those only two – how he dreaded both, how his crimson-bound fantasy life shuttled between them, seeking the releases. *You must choose, Charteris, the grim man said tight-lipped: one more deadly mission over the Mekong Delta, or else spend ten years in the hotel in Metz, full board!*

He was breathing hard by the time they reached the threshold of Zimmer Twenty. By opening his mouth, he could gasp in air without the girl hearing. She would be older than he – maybe twenty-two. Pretty enough. Took the long hard climb well. Dark. Rather angular calves but good ankles. Stifling here, of course.

Motioning her to stay, he marched past her into the room. As he crossed to one of the two tall windows, he threw his grip onto the bed, noting the loose-cash jingle of springs. He worked at the window-bar until it gave and the two halves of the window swung into the room. He breathed deep. Other poisons. France!

A great drop on this side of the hotel. Small in the street below, two *bambini* pulling a white dog on a lead. Looking up at him, they became merely two faces with fat arms and hands. Thalidomites. The images of ruin and deformity everywhere. England must be better. Nothing could be worse than France.

Buildings on the other side of the alley. A woman moving in a room, discerned through curtains. Further, a waste site, two cats stalking each other through litter, dryly computing the kinetics of copulation. A drained canal bed full of waste and old cans. Wasn't that also a crushed automobile? A notice scrawled large on a ruined wall: NEUTRAL FRANCE THE ONLY FRANCE.

Certainly they had managed to preserve their neutrality to the bitter end; their experience in the two previous world wars had encouraged that sort of tenacity.

Beyond the ruined wall, a tree-lined street of unnecessary wideness, with the Prefecture at the end of it. One policeman visible. A street light waking among bare winter branches. France!

Turning back into the room, Charteris surveyed its furnishings. He approved that they should be all horrible. Madame was consistent. The wash basin was grotesque, the lighting arrangements of a frankish hideousness, and the bed expressly designed for early rising.

'Combien, M'amselle?'

The girl told him, watching for his reaction. Two thousand six hundred and fifty francs including free lighting. He had to have the figure repeated. His French was poor and he was unused to the recent devaluation.

'I'll take the room. Are you from Metz, M'amselle?'

'No, I'm Italian.'

Pleasure rose in him, a sudden feeling of gratitude that not all good things had been eroded. In this rotten stuffy room, it was as if he breathed again the air of the mountains.

'I've been living in Italy since the war, right down south in Catanzaro,' he told her in Italian.

She smiled. 'I am from the south, from Calabria, from a little village in the mountains that you won't have heard of.'

'Tell me. I might have heard it. I was doing NUNSACS work down there. I got about.'

She told him the name of the village and he had not heard of it. They laughed.

'But I have not heard of NUNSACS,' she said. 'It is a Calabrian town? No?'

He laughed again, chiefly for the pleasure of doing it and seeing its effect on her. 'NUNSACS is a New United Nations organisation for settling and if possible rehabilitating war victims. We have several large encampments down along the Ionian Sea.'

The girl was not listening to what he said. 'You speak Italian well but you aren't Italian. Are you German?'

'I'm Serbian – a Jugoslav. Haven't been home to Serbia since I was a boy. Now I'm driving northwards to England.'

As he spoke, he heard Madame calling the girl impatiently. The girl moved towards the door, smiled at him – a sweet and shadowy smile that seemed to explain her existence – and was gone.

Charteris took his grip to the bamboo table under the window. He stood staring for a long while at the dry canal bed; the detritus in it made it look like an archaeological dig that had uncovered remains of an earlier industrial civilisation. He finally unzipped the bag but unpacked nothing.

Madame was working in the bar when he went down. Several of the little tables in the room were occupied by local people, jigsaw pieces. The room was large and dispiriting, the big dark wood bar on one side was dwarfed and somehow set apart from the functions it was supposed to serve, a tabernacle for pernod. In one corner of the chamber, a television set flickered, most of those present contriving to sit and drink so that they kept an eye on it, as if it were an enemy or at best an uncertain friend. The only exceptions to this rule were two men at a table set apart; they talked industriously to each other, resting their wrists on the table but using their hands to emphasise points in the conversation. Drab eyes, imperious gestures. One of these men, who grew a puff of beard under his lower lip, soon revealed himself as M'sieur.

Behind M'sieur's table, standing in one corner by a radiator, was a bigger table, a solemn table, spread with various articles of secretarial and other use. This was Madame's table, and to this she retired to work with some figures when she was not serving her customers behind the funereal bar. Tied to the radiator was a large and mangy young dog, who whined at intervals and flopped continually into new positions, as though the floor had been painted with anti-dog powder. Madame occasionally spoke mildly to it, but her interests clearly lay elsewhere.

All this Charteris took in as he sat at a table against the wall, sipping a pernod, waiting for the serving girl to appear. He saw these people as victims of an unworkable capitalistic system dying on its feet. They were extinct in their clothes. The girl came after some while from an errand in the back regions, and he motioned her over to his table.

'What's your name?'

'Angelina.'

'Mine's Charteris. That's what I call myself. It's an English name, a writer's name. I'd like to take you out for a meal.'

'I don't leave here till late – ten o'clock.'

'Then you don't sleep here?'

Some of the softness went out of her face as caution, even craftiness, overcame her; momentarily, he thought, she's just another lay, but there will be endless complications to it in this set-up, you can bet! She said, 'Can you buy some cigarettes or something? I know they're watching me. I'm not supposed to be intimate with customers.'

He shrugged. She walked across to the bar. Charteris watched the movement of her legs, the action of her buttocks, trying to estimate whether her knickers would be clean or not. He was fastidious. Italian girls generally washed more scrupulously than Serbian girls. Bright legs flashing behind torn windscreen. Angelina fetched down a packet of cigarettes from a shelf, put them on a tray, and carried them across to him. He took them and paid without a word. All the while, the M'sieur's eyes were on him, stains in the old poilu face.

Charteris forced himself to smoke one of the cigarettes. They were vile. Despite her neutrality in the Acid Head War, France had suffered from shortages like everyone else. Charteris had been pampered, with illegal access to NUNSACS cigars, which he enjoyed.

He looked at the television. Faces swam in the green light, talking too fast for him to follow. There was some excitement about a cycling champion, a protracted item about a military parade and inspection, shots of international film stars dining in Paris, something about a murder hunt somewhere, famine in Belgium, a teachers' strike, a beauty queen. Not a mention of the two continents full of nutcases who no longer knew where reality began or ended. The French carried their neutrality into every facet of life, with TV their eternal nightcap.

When Charteris had finished his pernod, he went over and paid Madame at her table and walked out into the square.

It was night, night in its early stages when the clouds still carried hints of daylight through the upper air. The flood-lighting was gaining on the cathedral, chopping it into alternate vertical sections of void and glitter; it was a cage for some gigantic prehistoric bird. Beyond the cage, the traffic on the motorway could be heard, snarling untiringly.

He went and sat in his car and smoked a cigar to remove the taste of the caporal, although sitting in the Banshee when it was motionless made him uneasy. He thought about Angelina and whether he wanted her, decided on the whole he did not. He wanted English girls. He had never even known one but, since his earliest days, he had longed for all things English, as another man he knew yearned for anything Chinese. He had dropped his Serbian name to christen himself with the surname of his favourite English writer.

About the present state of England, he imagined he had no illusions. When the Acid Head War broke out, undeclared, Kuwait had struck at all the prosperous countries. Britain had been the first nation to suffer the PCA Bomb – the Psycho-Chemical Aerosols that propagated psychotomimetic states, twilight ruptured its dark cities. As a NUNSACS official, he could guess the disorder he would find there.

Before England, there was this evening to be got through. . . . He had said such things so often to himself. Life was so short, and also so full of desolating boredom and the flip voluptuousness of speed-death. Acid Head victims all over the world had no problems of tedium; their madnesses pre-cluded it; they were always well occupied with terror or joy, which ever their inner promptings led them to; that was why one envied the victims one tried to 'save'. The victims never grew tired of themselves.

The cigar tasted good, extending its mildness all round him like a mist. Now he put it out and climbed from the car. He knew of two alternative ways to pass the evening before it was time to sleep; he could eat or he could find sexual companionship. Sex, he thought, the mysticism of materialism. It was true. He sometimes needed desperately the sense of a female life impinging on his with its unexplored avenues and possibilities, so stale, so explored, were his own few reactions. Back to his mind again came the riotous movements of the autostrada victims, fornicating with death.

On his way towards a lighted restaurant on the far side of the square, he saw another method by which to structure the congealing time of a French evening. A down-at-heel cinema was showing a film called SEX ET BANG-BANG. He glanced up at the ill-painted poster, showing a near-naked blonde with an ugly shadow like a moustache across her face, as he passed. Lies he could take, not disfigurements.

As he ate in the restaurant, he thought about Angelina and madness and war and neutrality; it seemed to him they were all products of different time-senses. Perhaps there were no human emotions, only a series of different synchronicity microstructures, so that one 'had time for' one thing or another. He suddenly stopped eating.

He saw the world – Europe, that is, precious, hated Europe that was his stage – purely as a fabrication of time, no matter involved. Matter was an hallucinatory experience: merely a slow-motion perceptual experience of certain time/emotion nodes passing through the brain. No, that the brain seized on in turn as it moved round the perceptual web it had spun, would spin, from childhood on. Metz, that he apparently perceived so clearly through all his senses, was there only because all his senses had reached a certain dynamic synchronicity in their obscure journey about the biochemical web. Tomorrow, responding to inner circadian rhythms, they would achieve another relationship, and he would appear to 'move on' to England. Matter was an abstraction of the time syndrome, much as the television had enabled Charteris to deduce bicycle races and military parades which held, for him, even less substance than the flickering screen. Matter was hallucination.

He recalled he had had a pre-vision of this illumination upon

18

entering the Hôtel des Invalides, although he could not precisely recall its nature.

Charteris sat unmoving. If it were so, if all were hallucination, then clearly he was not at this restaurant table. Clearly there was no plate of cooling veal before him. Clearly Metz did not exist. The autostrada was a projection of temporal confluences within him, perhaps a riverine duologue of his entire life. France? Earth? Where was he? What was he?

Terrible though the answer was, it seemed unassailable. The man he called Charteris was merely another manifestation of a time/emotion node with no more reality than the restaurant or the autostrada. Only the preceptual web itself was 'real'. 'He' was the web in which Charteris, Metz, tortured Europe, the stricken continents of Asia and America, could have their being, their doubtful being. He was God. . . .

Someone was speaking to him. Dimly, distantly, he became aware of a waiter asking if he might take his plate away. So the waiter must be the Dark One, trying to disrupt his Kingdom. He waved the man off, saying something vaguely – much later, he realised he had spoken in Serbian, his native tongue which he never used.

The restaurant was closing. Flinging some francs down on the table, he staggered out into the night, and slowly came to himself in the open air.

He was shaking from the strength and terror of his vision. For what passed as an instant, he had been God. As he rested against a rotting stone wall, its texture patterning his fingers, he heard the cathedral clock begin to chime and counted automatically. It was ten o'clock by whatever time-level they used here. He had passed two hours in some sort of trance.

In the camp outside Catanzaro, NUNSACS housed ten thousand men and women. Most of them were Russian, most had been brought from the Caucasus. Charteris had got his job on the rehabilitation staff by virtue of his fluent Russian, in many respects almost identical with his native tongue.

The ten thousand caused little trouble. Most of them were confined within the tiny republics of their own psyches. The PCA Bombs had been ideal weapons. The psychedelic drugs concocted by the Arab state were tasteless, odourless, colourless, and hence virtually undetectable. They were cheaply made, easily delivered. They were equally effective whether inhaled, drunk, or filtered through the pores of the skin. They were enormously potent. The after-effects, dependent on size of dose, could last a lifetime.

So the ten thousand wandered about the camp, smiling, laughing, scowling, whispering, still as bemused as they had been directly after the bombing. Some recovered. Others over the months revealed depressing character changes. Their guards were not immune.

The drugs passed through the human system unimpaired in strength. Human wastes had to be rigorously collected – in itself a considerable undertaking among people no longer responsible for their actions – and subjected to rigorous processing before the complex psychochemical molecules could be broken down. Inevitably, some of the NUNSACS staff picked up the contagion.

And I, thought Charteris, I with that sad and lovely Natrina...

I am going psychedelic. That godlike vision must have come from the drug. At least rainbows will flutter in those dark valleys where I shall tread.

He had moved some way towards the Hôtel des Invalides, dragging his fingers across the rough angles of the buildings as if to convince himself that matter was still matter. When Angelina came up to him, he scarcely recognised her.

'You were waiting for me,' she said accusingly. 'You are deliberately waylaying me. You'd better go to your room before Madame locks up.'

'I – I may be ill! You must help me!'

'Speak Italian. I told you, I don't understand German.'

'Help me, Angelina. I must be ill.'

'You were well enough before.'

She had sensed his strong angular body.

'I swear. . . . I had a vision. I can't face my room. I don't want to be alone. Let me come back to your room!'

'Oh no! You must think I am a fool, Signor!'

He pulled himself together, recalling the way of thought.

'Look, I'm ill, I think. Come and sit in my car with me for ten minutes. I need to get my strength back. If you don't trust me, I'll smoke a cigar all the time. You never knew a man kiss a pretty girl with a cigar in his mouth, did you?'

They sat in the car, she beside him looking at him warily. Charteris could see her eyes gleam in the thick orange light – the very hue of time congealed! – slicing off the walls of the cathedral. He sucked the rich sharp smoke down into his being, trying to fumigate it against the terrible visions of his psyche.

'I'm going back to Italy soon,' she said. 'Now the war's over and it is certain that the Arabs will not invade. I may work in Milano. My uncle writes that it's booming there again now. Is that so?'

'Booming.' A very curious word. Not blooming, not booing. Booming.

'Really, I'm not Italian. Not by ancestry. Everyone in our little village is descended from Albanians. When the Turks invaded Albania five centuries ago, many Albanians fled in ships across to the South of Italy to start life anew. The old customs were preserved from generation to generation. Did you hear of such a thing in Catanzaro?'

'No.' In Catanzaro he had heard the legends and phobias of the Caucasus, chopped and distorted by hallucination. It was a Slav, not an Illyrian, purgatory of alienation.

'As a little girl, I was bi-lingual. We spoke Tosk in the home and Italian everywhere else. Now I can hardly remember one word of Tosk! My uncles have all forgotten too. Only my old aunt, who is also called Angelina, remembers. She sings the old Tosk songs to the children. It's sad, isn't it, not to recall the language of your childhood? Like an exile?'

'Oh, shut up! I've never heard of Tosk. To hell with it!'

By that, she was reassured. Perhaps she believed that a man who took so little care to please could not want to rape her. Perhaps she was right.

They stared out at the tangerine stripes of the square. People passed slowly. The used cars slumped on their haunches listening to the distant noise of traffic, like new animals awaiting battle.

He asked. 'Did you have a mystical experience ever?'

'I suppose so. Isn't that what religion is?'

'I don't mean that stuff!' With his cigar, he indicated the illuminated stone outside. 'A genuine self-achieved insight, such as Ouspenski achieved.'

'I never heard of him.'

'He was a Russian philosopher.'

'I never heard of him.'

Already he was forgetting what he had seen and learned.

As he nursed his head and tried to understand what was inside it, she began to chatter, tongue delicate against teeth and lips redeeming the nonsense.

'I'll go back to Milano in the autumn, in September when it's not so hot. They're not good Catholics here in Metz. Are you a good Catholic? The French priests – ugh, I don't like them, the way they look at you! Sometimes I hardly seem to believe any more. . . . Do you believe in God any more, Signor?'

He turned and looked painfully at her orange eyes, trying to see what she was really saying. She was very boring, this girl, and without alternative.

'If you are really interested, I believe we each have gods within us, and we must follow those.' His father had said the same.

'That's stupid! Those gods would just be reflections of ourselves and we should be indulging in egotism to worship them.'

He was surprised by her answer. Neither his Italian nor his theology was good enough for him to reply as he would have liked. He said briefly, 'And your god – he is just an externalisation of egotism. Better to keep it inside!'

'What terrible, wicked blasphemy for a Catholic to utter!'

'You little idiot, I'm no Catholic! I'm a Communist! I've never seen any sign of your God marching about the world. He's a capitalist invention!'

'Then you are indeed sick!'

Angrily laughing, he grabbed her wrist and pulled her towards him. As she struggled, he shouted, 'Let's make a little investigation!'

She brought her skull forward and struck him on the nose. His head turned cathedral-size on the instant, flooded with pain. He hardly realised she had broken from his grip and was running across the square, leaving the Banshee's passenger door swinging open.

After a minute or two, Charteris locked the car door, climbed out, and made his way across to the hotel. The door was barred; Madame would be in bed, dreaming dreams of locked chests. Looking through the window into the bar, he saw that M'sieur still sat at his special table, drinking wine with his crony. Madame's dog sprawled by the radiator, still restlessly changing its position. The eternal recurrence of this evening, a morgue of life.

The enchanter Charteris tapped on the window to break their spell of sleeping wake.

After a minute or two, M'sieur unlocked the door from inside and appeared in his shirtsleeves. He stroked his tiny puff of beard and nodded to himself, as if something significant had been confirmed.

22

'You were fortunate I was still up, M'sieur! Madame my wife does not like to be disturbed when once she has locked and barred the premises. My friend and I were just fighting some of our old campaigns before bed.'

'Perhaps I have been doing the same thing.'

'You're too young! Not the pesky Arabs, the Bosche, boy, the Bosche! This very town was once under Bosche rule, you know!'

He went up to his room. It was filled with noise. As he walked over to the window and looked out, he saw that a lock gate on the dry canal had been opened. The bed of it was full of rushing water, coursing over the car body and other rubbish, slowly moving them downstream. All the long night, Charteris slept uneasily to the noise of the purging water.

In the morning, he rose early, drank Madame's first indifferent coffee of the day, and paid his bill. Angelina did not appear. His head was clear, but the world seemed less substantial than it had been. Something was awakening and uncoiling within him, making the very ground he trod seem treacherous, as if invisible snakes lay there. He could not decide whether he stood on the edge of truth or illusion, or a yet unglimpsed alternative to either. All he knew was his anxiety to escape from old battle pictures and stale caporal smells.

Carrying his grip out to the car, he climbed in, strapped himself up, and drove round the cathedral onto the motorway, which was already roaring with traffic. He turned towards the coast, leaving Metz behind at a gradually increasing speed, heading for his imagined England.

Metz Cathedral

Strong vertical lines familiarise
An alien love. Yet the cathedral
Escapes its statement after dusk
When for the tourist trade they floodlight
It and all-too-solid piety
Fragments in its own enormous shadows
Of buttresses, porches, peeling pillars.
Nothing familiar then: a cage
For something frightful? So you park
Outside and maybe make a joke
About the modern restorations
Being turned into a 3D Braque:
So much worse than it's bright:
And head towards the nearest bar, where
Horizontal lines familiarly
Provide the indifference of a bed.

NIGHT-TIME

Night-time
The town sleeps . . .
I pretend to sleep
By the cloaca maxima

The clock strikes
Midnight – yes, that's true
Enough. How goes the song?
A boy wanders across
The fields among the peonies

O Serbia I have another name
All things have other names
And will that change them

And will that change them
As I am changed?
Looking for his loved one's
House. . . . Let's hope her

Bed springs did not clang!
Night-time
The town sleeps
The springs strike

And I wander across
The midnight fields
Looking for the house

The house where dancing is

The Girl at the Inn

The city was open to the nomad
The fountain sparkled for his lips

But at the inn the girl who served there
Had nothing to spare a traveller

The traveller settled at the inn
Although he left his bill unpaid

The girl no longer held him strange
One day she let him clasp her lightly

And then that night he clasped her tightly
Now she lets him clasp her nightly
Wrongly rightly clasp her nightly

The traveller sang He loved the girl
And was captive of the city

This was their tiny personal story
Like perhaps to many others

Or why else should he say the curious thing
When smiling to her smiles one day

Although I love you dearly love
There's nothing personal in it

And then that night he clasped her tightly
Still she lets him clasp her nightly
Wrongly rightly clasp her nightly

The Knowledge That the Car is Going to Crash

The knowledge that the car is going to crash
The ponic jungle blowing through its tunnels
The certainty that bodies burst apart
Is with me as I put my foot down

And racial memory's the dangling chain
That earths me to a neolithic road
Earlier youths and stabs of unearned knowledge
Milano blinds my eyes its dust

Somebody said 'I knew the blazing plane
Was going to crash before I clambered in'
A premonition isn't quite the same
Thing as the suffering

What if I knew that every word I spoke
Fell into silence deep as any sea
Or sailed it drunken derelict should that
Stop up a throat others have used

I am not powerless even though the power
Was never mine the blazing plane came down
Though vulnerable I keep the power to wound
Draw blood from bloodless faces

The knowledge that my car is going to crash
Is my inheritance and monkeys take
Their seats before the jungle blurs again
Can't daunt me as I put my foot down

Zimmer Twenty

The glories of La Patrie in coloured lithographs
All up and down the airless stairs
The Huns are always running. Not my battle. But he laughs
Suppose that Zimmer Twenty really cares?

This bed's a battlefield for unconsumated doubts
Madame would charge more for it if she dared
It's so familiar worn sheets dry canal. Before she shouts
Suppose that Zimmer Twenty really cared?

To speak to him of childhood – and in my native tongue
Or foreign in my old aunt's prayers
Exiled committed in this beastly town and not so young
Suppose that Zimmer Twenty really cares?

How often Zimmer Twenty seems to care
The sluice gates open every midnight to the flood
Every dawning morn more debris thrown down there
They're not good Catholics in this rotten town
Fat old M'sieu with fingertips all brown
In Milano Milano there's better blood

Behind the other shutters neutrality is lying
I give myself defy them. There
My body's breath mists up the pane crying crying
Who's Zimmer Twenty? Should I care?

THE SERPENT OF KUNDALINI

AT the French port, they were sceptical, smiling, nodding, looking wizened, walking behind their barriers in a clockwork way. He stood there waving his NUNSACS papers which later, on the ferry going across to England, he consigned to the furtive waters.

They let him through at the last, making it clear he would find it harder to get back once he was out.

As yet he had nothing to declare.

Once the French coast and customs were left behind, he fell asleep.

When Charteris woke, the ship had already moored in Dover harbour and was absolutely deserted except for him. Even the sailors had gone ashore. Grey cliffs loomed above the boat. The quays and the sea were empty. The void was made more vacant by its transparent skin of flawless early spring sunshine.

The unwieldy shapes of quays and sheds did nothing to make the appearance of things more likely.

Just inside one of the customs sheds on the quay, a man in a blue sweater stood with his arms folded. Charteris saw him as he was about to descend the gangplank, and paused with his hand on the rail. The man would hardly have been noticeable; after all, he was perhaps thirty yards away; but, owing to a curious trick of acoustics played by the empty shed and the great slope of cliff, the man's every sound was carried magnified to Charteris.

The latter halted between ship and land, hearing the rasp of the waiting man's wrists as he re-folded his arms, hearing the tidal flow of his breath in his lungs, hearing the infinitesimal movement of his feet in his boots, hearing his watch tick through the loaded seconds of the day.

Very slowly, Charteris descended to the quay and began to walk towards the distant barriers, marching over large yellow painted arrows and letters meaningless to him, reducing him to a cipher in a diagram. Still water lay pallidly on his left. His course would take him close to the waiting man.

The noise of the waiting man grew.

The new vision of the universe which Charteris had been granted in Metz was still with him. All other human beings were symbols, nodes in an enormous pattern. This waiting man symbol could be death. He had come to England to find other things, a dream, white-thighed girls, faith. England, the million manarchies of ruined minds oerthrown.

'This deadness that I feel will pass,' he said aloud. The waiting man breathed by way of reply: a cunning and lying answer, thought Charteris. The motordeath images were gone from his crucible. Unstained porcelain. Bare. A flock of seagulls, white with black heads that swivelled like ball-bearings, sailed down from the cliff top, scudding in front of Charteris, and landed on the sea. They sank like stones. A cloud slid over the sun and the water was immediately the brown nearest black.

He reached the barrier. As he swung it wide and passed through, the noises of the waiting man died. To stand here was the ambition of years. Freedom from father and fatherland. Charteris knelt to kiss the ground; as his knees buckled, he glanced back and saw, crumpling over one of the yellow arrows, his own body. He jerked upright and went on. He recalled what Gurdjieff had said: attachment to things keeps alive a thousand useless I's in a man; these I's must die so that the big I can be born. The dead images were peeling from him. Soon he himself would be born.

He was trembling. Nobody wants to change.

The town was large and grand. The windows and the paintwork, Charteris thought, were very English. The spaces formed between buildings were also alien to him. He heard himself say that architecture was a kinetic thing essentially: and that photography had killed its true spirit because people had grown used to studying buildings on pages rather than by walking through them and round them and seeing them in relationship to other urban objects. In the same way, the true human spirit had been killed. It could only be seen in and by movement. Movement. At home in his father's town, Kragujevac, he had fled from stagnation, its lack of alternatives and movement.

Conscious of the drama of the moment, he paused, clutching

his chest, whispering to himself, *Zbogom*! For the thought was revelation. A philosophy of movement. . . . Sciences like photography must be used to a different purpose, and motion must be an expression of stillness. Seagulls rise from a flat sea.

A stony continental city in the grey prodigal European tradition, with wide avenues and little crooked alleys – a German city perhaps, perhaps Geneva, perhaps Brussels. He was arriving in a motor cavalcade, leading it, talking an incomprehensible language, letting them worship him. Movement. And a sullen English chick parting her white thighs, hair like clematis over white-washed wall, applause of multitudinous starlings, beaches, night groaning with weight-lifter strength.

Then the vision was gone.

Simultaneously, all the people in the Dover street began to move. Till now, they had been stationary, frozen, one-dimensional. Now, motion gave them life and they went about their chances.

As he walked through their trajectories, he saw how miscellaneous they were. He had imagined the English as essentially a fair northern race with the dark-haired among them as startling contrast. But these were people less sharp than that, parti-coloured, piebald, their features blunted by long inter-marriage, many stunted with blurred gestures, and many Jews and dark people among them. Their dress also presented a more tremendous and ragged variety than he had encountered in other countries, even his own Serbia.

Although these people were doing nothing out of the ordinary, Charteris knew that the insane breath of war was exhaled here too. The home-made bombs had splashed down from England's grey clouds; and the liquid eyes that turned towards him held a drop of madness. He thought he could still hear the breathing of the waiting man; but as he listened to it more closely, he realised that the people near him were whispering his name – and more than that.

'Charteris! Colin Charteris – funny name for a Jug!'

'Didn't he go and live in Metz?'

'Charteris is pretending that he swam the Channel to get here.'

'What's Charteris doing here? I thought he was going to Scotland!'

'Did you see Charteris kiss the ground, cheeky devil!'

'Why didn't you stay in France, Charteris – don't you know it's neutral?'

A woman took her small girl by the hand and led her hurriedly into a butcher's shop, saying, 'Come away, darling. Charteris raped a girl in France!' The butcher leant across the counter with a huge crimson leg in his hands and brought it down savagely on the little girl's head – Charteris looked round hastily and saw that the butcher was merely hanging a red boloney sausage on a hook. His eyes were betraying him. His hearing was probably not to be trusted, either. The arrows still worried him.

Anxious to get away from the whispering, whether real or imaginary, he walked along a shopping street that climbed uphill. Three young girls went before him in very short skirts. By slowing his pace, he could study their legs, all of which were extremely shapely. The girl on the outside of the pavement, in particular, had beautiful limbs. He admired the ankles, the calves, the dimpling popliteal hinges, the thighs, following the logic of them in imagination up to the sensuously jolting buttocks, the little swelling buds of fruit. Motion, again, he thought: without that élan vital, they would be no more interesting than the butcher's meat. An overpowering urge to exhibit himself to the girls rose within him. He could fight it only by turning aside into a shop; it was another butcher's shop; he himself hung naked and stiff on a hook, white, and pink-trottered. He looked directly and saw it was a pig's carcass.

But as he left the shop, he saw another of his discarded I's was peeling off and crumpling over the counter, lifeless.

A bright notice on a wall advertised the Nova Scotia Tread-mill Orchestra.

He hurried on to the top of the hill. The girls had gone. Like a moth, the state of the world fluttered in his left ear, and he wept for it. The West had delivered itself to the butchers. France Old Folks Home.

A view of the sea offered itself at the top of the hill. Breathing as hard as the waiting man, Charteris grasped some railings and looked over the cliff. One of those hateful phantom voices down in the town had suggested he was going to Scotland; he saw now that he was indeed about to do that; at least, he would head north. He hoped his new-found mental state would enable him to see the future with increasing clarity; but, when he made the effort, as if, it might be, his eyesight misted over at any attempt to read small print, the endeavour seemed bafflingly self-defeating: the small print of the future bled and ran – indeed, all he could distinguish was a notice reading something like LOVE BURROW which would not resolve into GLASGOW, some sort of plant with crimson blooms and . . . a road accident? – until, trying to grapple with the muddled images, he finally even lost the *direction* in which his mind was trying to peer. The breathing was in his head and chest.

Clinging to the railings, he tried to sort out his random images. LOVE BURROW was no doubt some sort of Freudian nonsense; he dismissed the crimson Christmas blooms; his anxiety clustered round the accident – all he could see was a great perspective of clashing and clanging cars, aligned down the beaches of triple-carriageways like a tournament. The images could be past or future. Or merely fears. Always the prospect of crashing and tumbling climaxes.

He had left his car on the ship. What was ahead was unknown, even to him with the budding powers – in a breathless moment like a ducking – and the sea was grey. Clutching the railings, Charteris felt the ground rock slightly. The deck. The deck rocked. The sea narrowed like a Chinese eye. The ship bumped the quay. A call to muster stations amid starling laughter.

He stood at the rail, trying to adjust, as the passengers left the ship and their cars were driven away from the under-deck. He looked up at the cliffs; gulls swooped down from them: and floated on the oily sea. He listened and heard only his own breathing, the rasp of his own body in his clothes. In or out of trance he stood: and the quay emptied of people.

'Is the red car yours, sir?'

'You are Mr Charteris, sir?'

Slowly he turned towards the English voice. He extended a hand and touched the fabric of the man's tunic. Nodding without speaking, he made his way slowly below deck. Slowly, he walked down the echoing belly-perspective of the car deck to where his Banshee stood. He climbed in, searched in his pocket for the ignition key, slowly realised it was already in the ignition, started up, and drove slowly over the ramp onto English concrete, English yellow arrows.

He looked across to the customs shed. A man stood there half in shadow, in a blue sweater, arms folded. He beckoned. Charteris drove forward and found it was a customs man. A small rain began to fall as the man looked laconically through Charteris's grip.

'This is England, but my dream was more true,' he said.

'That's as may be,' said the man, in surly fashion. 'We had a war here, you know, sir, not like you lot in France. You'd expect a bit of dislocation, sort of, wouldn't you?'

'Dislocation, my God, yes!'

'Well, then. . . . '

As he rolled forward, the man called out, 'There's a new generation!'

'And I'm part of it!'

He drove away, enormously slow, and the slimy yellow arrows licked their way under his bonnet. TENEZ LA GAUCHE. LINKS FAHREN. DRIVE ON THE LEFT. WATNEY'S BEER. The enormous gate swung open and he felt only love. He waved at the man who opened the gate; the man stared back suspiciously. England! Brother we are treading where the Saint has trod!

The great white lumpish buildings along the front seemed to settle. He turned and looked back in fear at the ship – where – what was he? In the wet road, crumpled over one of the arrows, lay one of his I's, just as in the vision, discarded.

Only now did he clearly recall the details of the vision.

To what extent was a vision an illusion, to what extent a clearer sort of truth?

He recollected the England of his imagination, culled from dozens of Saint books. A sleazy place of cockneys, nursemaids, policemen, slums, misty wharves, large houses full of the vulnerable jewellery of beautiful women. That place was not this. Well, like the man said, there had been a war, a dislocation. He looked at these people in these streets. The few women who were about moved fast and furtive, poorly and shabbily dressed, keeping close to walls. Not a nursemaid among them. The men did not stir. A curse of alternate inertia had been visited upon the English sexes. Men stood waiting and smoking in little groups, unspeaking; women scurried lonely. In their eyes, he saw the dewy glints of madness. Their pupils flashed towards him like animal headlights, feral with guanin, the women's green, the men's red like wolfhounds or a new animal.

A little fear clung to Charteris.

'I'll drive up to Scotland,' he said. Bombardment of images. He was confusing his destiny: he would never get there. Something happened to him . . . would happen. Had happened – and he here and now was but a past image of himself, perhaps a dead image, perhaps one of the cast-off I's that Gurdjieff said must be cast off before a man could awaken to true consciousness.

He came to the junction where, in his vision, he had turned and walked up the steep shopping street. With determination, Charteris wrenched the wheel and accelerated up the hill. Under sudden prompting, he glanced over his shoulder. A red Banshee with himself driving had split away and was taking the other turning. Did that way lead to Scotland or to .... Love Burrow? His other I caught his gaze just momentarily, pupils flashing blank guanin red, teeth bright in a wolf snarl.

That's one I I'm happy to lose ...

As he climbed up the hill, he looked for three girls in mini-skirts, for a butcher's shop. But the people were the shabby post-catastrophe crowd, and most of the shops were shuttered: all infinitely sadder than the vision, however frightening it had been. Had he been frightened? He knew he embraced the new strangeness. Materialism had a silver psychedelic bullet through its heart; the incalculable took vampire-flight. The times were his.

Already, he felt a cooler knowledge of himself. Down in the south of Italy, that was where this new phase of life had festered for him, in the rehabilitation camp for the slav victims, away from his paternal roof. In the camp, he had been forced to wander in derangements and had learnt that sanity had many alternatives, a fix for individual taste.

From his personal revolt, definition was growing. He could believe that his forte was action directed by philosophy. He was not the introspective; on the other hand, he was not the simple doer. The other I's would be leaves from the same tree.

And where did these thoughts lead? Something impelled him: perhaps only the demon chemicals increasing their hold on him; but he needed to know where he was going. It would help if he could examine one of his cast-off I's. As he reached the top of the hill, he saw that he still stood gripping the railings and staring out to sea. He stopped the car.

As he walked towards the figure, monstrous things wheeled in the firmament.

His hearing became preternaturally acute. Although his own footsteps sounded distant, very near at hand were the tidal flow of his breathing, the tick of his watch, the stealthy rustle of his body inside its clothing. Like the man said, there had been a war, a dislocation.

As his hand came up to touch the shoulder of the Gurdjieffian I, it was arrested in mid-air; for his glance caught the sight of something moving on the sea. For a moment, he mistook it for some sort of a new machine or animal, until it resolved itself under his startled focus into a ship, a car ferry, moving close in to the harbour. On the promenade deck, he saw himself standing remote and still.

The figure before him turned.

It had broken teeth set in an indefinite mouth, and dark brown pupils of eyes gripped between baggy lids. Its nose was brief and snouty, its skin puffed and discoloured, its hair as short and tufted as fur. It was the waiting man. It smiled.

'I was waiting for you, Charteris!'

'So they were hinting down in the town.'

'You don't have any children, do you?'

'Hell, no, but my ancestry goes right back to Early Man.'

'You'll tell me if you aren't at ease with me? Your answer reveals, I think, that you are a follower of Gurdjieff?'

'Clever guess! Ouspenski, really. The two are one – but Gurdjieff talks such nonsense.'

'You read him in the original, I suppose?'

'The original what?'

'Then you will realise that the very times we live in are somewhat Gurdjieffian, eh? The times themselves, I mean, talk nonsense – but the sort of nonsense that makes us simultaneously very sceptical about the old rules of sanity.'

'There were no rules for that sort of thing. There never were. You make them up as you go.'

'You are not much more than a kid! You wouldn't understand. There are rules for everything once you learn them.'

Charteris was feeling almost no apprehension now, although his pulse beat rapidly. Far below on the quay, he could see himself climbing into the Banshee and driving towards the customs shed.

'I must be getting along,' he said formally. 'As the Saint would say, I have a date with destiny. I'm looking for a place called . . . ' He had forgotten the name; that image had been self-cancelling.

'My house is hard by here.'

'I prefer a softer kind.'

'It is softer inside, and my daughter would like to meet you. Do come and rest a moment and feel yourself welcome in Britain.'

He hesitated. The time would come, might even be close, when all the gates of the farmyard would be closed to him; he would fall dead and be forgotten; and continue to stare for ever out through the window at the blackness of the garden. With a simple gesture of assent – how simple it yet remained to turn the wrist in the lubricated body – he helped the waiting man into the car and allowed him to direct the way to his house.

This was a middle-class area, and unlike anywhere he had visited before. Roads of small neat houses and bungalows stretched away on all sides, crescents curved off and later rejoined the road, rebellion over. All were neatly labelled with sylvan names: Sherwood Forest Road, Dingley Dell Road, Herbivore Drive, Woodbine Walk, Placenta Place, Honeysuckle Avenue, Cowpat Avenue, Geranium Gardens, Clematis Close, Creosote Crescent, Laurustinus Lane. Each dwelling had a neat little piece of garden, often with rustic work and gnomes on the front lawn. Even the smallest bungalows had grand names, linking them with a mythical green nature once supposed to have existed: Tall Trees, Rolling Stones, Pan's Pantiles, Ocean View, Neptune Tiles, The Bushes, Shaggy Shutters, Jasmine Cottage, My Wilderness, Solitude, The Laurustinuses, Our Oleanders, Florabunda.

Charteris grew angry and said, 'What sort of a fantasy are these people living in?'

'If you're asking seriously, I'd say, Security masquerading as a little danger.'

'We aren't allowed this sort of private property in Jugoslavia. It's an offence against the state.'

'Don't worry! This way of life is dead – the war has killed it. The values on which this mini-civilisation has been built have been swept away – not that most of the inhabitants realise it yet. I keep up the pretence because of my daughter.'

The waiting man began to breathe in a certain way. Charteris regarded him curiously out of the corner of his eye, because he fancied that the man was accomplishing rather an accurate parody of his daughter's breathing. So good was it that the girl was virtually conjured up between them; she proved to be, to Charteris's delight, the one of the three girls in a mini-skirt he had most admired while walking up the hill, perhaps a year younger than himself. The illusion lasted only a split second, and then the waiting man was breathing naturally again.

'All pretence must be broken! Maybe that is the quest on which I came to this country. Although we are strangers and should perhaps talk formally together, I must declare to you that I believe very deeply that there is a strange force latent in man which can be awakened.'

'Kundalini! Turn left here, down Petunia Park Road.'

'What?'

'Turn left.'

'What else did you say? You were swearing at me, I believe?'

'Kundalini. You don't know your Gurdjieff as well as you pretend, my friend. So-called occult literature speaks of Kundalini, or the serpent of Kundalini. A strange force in man which can be awakened.'

'That's it, then, yes! I want to awaken it. What are all these people doing in the rain?'

As they drove down Petunia Park Road, Charteris realised that the English middle-classes were standing neatly and attentively in their gardens; some were performing characteristic actions such as adjusting ties and reading big newspapers, but most were simply staring into the road.

'Left here, into Brontosaurus Broadway. Listen, my boy, Kundalini, that serpent, should be left sleeping. *It's nothing desirable!* Repulsive though you may find these people here, their lives have at least been dedicated – and successfully, on the whole – to mechanical thought and action, which keep the serpent sleeping. I mean, security masquerading as a little danger is only a small aberration, whereas Kundalini – '

He went into some long rigmarole which Charteris was unable to follow; he had just seen a red Banshee, driven by another Gurdjieffian I, slide past the top of the road, and was disturbed by it. Although there was much he wanted to learn from the waiting man, he must not be deflected from his main north-bound intention, or he might find himself in the position of a discarded I. On the other hand, it was possible that going north might bring him into discardment. For the first time in his life, he was aware of all life's rich or desiccating alternatives; and an urge within him – but that might be Kundalini – prompted him to go and talk to people, preach to them, about cultivating the multi-valued.

'Here's the house,' said the waiting man. 'Pear Tree Palace. Come in and have a cup of tea. You must meet my daughter. She's your age, no more.'

At the neat little front gate, barred with a wrought-iron sunset, Charteris hesitated. 'You are hospitable, but I hope you won't mind my asking – I seem myself to be slightly affected by the PCA bombs – hallucinations, you know – I wondered – aren't you also a bit – touched – '

The waiting man laughed, making his ugly face look a lot

uglier. 'Everyone's touched! Don't be taken in by appear-
ances here. Believe me, the old world has gone, but its shell
remains in place. One day soon, there will come a breath of
wind, a new messiah, the shell will crumple, and the kids will
run streaming, screaming, barefoot in the head, through lush
new imaginary meadows. What a time to be young! Come on,
I'll put the kettle on! Wipe your shoes!'

'It's as bad as that?' – '

The waiting man had opened the front door and gone
inside. Uneasy, Charteris paused and looked about the garden
suburb. Kinetic architecture here had spiked the viewpoint
with a crazy barricade of pergolas, patios, bay windows,
arches, extensions, all manner of dinky garages and outhouses,
set among fancy trees, clipped hedges, and painted trellis.
Watertight world. All hushed under the fine mist of rain.
Neighbourhood of evil for him, small squares of anaemic
fancy, wrought-iron propriety.

He found himself at the porch, where the gaunt rambler
canes already bore little snouts of spring growth. There'd
be a fine show of New Dawn in four more months. An en-
chantment waited here. He went in, leaving the door open.
He wanted to hear more about Kundalini.

At the back of the house, the waiting man pottered in a
small kitchen, all painted green and cream, every surface
covered with patterned stuff and, on a calendar, a picture of two
people tarrying in a field. Behind the frozen gestures of the
couple, sheep broke from their enclosure and surged among
the harvest wheat to trample it with delight.

'My daughter'll be back soon.' The waiting man switched
on a small green-and-cream dumpy streamlined radio from
which the dumpy voice of a disc-joker said, 'And now for those
who enjoy the sweet things of life, relax right back for the great
all-time sound of one of the great bands of all time and we're
spinning this one just especially for Auntie Flora and all the
boys at "Nostalja Vista", 5 The Crossings, The Tip, Scrawley,
in Bedfordshire – the great immortal sound of you guessed it the
Glenn Miller Orchestra playing "Moonlight Serenade".'

Out in the garden winter birds plunged.

' "All time sound" – you are for music?' asked the waiting
man as he beat time and watched the treacly music as it rose
from the kettle spout and steamed across the withered ceiling.

'My daughter isn't in. I expect she'll be back soon. Why
don't you settle down here with us for a bit? There's a nice

little spare room upstairs – a bit small but cosy. You never know – you might fall in love with her.'

He remembered his first fear of the waiting man: that he would detain Charteris in the customs shed. Now, more subtly, the attempt at detention was again being made.

'And you're a follower of Gurdjieff, are you?' Charteris asked.

'He was rather an unpleasant customer, wasn't he? But a magician, a good guide through these hallucinatory times.'

'I want to waken a strange force that I feel inside me, but you say that is Kundalini, and Gurdjieff warns against waking it?'

'Very definitely! Most definitely! G says *man* must awake but the snake, the serpent, must be left sleeping.' He made the tea meticulously, using milk from a tube which was lettered Ideal. 'We've all got serpents in us, you know!' He laughed.

'So you say. We also have motives that make our behaviour rational, that have nothing to do with any snakes!'

The waiting man laughed again in an offensive way.

'Don't laugh like that! Shall I tell you the story of my life?'

Amusement. 'You're too young to have a life!' He dropped saccharine pills into the tea.

'On the contrary! I've already shed many illusions. My father was a stone-mason. Everyone respected him. He was big and powerful and harsh and sad. Everyone said he was a good man. He was an Old Communist, a power in the Party.

'When I was a small boy, there was a revolt by the younger generation. They wanted to expel the Old Communists. Students everywhere rose up and said, "Stop this antique propaganda! Let us live our lives!" And in the schools they said, "Stop teaching us propaganda! Tell us facts!" You know what my father did?'

'Have your tea and be quiet!'

'I'm talking to you! My father went boldy out to meet the students. They jeered him but he spoke up. "Comrades," he said, "You are right to protest – youth must always protest. I'm glad you have the courage to speak up because for a long while I have secretly felt as you do. Now I have your backing, I will change things. Leave it to me!" I heard him say it and was proud.'

And he heard now the all-time orchestra never dead.

'I became fervent then myself. Sure enough, father made

40

changes. Everyone said that the young idealists had won and in the schools they taught how the Old Communism had been okay but the new non-propagandist kind was better. The young ringleaders of the revolt were even given good jobs. It was wonderful.'

'Politics don't interest me,' said the waiting man, stirring his tea. 'Do you care for music?'

'Five years later, I had my first girl. She said she would let me in on a secret. She was part of a revolutionary group of young men and girls. They wanted to change things so that they could live their lives freely, and they wanted the schools and newspapers to stop all the propaganda. They determined to expel the Young Communists.

'For me, it was a movement of terrible crisis! I realised that Communism was a just system for hanging on to what you had, no better than Capitalism. And I realised that my father was just a big fraud – an opportunist, not an idealist. From then on, I knew I had to get away, to live my own life.'

The waiting man showed his furry teeth and said, 'That's hardly as interesting to me as what I was telling you about the serpent, I think you must admit. There's no such thing as an "own life".'

'What is this serpent of Kundalini then? Come on, out with it, or I could pretty easily brain you with this kettle!'

'It's an electric kettle!'

'I don't care!'

At this proof of Charteris's recklessness, the waiting man backed away, helped himself to a saccharine pill, and said, 'Enjoy your tea while it's hot! Forget your father – it's something we all have to do!'

'Yes siree, one of the great ones in the Miller style. And now for a welcome change of pace –'

Charteris was conscious of a mounting pressure inside him. Something was breathing close to his left ear and stealing away.

'Answer my question!' he said.

'Well, according to G, the serpent is the power of the imagination – the power of fantasy – which takes the place of a real function. You get my meaning? When a man dreams instead of acting, when he imagines himself to be a great eagle or a great magician . . . that's the force of Kundalini acting in him . . .'

'Cannot one act and dream?'

The waiting man appeared to double up, sniggering in

repulsive fashion with his fists to his mouth. Love Burrow – that was the sign, and a pale-thighed wife beside him. . . . His place was there, wherever that was. This Pear Tree Palace was a trap, a dead end, the waiting man himself an ambiguous either/or/both/and sign, deluding yet warning him: perhaps a manifestation of Kundalini itself. He had got his tasks in the wrong order; clearly, this was a dead end with no alternative, a corner of extinction. What he wanted was a new tribe!

Now the waiting man's sniggers were choking him. Above their bubbling din, he heard the sound of a car engine outside, and dropped his teacup. The tea sent a dozen fingers across the cubist lino. Over his fists, the little doubled figure glared blankly red at him. Charteris turned and ran.

Through the open door. Birds leaped from the lawn to the eaves of the bungalow, leaden, from motionlessness to instant motionlessness.

His heart's beat dragged in its time-snare like a worn serenade.

Down the path. The rain had lured out a huge black slug which crawled like a torn watch-strap before him. The green-and-cream radio still dialled yesterday.

Through the gate. The sun, set for ever with its last rays caught in mottled iron.

To the road. But he was a discarded alternative. A red Banshee was pulling away, with one of his glittering I's at the wheel, puissant, full of potential, multi-valued, saviour-shaped.

He ran after it, calling from the asphalt heart of Brontosaurus Broadway, leaping over the gigantic yellow arrows. They were becoming more difficult to negotiate. His own powers, he knew, were failing. He had chosen wrongly, become a useless I, dallying with an old order instead of seeking new patterns.

Now the arrows were almost vertical. LINKS FAHREN. The red car was far away, just a blur moving through the barrier, speeding unimpeded for. . . .

He still heard breathing, movements of clothes, the writhing of toes inside shoe-caps. But these were not his. They belonged to the Charteris in the car, the undiscarded I. He no longer breathed.

As he huddled over the arrow, gulls tumbled from the cliff and sank into the water. Over the sea, the ship came. Up the hill, motors sounded. In the head, barefoot, a new age.

There had been a war, a dislocation.

TIME NEVER GOES BY

You must remember this
That beds get crumpled skirts get rumpled
And hedges grow up into trees
Cinemas close and the parking lot
Loses its last late Ford
Everything goes by the board
But Time Never Goes By

And when true lovers screw
Novelty wears off the affair's off
Perfume fades from the air
The bright spinning coin will tarnish and
The miser forget his hoard
Everything goes by the board
But Time Never Goes By

The watch keeps ticking true enough
But time's glued down to something stronger
It's a fixture   Do enough
But every second's a second longer
Try your best you'll be impressed
Every minute has centuries in it

It's still the same old story
Characters change events rearrange
Plot seems to wear real thin
Coffins call for running men
Hated or adored
Everything goes by the board
But Time Never Goes By

NOVA SCOTIA TREADMILL ORCHESTRA

ROSEMARY LEFT ME

Beyond the buildings the buildings
Begin again
Beyond recording the old records
Spin again

It's sort of sad its kind of safe
It seems so sour
The things that are past will fortify
The menace of the coming hour

My Rosemary left me outside The Fox
Said I smelt said I didn't care
Then why do I keep her pubic hair
Tied up in ribbon in a sandalwood box

Now I've found Jeanie cute as you please
Tight little skirt and leather jerkin
Soon I'll get the scissors working
History comes bobbing on back like knees

So I go ahead tho I know ahead
Winds blow ahead
Two steps forward one step back
Trodden in another tread

Beyond recording the old records
Spin again
Beyond the buildings the buildings
Begin again

THE GENOSIDES

LITTLE PAPER FACES

He goes through the land
His tomorrow in his pocket
He seeks a land
Where the faces fit the heads

Little paper faces
Little paper faces
Little paper faces
Yeh, with hand-drawn expressions

He crosses over the sea
Pilgrim of the Pilgrim Age
He hopes to see
A different mask beneath the skull

Little paper faces
Little paper faces
Little paper faces
Yeh, with crayoned experience

Little paper faces
Little paper faces
Little paper faces
Yeh, papered on the paper bone

THE ESCALATION

DRAKE-MAN ROUTE

So maybe this was the real Charteris or a personal photograph of him wire-wheeling towards the metropolis none
too sure if matter was not hallucination, smiling and speaking
with a tone of unutterable kindness to himself to keep down
the baying images. Uprooted man. Himself a product of time.
England a product of literature. It was a good period and to
dissolve into all branches – great new thing with all potentials,
prosperity and prenury.

He saw it, see-saw the new thing, scud across the scudding
road before him, an astral projection perhaps, all legs, going all
ways at once. A man could do that.

He wanted to communicate his new discoveries, pour out
the profusion of his confusion to listeners, in madness never
more nerved or equilustral, all paradised by the aerosols
until the unclipped hedges of mind grew their own utopiary.

His car snouted out one single route from all the possible
routes and now growled through the iron-clod night of London's
backyards: papiermâché passing for stone, cardboard passing
for brick, only in the yellow fanning wash of French headlights;
pretence all round of solidity, permanence, roofs and walls and
angles of a sly geometry, windows infinitely opaque on seried
sleepers, quick corners, snickering bayonets at vision's angles,
untrodden pavements, wide eyes reflected from blind shops,
the ever-closing air, the epic of unread signs, and under the bile
blue fermentation of illumination, roundabouts of concrete
boxed by shops and a whole vast countryside rumpling upwards
into the night under the subterranean detonation of unease.
The steering wheel swung it all this way and that, great raree
show-down for foot-down Serbs. Song in the wings, other
voices.

Round the next corner FOR YOUR THROAT'S SAKE SMOKE
a van red-eyed – a truck no *trokut*! – in the middle of the
guy running out waving bloody leather – Charteris braked

spilling hot words as the chasing thought came of impact and splat some clot mashed out curving against a wall of shattered brick so bright all flowering: a flowering cactus a christmas cactus rioting in an anatomical out-of-season.

Car and images dominoed into control as the man jumped back for his life and Charteris muscled his Banshee past the van to a halt.

All along the myriad ways of Europe that sordid splendid city in the avenues Charteris had driven hard. He thought of them spinning down his window thrusting out his face as the vanman came on the trot.

'You trying to cause a crash or something?'

'You were touching some speed, lad, come round that corner like you were breaking the ruddy speed record, can you give me a lift I've broken down?'

He looked broken down like all the English now narrowly whooping up the after-effects of the Acid Head War, with old leather shoulders and elbows and a shirt of macabre towelling, no tie, eyes like phosphorescence and a big mottled face as if shrimps burrowed in his cheeks.

'Can you give me a lift, I say? Going north by any chance?'

The difficulty of the cadence of English. Not the old simple words so long since learnt by heart as the gallant saint slipped into the villainous captain's cabin pistol in hand but simply the trick of drawing it vocal from the mouth.

'I am going north yes. What part of it are you wanting to reach?'

'What part are you heading for?'

'I – I – where the christmas cactus blooms and angelina flowers –'

'Heck, another acid nut, look, lad, are you safe to be with?'

'Forgive me I it's they you see I take you north okay, only I'm just a bit confused by anywhere you want I go why not?'

He couldn't think straight, couldn't aim straight though he sighted his intellect at the target the bullets of thought were multi-photographed and kept recurring and stray ricochets spanged back again and again like that succulent image that perhaps he thought sniped him from his future – and why not if the Metz vision was true and he no more than a manifestation on a web of time in which matter was the hallucination. Bafflement and yet suffusing delight as if a great havering haversack was lifted off his back simplifying under its perplexities such personal problems as right or wrong.

47

'If you feel that way. You are a foreigner? France was not affected they say played it cool stayed neuter. Friend to the Arab world. Lost all loot, I say. Okay I'll get my gear name's Banjo Burton by the way.'

'Mine's Charteris. Colin Charteris.'

'Good.'

Burly of shoulder he ran back to the van all conked and hunched fifty yards back, struggled at the rear and then returned for help. So Charteris not unloath climbed into the silent stage set of this *quartier* looking about licking the desolation – London London at last this ouspenskian eye beholds this legendary if meagre exotic scene. Lugging at the back of the van the other man Banjo Burton pulls at something and between them they drag it machinery across the indoor road: a passing speedster and for a moment they are both outdoors again.

'What you got here?'

'Infrasound equipment,' as they load it into the back of Charteris's car backs bending grunting in work lonely company under the night eyes. Then stand there half-inspecting each other in the semi-dark you do not see me I do not see you: you see your interpretation of me I see my interpretation of you. Moving to climb into the front seats heftily he swinging open the door with unrecorded muscling asks, 'So you're French then are you?'

'I am Serbian.'

Great conversation stopper slammer of doors internally quasi-silent revving of engines and away. The start and bastion of Europe oh they know not Serbia. O Kossovo the field of blackbirds where the dark red peonies blow but then on into the Turkish night of another era of the mobility soothed soon the shouldered man begins to manifest his flat voice as if speed harmonised it.

'I'll not be sorry to get out of London and home again though mind you you certainly see some funny things here make you laugh if you feel that way I mean to say people are more open than they used to be.'

'Open? Minds open? You don't mean thoughts flowing from one to another like a net a web?'

'I don't mean that as far as I know. I don't get what goes on in the heads of you blokes though I don't mind telling you. And when I say laugh it's really enough to make you cry. I was up in Coventry when they dropped the bombs.'

48

The light and lack of it played across his cragged face as he fumbled for a cigarette and lit it very close to his face between a volcano crater of cupped hands all afire to the last wrinkle and looking askance with extinct pits said through smoke, 'I mean to say this is the end of the world take it or leave it.'

But this goblin had no hex on the charmed Charteris who sang 'In English you have a saying where there's life there's hope and so here no end – one end maybe but a straggle of new starts.'

'If you call going back to caveman level new start, look mate I've been around see I got a brother was in the army he's back home now because why because the forces all broke up – no discipline once the air is full of this cyclodelic men'll fall about with laughing rather than stand in a straight line like they don't get it, eh? So similarly where's your industry and agriculture going without discipline I tell you this country and all the other countries like Europe and America they're grinding to a standstill and only the bloody wogs fit to hold a spoon and fork.'

As they clattered up a long forlorn street built a century back archaic blind shuttered shattered in the stony desert just for the sheer delight of going Charteris thus: 'New disciplines grind from the stand only the old bind gone I can't argue it but industrial's a crutch thrown away.'

Can't argue it but one day with a tuned tongue I will my light is in this darkness as his face splashes flame so the sweet animal lark of my brain will be cauterise a flamingot of golden flumiance.

Though by the deadly nightshade sheltered figures rankled in vacant areas moving in groups with new instinct and on missing slates derisive the city's cats also tabbled in doubled file for every shadow a shadower.

'Your army brother got the aerosolvent?'

'Got some sort of religious kick like his whole brain's snarled up. Wide open to what ever comes along.'

'As we were meant to be.'

Banjo Burton laughed and coughed at the same time pouring smoke as if it were all he had to give.

'Bust open I'd say that's no way to go on like. Mark my words it's the end and cities hit real bad like London and New York and Brussels they copped it worst they're sinking with all hands and feet. Still a man does what he can so I run the group and hope like I mean not much one man can do after all if people aren't going to work proper they've got to do something so they trace for the sparky sound right?'

Tunnelling in his own exploding reverie where a whole sparse countryside under the sun rustled with the broken dreams of Slavs he signalled 'Sound?'

'I got a group. I manage them. I also launched the Nova Scotia Treadmill Orchestra. Used to be the Genosides. Remember their "Deathworld Boy"?'

'I was thinking your van should you just leave it?'

'It wasn't mine. I picked it up.'

Silence and night fading between them and between furry teeth the jaded taste of another sunrise until Burton huddled deeper and said again, 'I got this group.'

The camp had been full of eyes and there it had all started his first promptings on this solitary migration. 'What group?'

'A group like. Musicians. You know. . . . We used to be called the Dead Sea Sound now we changed to The Escalation now we're going to have infrasound like and the great roar tiding in over the heady audience in surges of everyone doing, his fruit-and-nutmost.' He waved his hand at the sky and said, 'There's no equation for a real thing what you think?'

'Musicians eh?'

'Aye damned right musicians.' He began to sing and the lost references added one more stratum to Charteris' tumbled psychogeology where many castled relics of experience lay. Untaught by his old politico-philosophical system to dig introspection he now nevertheless eased that jacket and shovelled down into his uncommon core to find there ore and always either/or, and on that godamnbiguity to snag his blade and whether there in the subsoil did not lie Kidd's treasure of all possibility, doubloons, pistoles for two, and gold moidores to other ways of thought.

Blinded by this gleam of previous metal he turned upon the singer huddled in his shadow and said, 'You could be another strand to the web or why not if all routes I now sail are ones of discovery and screaming up this avenue I also circumnavigate myself with as much meaning as your knighted hero Francis Drake.'

'I reckon as you've gone wrong somewhere this is the Portobello Road.'

'In my hindquarters reason's seat I see I sit sail unknowing but that Christmas cactus may be a shore and is there not a far

50

peninsula of Brussels?' Trying to look into a possible future port.

'I don't know what you mean man look where you're going.'

'I think I look I think I see. Enchanted mariner ducks into unknown bays and me with a laurel on my brow I see. . . . '

Charteris could not say what he saw and fell silent in a daze of future days; but what he had said moved Burton from his trental mood to say, 'If you're keeping on down the Harrow Road I have a friend in St John's Wood name of Brasher who would also be glad of a lift north like a sort of religious chap in many ways a prophet with strange means about him and god's knuckleduster when he's crossed.'

'He wants to go north?'

'Aye his wife and all that that. And my brother that I told you he was in the army well he acts as sort of disciple to Phil that's this bloke Brasher he's a bit of a touch nut but he's reckoned a bit of a prophet and he was in this plane crash and don't tell me it wasn't god's luck he managed to escape. . . . '

The slow bonfire of unaccustomed words flickered on the tired minds consuming and confusing leaves of yesterday but for Charteris no meaning sunk low in the cockpit of his pre-destined dreams where the ashes of father domination were a trance-element and just said lazily 'We can pick him up.'

'He's in St John's Wood I've got his address here on a bit of paper wait a bit like he's shacked up with some of his disciples. I tell you saints and seers are two a penny just lately, better turn off at this next traffic signals.'

Weren't these lay songs and carnal fictions a brighter fire than any burning in a regulation grate blessed by clergy or a funeral just the darker extension of forests lights illusions the frustration of material branches in leaf-fall or flooded delight where my dad went down.

The whole town had turned out to attend his father's funeral. Only he stayed at home. Finally, impulses of guilt and love sent him out, dressed as he was, to join the mourners.

Heavy rains had caused flooding, and the floods had delayed the progress of the funeral. It was growing dark. He drove along the winding valley road in the car: lately his father's car now his by inheritance. His father's old raincoat lay on the back seat. He did not like to throw it out. The car held the smell of his father.

It was dark under the mountain. The swollen river glinted. Between him and the river were broken and twisted trees where people went to laze on summer afternoons; lately, parties of picnickers had taken to driving over here from Svetozarevo, leaving their beer cans under the bushes. Now the beer cans were afloat. It was not easy to see where the deeps of the river began. The water was running fast and stern.

He could see solitary people walking on the other side of the river. The bridge was down; he could not get across. He drove on, winding and twisting round the rumps of mountainside.

A few lamps marked the other bank of the river now. A small rain began to fall, smearing the lights. He could just make out knots of people. When he came to the second bridge, he saw that a large area in front of it had flooded; he could not drive across. Stopping the car on a bank, he climbed out and started to wade through the flood. Music was playing on the far bank, coming to him fitfully. He caught his foot on something submerged under the dark water and fell, landing on hands and knees. With a curse, he got up and went back to the car. He drove on.

Now he could see the cemetery across the intervening waste of waters. His father had been a good Communist; he was going to get a good funeral, with an Orthodox priest presiding, and members of the Party present, humble in their raincoats.

The light was ragged from wild clouds. An island, a mere strip crowned with elders and beeches, stood between him and a clear view of the funeral party opposite. When he stopped the engine, he could just hear the voice of the priest, and could make out the man's head under a lantern.

He drove farther down the road, then back, looking for a better vantage point. There was none. He contemplated going all the way back to the village and then starting again down the other road; but it would take too long, and by then the ceremony might be entirely over. Painfully lack of alternative. Eventually, he backed the car across the road – there would be no more traffic on it today – so that its nose faced out towards the flood.

He turned on the headlights, letting them glare across the river, and stood by the car with the door hanging open, staring across himself. Rain clung to his face. It was really impossible to distinguish what was going on. He paddled among the flooded trees, staring, staring, at the far bank.

'Daddy!' he cried.

And past the greeneyes swinging right past Stones with headlights and Leeds Permanent all bordered up a glimpsed group of girls running down a dark turn legs and ankles what the blackbirds on the bloody field or through my poppied dark autobreasted antiflowered the desired succubae come to me with their dark mandragoran flies.

Lost vision. Other avenues. The natural density of loins.

And all these drunken turnings as again they lost themselves a simplified pantographic variablegeometric seedimensional weltschmerzanschauungerstrasshole of light-dashed caverns rumpussed in the stoned night were names to beat on inner ears with something more than sense: Westbourne Bridge Bishop's Bridge Road Eastbourne Terrace Praed Street Norfolk Place South Wharf Road Praed Street again and then more confidently up the Edgware Road and Maida Vale and St John's Wood Road and past Lord's with the unread signs and now more rubbish in the streets and on the rooftops gliding unobtrusively another turning worlds day and so to where the man called Brasher lived.

Here so long had been his drive that when the man called Burton left to give a call Charteris dozed in a dover head down upon the steering wheel and let this longplanned city substantiate itself around him in dawning colour. In his shuttered sleep he saw himself drawn from the ground multi-pronged and screaming with several people standing ceremonially but their heads averted or under cowls to whom he was then able to speak so that they moved through whole sparse countrysides of rooms and chambers and compartments, always ascending or descending stairs. Though all was malleable it seemed to him he had a winged conversation with two two women but one of them was maimed and the other took wings and burst out from a window for some sort of freedom although they heard an old man cry that beyond the sprawling giant of a building the buildings began again.

When he was aroused he could not say whether it was he that woke or the serpent within him.

Banjo Burton was talking at the car window without making himself understood his face landscaping so Charteris followed him towards crumbling semi-daylight house and that appeared the correct procedure. Mention of breakfast chill cramped in the dull limbs part still down in cup of coffee at least hospitally south of Italy and my nose still smarting from that blow in Metz they're upstairs he went after along the million gravel.

Old grey steps to the old brown building tucked in iron railings curled to a dilute Italian mode and in the grey-brown hall black-and-red tiles of the same illusory epoch and everywhere on every side apart from the murmuring of voices rich dull rich dull patterning making claims delaying senses – asking always of each moment was it eternal could one walk through the hall and walk forever through the hall: become no more than an experience of the hall as stiff-legged from the car one in the hall's embrace and the murmuring these ephemeral halls eternally retaining.

Then again another sumptuous time-bracket and the millenial-ephemeral world of the worn stair-carpet asking always what can be the connection between this and that moment except deep in the neovortex of old apemen in masquerading mansions and the smell of England tea old umbrellas jam trees and maybe corsets? And the voices nestlings at the rocking lifetop.

Utters at the top of the stairs and another time-bracket somehow one comes through them with people milling and what really goes on who sees or in my father's head. Patterny people all minority men and women with hands Byzantine and kindly expressions born to ingenuflect. Pinkness below the high hair. Dove voices with one voice angry madbulling the china-shoppers about it: the bullman for the crestfallen times all head and shoulders all bitumen surface blunt as a block shaking Charteris' hand saying 'My name's Phil Brasher I'm you will have heard of me I lead the people the new Proceed making extricate from the dull weavings of mundanity –'

'Proceed what?'

'The name of the new religion you should of heard of it they know me better in Loughborough a failed saint there Robbins announced me inadvertently in the market with crowds howling like dogs in great schemuzzle of relevation I was born.'

And now they gazed at each other under a naked bulb with Charteris all a smooth man but for the starting English whiskers his tongue always in an easy niche and only sound within the eternal squeal of tyres too late and the erotic gridlestone of bodies lying lively on the highway jumped up and jerked off speedwise. Opposed to him Brasher everywhere chunky and wattled from suit or cheeks or breeks a fine managerie odour and premeating him no favourable aspect of the future. They were both betrayed as beyond the recording old records began again.

How they saw each other. Each in isolation shipwracked. Always a farther coast beneath the coastline. I now my own mariner seized from sealess Serbia crossed at last the saint rowing with muffed oars down foggy Port of London to the

54

crimeship or Sir Francis circumaggraving the globe under my own prowess crossed the eggless waters to these shores this man this mantle.

They saw each other in a frost of violence crystallised recognised – a thousand self-photographing photographs fell about them on each a glimpse without its clue a fist a wrist a shoe a wall a word a cry Charteris we cry we hear his voice cry Paradise. What crazed triumph as Charteris foresuffers in utter puzzlement but yet did he not already do it all in menace of future hour.

In contrast Brasher he. Ashen he mounts back his anger on an unsound rampant saying, 'I'll not ride anywhere with you or where the lorries sweep. Isn't there's a limit a limbo a limit somewhere isn't there? You must know that I am the great Sayer and cannot in my mouth's teeth be dumb before these my fellowers.' They cheer and bring thin coffee always offstage like little paper faces. 'Now you arrive here and fatal events begin spreading forward along my trail and every premonition to an ashtip. See all how even death is multi-valved and in its colour black nearest brown. Back into the traffic no not I! No more moving no more movement only to still and take what I teach.'

And all those present said, 'Not the ashtits. Sickle ourselves on stillnesss,' like the backrow of the chorus.

But Burton drew Charteris aside and said, 'It's the PCA bombs he's not too bad will be glad to get home to his wife it's just he's psychic sees a bad image in you like and the menuts of a future hour.'

Bombardment of images. Peltocrat. White thighs with peonies curling between and the walk up narrow stair, *božur m'sieur*. All that he took and let the others burst about and drank his thin naked carcinomatous London coffee as they milled and mixed paper lips over china lip all textures communicasement.

And Brasher came near again something in a suit and narrowly said encouraged by Charteris' absence of aggression, 'You also pedal a belief, my foreign friend? From France if my infirmation is correct.'

'Now I arrive here and fatal events spread forward along the trails. I am quoting, but we are nothing to each other and I have no word yet. I was a member in my own country of the party, but enough of that, I'm dazed here maybe not fully awake the afflict of that Arabian nightmoil.'

The heavy man now pressed against him against the banisters.

'Tell me nothing you parisher this is my perish get it I had a miraculous survival from the air crash we're going to hit great wheeling scabs of metropolis mouths teeth and you keep quiet. I'm the Sayer here.' As panic stammer as if he still fell.

'I'll be getting on if you object. Objectivity of speeches. I have no feelings and the day spurs me, or Burton if he still wants to come.'

Tremor by the side of the mouth speaking independently.

'Come on Phil,' says Burton and to Charteris, 'He's coming but he's just suspicious of you because he saw you in the crashing plane, an apparition. On him rides the word like.'

'Nonsense,' said Charteris. 'That countryside rumpling upwards your distorted vision it was Brasher that interweaves my thoughts! I get it now the plane diving down to, well. I'm going thanks. I want no part of this man's dream nor did I ever fly with him in any plane.'

As if this abdication soothed Brasher he came forward again and barred Charteris' way brushing aside Burton saying, 'On that plane among the vestal virgings southwards you usurped my sodding seat and as we came – '

'Driving, driving, I have not flown, now get that through your acid head – '

'I only spared the flashing plashing, and all those cute little bits of stuff – now look here my foreign friend, I have a right to my share of any bits of crumpet as suffer conversion to Proceed and you – '

'Let him go Phil, he only offered you a lift to Lough along with me so are you coming, and this lot and your harum can come on after.' Thus Burton and in a closed sentence for Charteris, 'He's an old mate of mine or was till religion got him – now he's worse to manage than the Escalation. Everyone's the solo instrument in this scene.'

So was it that with papered-on cheers from the walk-on parts they took the legend down the dirty creaking stairs and to the floor below the tiles returning and in the darkness waited for a moment unknowing within the shelter of the judas house before the inward-gazing judas-hole: and then went forth.

Precognition is a function of two forces he told himself and already wished that he might record it in case the thought drifted from him on the aerosolar light. Precognotion. Two forces: mind of course and also time: the barriers go down and somewhere a white-thighed woman waits for me –

These are not my images. Bombardment of others' images. Autobreasted succubae again from Disflocations.

Yet my image the white-thighed, although I have not seen them already familiar like milk inside venetian crystal all the better to suck you by. But my precognotions slipping.

It's not only that mind can leap aside from its tracks but that the tracks must be of certain property: so there are stages I have crossed to reach this point the first being the divination of time as a web without merely forward progress but all directions equally so that the essential I at any moment is like a spider sleeping at the centre of its web always capable of any turn and the white thorn thighs turning. Only that essential Gurdjieffian I aloof. And secondly the trip-taking soaked air of London tipping me off my traditional cranium so that I allow myself a multi-dimensional way.

Zbogom, what am I now if not more than man, mariner of my seven seizures.

More than pre-psychedelic man.

Me homo viator

She homo victorine

She haunts me as I hope to haunt her. Not so far north as Scotland.

In his treadmillrace he was on her thought scent moving along the web taking a first footfall consciously away from antique logic gaining gaining and losing also the attachment to things that keeps alive a thousand useless I's in a man's life seeing the primary fact the sexual assertion that she took wing whoever she was near to these two strange men.

Then he knew that he was the last trump of his former formal self to ascend from the dealings at Dover by the London lane and the other caught cards of his pack truly at discard trapped in old whists and wists.

He had a new purpose that was no more a mystery only now in this moment of revelation was the purpose yet unrevealed. Magical now he played the car scudding and leaping and bouncing from the surface of the road to the madland of the midlands. He wondered if voices cried his name or a paper face tore screaming down to living flesh.

Low hills whirled by like bonfires.

And while Charteris took his frail barque into strange seasoned seas, life on the textbook level continued in the back of the Banshee where Brasher uncomfortably crouched next to the group's equipment held forth to Burton once more of his traumatic trip when the wings failed the pilot's part of reason.

'I knew the flaming plane was going to crash before ever I got into it.' Brasher reliving the drama of his predictive urges all terror cotta at his wattles.

As his simple sentence speared a few facts on the material surface, they twisted under and swam to Charteris through the accumulating fathoms of his flooding newness, garbed in beauty and madness speckled.

Brasher's plane was one of the last to fly. It brought the members of the Stockholm Precognitive Congress back to Great Britain on flight S614 leaving Arlanda Airport from Runway 3 at 1145 hours local time or maybe it was later because the airport clock had taken to marking an imperceptible time of its own and your pilot was Captain Mats Hammarström who welcomes you a bored-looking man whose wooden face conceals a maelstrom of beauty caught from the falling aerosoused air.

Takeoff kindly fasten

And soon we're over the frosty snowy terrain astonishing

Suggestive contours showing through the ecological extract a Ben Nicholson low relief with public hair

Frosted lakes new formations tracks to abstracks spoor of industry neat containments of terrain scarred forests pattern appearing as we rise where no pattern was where no pattern was intended. Models too precise for truth marvellous

Clouds scraping ground. As clouds thicken sun lights them draws a screen over the world so on the fantastic stage-set a new world solid appears untrodden by man whiter-than-white more-than-arctic world of cloudbergs where nothing polar could survive miraculous

All this mindmoving while trim succulent young air-hostesses minister to the passengers pretending in their formal blue uniforms courtesy SAS that they know nothing of ersex. To nobody's deception. The masquerade keeps the serpent sleeping forms part of the formalised eroticism of pre-psyche-delic times that these nubile and gleaming maidens should minister to men above the cloud formations incredible

Old concepts of godliness harnessed to conceits of airline schedules

What price the crack-up Brasher

The maidens are antidotes to this bleak world of freedom and their secret confined spaces stand alone against the idiot acreage of sky tremendous

Their suggestive contours show through the uniformal abstracts low reliefs in high style delicious

Delicate unpruned lips offer small torque before a tailspin

Plane begins to descend perhaps Brasher flinches at the white land as it rushes up but no impact. Is plane or cloud intangible. So swallowed by these mountains and valleys on which nobody ever built erewhonderful

Great wheeling scab of metropolis below thirty thousand streetscars cutting through the primaeval concrete crust. Silver paternal Thames threading through it a curling crack of sky and your Captain Mats Hammarström takes it into his capital notion to land upon it

All Brasher had lumbered in his bare cranian retort were an old Cortina and a lorry with Glasgow numberplate. So much for precognition. Next second. Your Captain got. Tower Bridge. Slap. In. The. Owspenskian Eye.

'The plane sank in the flaming river like a stone and I was the only one who survived,' concluded Brasher.

Charteris nearly ran into a group of people he swerved they scattered and adrenalin generated cleared his brain.

'People all group,' he said. 'Changed living pattern.'

'Aye, well, it's the bombs,' said Banjo Burton. 'They're regrouping, lost all loot. Ideas of solitude and togetherness have changed. They listen to a new sound semi-entirely.'

'I was lucky to get away. I nearly drowned,' Brasher insisted.

'It's a new world,' said Charteris. 'I can begin to hear it like an earquake.'

'The group will be glad to see me back,' said Burton. 'The Escalation.'

'My exploration of it,' said Charteris with the vehicle vibrant.

'Loughborough will welcome me,' said Brasher. 'And my wife of course.'

Charteris was laughing with a random note to mesh into the engine noise. The silver thread of road his narrow sea and he Sir Francis? Then where these Englishmen went might well prove his cape of good hope.

'This infrasound really breaks people up,' said Burton.

'Robbins is no more than a feeble pseudo-saint,' said Brasher. 'I must train up a new disciple, find someone to master the illogic of the times or generally clamp a baffle onto the flux.'

'Train me,' said Charteris.

The road ran north and north and always on never homesick its own experience. They saw towns and houses and sometimes people in groups but more often trees heavy with a new black wooden winter growth and everything stretched very thin over the great drum of being. Juiced the car caperilled frowards northwoods. And the three men sat in the car, close together, also apart, with their wits about them knowing very little indeed of all the things of which they were entirely aware. Functioning. Of a function. Existing in more ways than they could possibly learn to take advantage of.

Fragment of a Much Longer Poem

Oh one day I shall walk ahead
Up certain sunken steps into a hall
Patterned with tiles in black and red
And recognise the colour and the place
As well as if I once walked back
In time up certain sunken steps
And came into a hall with black
And red tiles in a certain coded
Pattern that makes me think I tread
Up sunken steps into a hallway and
Confront a tiled floor patterned red
And black which makes me think I stand

Circadian Rhythm

I've got circadian rhythm
You've got circadian rhythm
We've got circadian rhythm –
   So the town-clock's stopped for good

In the night-time I see daylight
And my white nights outshine daytime –
It beats the living daylight
Out of one-time lifetime

Spill my living daylights down my shirt-front
Chase my living nightmares round my shirt-tail
All my trite cares
They're just rag and bob-tail

So I've got circadian rhythm
You've got circadian rhythm
We've got circadian rhythm –
   So we ain't going home no more

THE DEAD SEA SOUND

The First and Future Paradise

We all know it –
There was primordial epoch
In which everything was decided
An exemplar for future ages.

Let's say it again –
You glimpse it sometimes behind bedroom
Curtains – a paradise and then
Catastrophe! They constitute the present.
Meaning what we do now is an end trajectory
Trajectory.
When I love you love
There's nothing personal in it.

The decisive deed took place before us
Essential preceeding actual.
We must confront mythic ancestors
Unless we wish for ever
To be driven by our whirlwinds
To live in their old nostalgias.

Paradise is lingering legend in our day
The world's smiles are few and wintry.
And the mountains no longer shore the sky.
But one may be a mountain even now –
It's not too late! – if you pursue your self
If you can make cosmic journeys
Be a shaman not a sham man.

Dangers lie in the self, serpents
Lurk but there are new animals
And auxiliaries and tongues
To help psychopomps and singers
(Listen to birds and the throat of the cockatoo!)

Friendship with the animals who are
Beyond broken time, and schizophrenics:

Bliss of other bodies: the paradisiac
Journeys beyond life and
Death: pushing of utterance into
Mystery of myth: these are the four known ways

To the seat of the Free | Death is the sin
The Free who live in the Tree | And on the many motor-roads
The Cosmic Tree | Until we attain incombustibility
Above the Sea | We fly in its qualifying fact
Of Being | Man the driver close
 | To the ultimate tick
We all know it | And abolition of that curtain time
All we have to do is | Which killed
Wake and know it. | The primordial epoch.

Fall About Laughing

When we tell them that we're in love
Men'll fall about laughing
When the lion gets around to lying down with the dove
Men'll fall about laughing

When they try to work the machines
Men'll fall about laughing
Ride a bike or open a can of sardines
Men'll fall about laughing

What happened to the old straight line
Is no affair of yours or mine
Or the guys who run the place
It's such an awful disaster
When the mind's not the master
You can't even keep a straight face

When we say that the wild days are back
Men'll fall about laughing
When they find out that we're sharing a sack
Men'll fall about laughing
Men'll fall about laughing

THE DEAD SEA SOUND

```
                      L
                   BLISS
                      F
                      E
                   ANGEL
                   U   I O
                   T   V U
                   O   E G
                   BIRTH
                   R       B
                   E       O
                   A   AFTER O
                   S       R O
                   T       O U
       ANTIFLOWERED        G
       N    I    DEATH
       VIGIL    V    A
       I    T    E    T
       LOUGHBOROUGH
```

Love's Nocturnal Entry into Bombed Coventry

```
                        C
     L  M            CASH
    LOSE             CHARTERS                    C
  COVENTRY           REVEAL  H                    L
 TUNER  R            CAPERIL A                    U
 AND  BYE            NOR NORD                     O
   TO   A            I  N    E                    U
    NIGHT            ASSUAGES        SILENCED
```

Topography of an Unrealised Affair

```
        C
H E L L O
E     O   O
A     V   L
S T R E S S
```

An Anagrammatical Small Square
Palinaromic Vision

War was:
Sin ran:
S saw a rani
In a raw ass.
W A R
A   A
S I N

```
    DACIDAC
   DACIDACID
   ACIDACIDA
  ACID       ACI
        HEAD
   CI      ID      DA
ID        DA        AC
  ACIDACIDAC
   IDACIDAC
   DACIDACI
    CIDACI
    DACI
    ACID
```

A I I I I I I I I
I I I I I I I I I I   I
I I I I I I I I I I I I
I I I I I I I I I I I I
I I I I I I I I I I I I
I I I I I I c I I I I I I
I I I I I I I I I I I I
I I I I I I I I I I I I
I I I I I I I I I I I
I   I I I I I I I I
I I I I I I I I
I I I I I I I I D

MULTI-VALUE MOTORWAY

SHE too was obsessed with pelting images. Phil Brasher, her husband, was growing more and more violent with Charteris, as if he knew the power was passing from him to the foreigner. Charteris had the certainty Phil lacked, the *gestalt*. Certainty, youth, handsome. He was himself. Also, perhaps, a saint. Also other people. But clearly a bit hipped, a heppo. Two weeks here, and he had spoken and the drugged Loughborough crowds had listened to him in a way they never did to her husband. She could not understand his message, but then she had not been sprayed. She understood his power.

The pelting images caught him sometimes naked.

Nerves on edge. Army Burton, played lead guitar, passed through her mind, saying, 'We are going to have a crusade.' Lamp posts flickered by, long trees, a prison gate, furry organs. She could not listen to the two men. As they walked over the withdrawn meaning of the wet and broken pavement, the hurtling traffic almost tore at their elbows. That other vision, too, held her near screaming pitch; she kept hearing the squeal of lorry wheels as it crashed into her husband's body, could see it so clear she knew by its nameboards it was travelling from Glasgow down to Naples. Over and over again it hit him and he fell backwards, disintegrating, quite washing away his discussion, savage discussion of multi-value logic, with Charteris. Also, she was troubled because she thought she saw a dog scuttle by wearing a red and black tie. Bombardment of images. They stood in a web of alternatives.

Phil Brasher said, 'I ought to kill Charteris.' Charteris was eating up his possible future at an enormous pace. Brasher saw himself spent, like that little rat Robbins, who had stood as saint and had not been elected. This new man, whom he had at first welcomed as a disciple, was as powerful as the rising sun, blanking Brasher's mind. He no longer got the good images from the future. Sliced bread cold oven. It was dead, there was a dead area, all he saw was that damned Christmas cactus which he loathed for its meaninglessness, like flowers on a grave. So he generated hate and said powerfully and confusedly to Charteris, 'I ought to kill Charteris.'

'Wait, first wait,' said Colin Charteris, in his own English, brain cold and acid. 'Think of Ouspenski's personality photographs. There's a high gloss. You have many alternatives. We are all rich in alternatives.' He had been saying that all afternoon, during this confused walk, as he knew. Ahead a big blind wall. The damp smudged crowded city, matured to the brown nearest black, gave off this rich aura of possibilities, which Brasher clearly was not getting. Charteris had glimpsed the world-plan, the tides of the future, carried with them sailor-fashion, was not so much superior to as remote from the dogged Brasher and Brasher's pale-thighed wife, Angelina, flocking on a parallel tide-race. Many alternatives; that was what he would say when next he addressed the crowds. Power was growing in him; he stood back modest and amazed to see it and recognise its sanctity like his father had. Brasher grabbed his wet coat and waved a fist in his face, an empty violent man saying 'I ought to kill you!' Traffic roared by them, vehicles driven by drivers seeing visions, on something called Inner Relief Road.

The irrelevant fist in his face; teeth in close detail; in his head, the next oration. You people – you midland people are special, chosen. I have come from the south of Italy from the Balkans to tell you so. The roads are built, we die on them and live by them, neural paths made actual. The Midlands of England is a special region; you must rise and lead Europe. Start a new probability. Less blankly put than that, but the ripeness of the moment would provide the right words, and there would be a song, Charteris we cry! He could hear it although it lay still coiled in an inner ear. Not lead but deliver Europe. Europe is laid low by the psychedelic bombs; even neutral France cannot help, because France clings to old nationalist values. I was an empty man, a materialist, failed Communist, waiting for this time. You have the alternatives now to wake yourselves and kill the old serpent.

You can think in new multi-value logics, because that is the pattern of your environment. The fist swung at him. The entire sluggish motion of man aiming it. Angeline's face was taking in the future, traffic-framed, dark of hair, immanent, luminous, freight-ful. It seemed to me I was travelling aimlessly until I got here stone cold from hotter beds too young father I called you from that flooded damned bank.

'I was just passing through on my way to Scotland, belting up the motorway in expedition. But I stopped here because of premonitions shy as goldfish thought. Think in fuzzy sets. There is no either-or black-white dichotomy any more. Only a spectrum of partiallys. Live by this, as I do – you will win. We have to think new. Find more directions make them. It's easy in this partially country.'

But Brasher was hitting him. World of movement lymphatic bursting. He looked at the fist, saw all its highways powerlines and tensions as Brasher had never seen it, fist less human than many natural features of the man-formed landscape in this wonderful traffic-tormented area. A fist struck him on the jaw. Colliding systems shock lost all loot.

Even in this extreme situation, Charteris thought, multi-value logic is the Way. I am choosing something between being hit and not being hit; I am not being hit very much.

He heard Angeline screaming to her husband to stop. She seemed not to have been affected by the PCA Bombs, carrying her own neutrality through the brief nothing hours of the Acid Head War. But it was difficult to tell; bells rang even when classrooms looked empty or birds startled from cover. Charteris had a theory that women were less affected than men. Stridulations of low tone. He would be glad to measure Angeline's rhythm but disliked her screaming now. Bombardment of images, linked to her scream – theory of recurrence? – especially toads and the new animal in the dead trees at home.

There was a way to stop her screaming without committing oneself to asking her to cease. Charteris clutched at Brasher's ancient blue coat, just as the older wattled man was about to land another blow. The great wheeling scab of metropolis. Behind Brasher, on the other side of Inner Relief, lay an old building made of the drab ginger stone of Leicestershire, to which a modern glass-and-steel porch had been tacked. A woman was watering a potted plant in the porch. All was distinct to Charteris while he pulled Brasher forward and then heaved him backward into Inner Relief little watering can of copper she had.

The lorry coming from the north swerved out to avoid. The old Cortina blazing along towards it spun across the narrow verge, swept away lady's glass-and-steel porch, copper can gone like that, and was itself hit by a post office van which had swerved to avoid the lorry. The lorry still bucking across the road hit

74

another oncoming car which could not stop in time. The world's noise on granite. Another vehicle its brakes squealing ran into the wall within feet of where Charteris and Angeline stood, and crumpled to a prearranged device too quickly, cicatrices chirping open. A series of photographs, potentialities multiplying or cancelling, machines as bulls herded.

'So many alternatives,' Charteris said wonderingly. He was interested to see that Brasher had disappeared, bits of him distributed somewhere among the wreckage. He remembered the multiple crash on the autostrada near Milano. Or was it a true memory? Was the Milano crash merely a phantasm of a mind already on the swerge of delision or some kind of dream-play-back awry both the crashes the same crash or another his own predestination already in the furniture maybe wrong delivery wrong addrents from the dreamvelope where that stamping grind unsorted the commutations of the night's post orifices or who knew who was in serge of what when on.

At least the illusion was strong on particularity with the photograves unblurred. If it happened or not or would or did it on this internal recurrence was a jolt, sparky as all algebra, and he saw a tremendous rightness in the blossom of the implact and shapes of wreckage; it was like a marvellous – he said it to the girl, 'It is like a marvellous complex work of sculpture, where to the rigorous manformed shapes is added chance. Wider theory of numbers aids decimation. The art of the for-tuitous.'

She was green and drab, swaying on her heels. He tried looking closely at the aesthetic effect of this colour-change, and recalled from somewhere in his being a sense of pity like a serpentstir. She was hurt, shocked, although he saw a better future for her. He must perform a definite action of some sort: remove her from the scene and the blood-metal steaming.

She went unprotestingly with him.

'I think Charteris is a saint. He has spoken with great success in Rugby and Leicester,' Army Burton said.

'Wide to whatever comes along,' Banjo Burton said. 'Full of loot.'

'He has spoken with great success in Rugby and Leicester,' Robbins said, thinking it over. Robbins was a faded nineteen, the field of his hair unharvested; he was the eterminal art student; his psychedelic-disposed personality had disintegrated under the efflict of being surrandied by acid heads, although

75

not personally caught by the chemicals of Arab design.

They sat in an old room dark bodies curtains drawn tight and light a blur on the papered walls.

Outside in the Loughborough streets night and day kept to the dialogue. Small dogs ran between stone seams.

Army used his uniform as barracks. Banjo had been a third-yearer, had turned agent, ran the pop group, the Escalation, operated various happenings; he had run Robbins as a saint with some reward, until Robbins had deflated one morning into the role of disciple cold cracked lips on the blue doorstep. They all lived with a couple of moronic girls in old housing in the middle of tumbletown, overlooking the square high moronic rear of F. W. Woolworth's. All round the town waited new buildings designed to cope with hypothetical fast-growing population; but conflicting eddies of society had sent people hearing echoes in each other's rooms gravitating towards the old core. The straggle of universities and technical colleges stood in marshy fields. It was February.

'Well, he spoke with great success in Leicester,' Burton said, 'made them believe in a sex-style.'

'Ay, he did that. Mind you, I was a success in Leicester,' Robbins said, 'Apathy's like bricks there to build yellow chapels on some fields you care to name.'

'Don't run down Leicester,' Greta squeaked. 'I came from there. At least, my uncle did the one with the dancing cat I told you about ate the goldfish. Did I ever tell you my Dad was a Risparian? An Early Risparian. My Mum would not join. She only likes things.'

Burton dismissed all reminiscence with a sweep of his hand. He lit a reefer and said, 'We are going to have a crusade, burn trails, make a sparky party of our Charter-flightboy, really roll. Play the noise-game.'

'Who's gone off Brasher then?'

'Stuff Brasher. You've seen our new boy. He's a song!'

He could see it. Charteris was good. He was foreign and people were ready for foreigners and exotic toted even in a tuning eyeball. Foreigners were exotic. Charteris had this whole thing he believed in some sort of intellectual thing fitted the machine-scene. People could take it in or leave it and still grab the noise of his song. Charteris was writing a book too. You couldn't tell he was real or phoney it didn't matter so he couldn't switch off.

The followers were already there. Brasher's following.

Charteris beat Brasher at any meeting. You'd have to watch for Brasher. Big munch little throat. The man thought he was Jesus Christ. Even if he is Jesus Christ, my money's on Charteris. He's got loot! Colin Charteris. Funny name for a Jugoslav!

'Let's make a few notes about it,' he said. 'Robbins, and you, Gloria.'

'Greta.'

'Greta, then. A sense of place is what people want – something to touch among all the metaphysics, big old jumbos in the long thin grass. Charteris actually likes this bloody dump its dogshitted lanes. I suppose it's new to him. We'll take him round the houses, tape-record him. Where's the tape-recorder?' He was troubled by images and a presentiment that they would soon be driving down the autobahns of Europe. He saw a sign to Frankfurt, rubbed hands over his Yorkskull pudding eyes.

'I'll show him my paintings,' Robbins said. 'And he'll be interested about the birds all close local stuff.'

'What about the birds in all areas?'

'A sense of place, you said with the jumbos in the long grapes. What they do, you know, like the city, the birds like the city.' They liked the city, the birds. Took its bricks for leaves. He had watched, down where the tractor was bogged down in the muddy plough, stood himself bogged all day in content, the landscape the brown nearest black under the thick light. It was the sparrows and starlings, mainly. There were more of them in the towns. They nested behind neon signs, over the fish and chip shops, near the chinese restaurants, by the big stores, furniture stores, redemption shops, filling stations, for warmth, and produced more babies than the ones in the country, learning a new language. More broods annually. The seagulls covered the ploughed field. They were always inland. You could watch them, and the lines of the grid pencilled on the sky. They were evolving, giving up the sea. Woodgulls. The Greater Mole Gull. Or maybe the sea had shrivelled up and gone. Shrunk like melted plastic. God knows what the birds are up to, acid-headed like everything else. Doing the pattern-thing themselves. 'City suits the birds. It has built-in pattern.'

'What are you talking about?' She loved him really, but you had to laugh. His dandy lion-yellow hair.

'We aren't the only ones with a population expulsion. The birds too. Remember that series of painting I did of birds, Banjo? Flowers and weeds, too. Like a tide. Pollination expulsion.'

77

'Just keep it practical, sonny. Stick to buildings, eh?' Maybe he could unzip his skull, remove the top like a wig, and pull that distracting Frankfurt sign dripping out of his brain batter.

'The Pollination Explosion,' Charteris said. 'That's a good title. I write a poem called The Pollination Explosion, about the deep pandemic of nature. The idea just came into my head. And the time will come when you try to betray me to leave me desolate between four walls.'

She said nothing.

'There could be trees in our future if the brain holds up.'

Angeline was walking resting on his arm, saying nothing. He had forgotten where he had left the Banshee; it was pleasure padding through the wet, looking for it. They strolled through a new arcade, where one or two shops functioned on dwindling supplies. A chemist's; Get Your Inner Relief Here; a handbill for the Escalation, Sensational and Smelly. Empty shells where the spec builder had not managed to sell shop frontage, all crude concrete, marked by the fossil-imprints of wooden battens. City pattern older than wood stamped by brainprint. Messages in pencil or blue crayon. YOUNG IVE SNOGED HERE, BILL HOPKINS ONLY LOVES ME, LOVES LOST ITS LOOT, CUNT SCRUBBER. What was a cunt scrubber? Something like a loofah, or a person? Good opening for bright lad!

The Banshee waited in the rain by a portly group of dustbins exchanging hypergeometic forms, moduli of the cosmic run-down. It was not locked. They turned out an old man sheltering inside it.

'You killed my husband,' Angeline said, as the engine started. The filling station up the road gave you quintuple Green Shields on four gallons. Nothing ever changed except thought. Thought was new every generation, or they thought it was new, and she heard old wild music playing.

'The future lies fainting in the arms of the present.'

'Why don't you listen to what I'm saying Colin? You're not bloody mad, are you? You killed my husband and I want to know what you're going to do about it!'

'Take you home.' They were moving now. Although his face ached, he felt in a rare joking mood as after wine in the deep home forests.

'I don't live out this direction.'

'Take you to my home. My place. Where I build a sort of project from. I've started making a new model for thought. You came once, didn't you, with Brasher in some untidy evening? It's not town, not country. You can't say which it is; that's why I like it – it stands for all I stand for. In the mundane world and France, things like art and science have just spewed forth and swallowed up everything else. There's nothing now left that's non-art or non-science. A lot of things just gone. My place is neither urban nor non-urban. Fuzzy set, its own non categorisable catasgory. Look outwards, Angeline! Wonderful!' He gave a sort of half-laugh by a wall, his beard growing in its own silence.

'You Serbian bastard! There may have been a war, the country may be ruined, but you can't get away with murder! Justice doesn't just fuzz off! You'll die, they'll shoot you!' There was no conviction in her voice; his sainthood was drowning her old self, or whatever he had behind eyes.

'No, I shall live, be justice. I haven't fulfilled any purpose yet, a sailor but the ocean's still ahead, hey?' The car was easing on to the Inner Relief. Behind them, ambulances and a fire engine and police cars and breakdown vans were nuzzling the debris. 'I've seen reality, Angeline – Kragujevac, Metz, Frankfurt – it's lying everywhere. And I myself have materialised into the inorganic, and so am indestructible, auto-destruct!'

The words stoned him. Since he had reached England, the psychedelic effect had gained on him daily in gusts. Cities had speaking patterns, worlds, rooms. He had ceased to think what he was saying; the result was he surprised himself, and this elation fed back into the system. Every thought multiplied into a thousand. Words, roads, all fossil tracks of thinking. He pursued them into the amonight, struggling with them as they propagated in their deep burrows away from the surface. Another poem: On the Spontaneous Generation of Ideas During Conversation. Spontagions Ideal Convertagion. The Conflation of Spongation in Idations. Agenbite of Auschwitz.

'Inwit, the dimlight of my deep Loughburrows. That's how I materialised, love! Loughborough is me, my brain, here – we are in my brain, it's all me. The nomad's open to the city. I am projecting Loughborough. All its thoughts are mine, in a culmination going.' It was true. Other people, he hardly saw them, caught in bursts, crossflare, at last shared their bombardment of images.

'Don't be daft – it's raining again! Don't go daft. Talk proper.' But she sounded frightened.

They swerved past factories, long drab walls, filling stations, long ochre terraces, yards, many genera of concrete.

Ratty little shops now giving up; no more News of the World, Guinness. Grey stucco urinal. Coal yard, Esso Blue. A railway bridge, iron painted yellow, advertising Ind Coope, sinister words to him. More rows of terrace houses, dentured, time-devoured. A complete sentence yet to be written into his book; he saw his hand writing the truth is in static instants. Then the semis, suburbanal. More bridges, side roads, iron railings, the Inner Relief yielding to fast dual-carriage, out onto the motorway, endless roads crossing over it on primitive pillars. Railways, some closed, canals, some sedge-filled, a poor sod pushing a sack of potatoes on the handlebars of his bike across a drowning allotment, footpaths, cycle-paths, catwalks, nettlebeds, waste dumps, scrap-pits, shortcuts, fences.

Geology. Strata of different man-times. Tempology. Each decade of the past still preserved in some gaunt monument. Even the motorway itself yielding clues to the enormous epochs of pre-psychedelic time: bridges cruder, more massive in earliest epoch, becoming almost graceful later, less sick-orange; later still, metal; different abutment planes, different patterns of drainage in the under-flyover bank, bifurcated like enormous Jurassic fern-trees Here we distinguish by the characteristics of this medium-weight aggregate the Wimpey stratum; while, a little further along, in the shade of these cantilevers, we distinguish the beginning of the McAlpine seam. The layout of that service area, of course, belongs characteristically to the Taylor Woodrow Inter-Glacial. Further was an early electric generating station with a mock-turkish dome, desolate in a field. All art, assuaging. Pylons, endlessly, too ornate for the cumbersome land, assuaging. Multiplacation.

The skies were lumped and flaky with cloud, Loughborough skies. Squirting rain and diffused lighting. No green yet in the hedges. The brown nearest black. Beautiful. . . .

'We will abolish that word beautiful. It carries implications of ugliness in an Aristotelian way. There are only gradations in between the two. They pair. No ugliness.'

'There's the word "ugliness", so there must be something to attach it to, mustn't there? And don't drive so fast.'

'Stop quoting Lewis Carroll at me!'

'I'm not!'

'You should have allowed me to give you the benefit of the doubt.'

'Well, steer properly! You lost your loot or something?'

He flicked away back onto his own side of the motorway,

narrowly missing an op-art Jag, its driver screaming over the wheel. I also drive by fuzzy sets, he thought admiringly. The two cars had actually brushed; between hitting and not-hitting were many degrees. He had sampled most of them. The lookout to keep was a soft watch. It was impossible to be safe – watering your potted plant, which was really doing well, impossible. A Christmas cactus it could be, you were so proud of it. The Cortina, Consortina, buckling against – you'd not even seen it, back turned, blazing in a moment's sun, Christ, just sweeping the poor woman and her pathetic little porch right away in limbo!

'Never live on Inner Relief.' Suddenly light-hearted and joking.

'Stop getting at me! You're really rather cruel, aren't you?'

'*Jebem te sunce!* Look, Natrina – I mean, Angelina, I love you, I dream you.'

'You don't know the meaning of the word!'

'So? I'm not omniscient yet. I don't have to know what it is to do it, do I? I'm just beginning, the thing's just beginning in me, all to come. I'll speak, preach! Burton's group, Escalation Limited, I'll write songs for them. How about Truth Lies in Static Instants? Or When We're Intimate in the Taylor Woodrow Inter-Glacial. No, no – Accidents and Aerodynamics Accrete into Art. No, no! How about . . . Ha, I Do My Personal Thinking In Pounds Sterling? Or Ouspenski Has It All Ways Always. Or The Victim and the Wreckage Are The Same. The Lights Across the River. Good job I threw away my NUNSACS papers. Too busy. I'll fill the world till my head bursts. Look – *zbogom*, missed him! What a driver! Maybe get him tomorrow! Must forget these trivialities, which others can perform. Kuwait was the beginning! I'm just so creative at present, look, Angelina – '

'It's Angeline. Rhymes with "mean".' She couldn't tell if he was joking.

'My lean angel mean, Meangeline. I'm so creative, feel my temple! And I sense a gift in you too as you struggle out of old modes towards creams of denser feeling. What's it going to be we got to find together eh?'

'I've got no gifts. My ma told me that.'

'Anyhow, see that church of green stone? We're there. Almost. Partially there. Fuzzy there. Kundalinically there. *Etwas there.*'

But this *etwas* country was neither inhabitable nor uninhabitable. It functioned chiefly as an area to move through a dimensional passage, scored, scarred, chopped by all the means the centuries had uncovered of annihilating the distance between Loughborough and the rest of Europe, rivers, roads, rails, canals, dykes, lanes, bridges, viaducts. The Banshee bumped over a hump-backed bridge, nosed along by a municipal dump, and rolled to a stop in front of a solitary skinned house.

Squadrons of diabolical lead birds sprang up to the roof of the house, from instant immobility to instant immobility on passage from wood to city. Slates were broken by wind and birds. Sheer blindness had built this worthy middle-class house here, very proper and some expense spared in the days before currency had gone decimal. It stood in its English exterior pluming as if in scaffolding. A land dispute perhaps. No one knew. The proud owner had gone, leaving the local council easy winners, to celebrate their triumph in a grand flurry of rubbish which now lapped into the front garden, eroded, rotting intricate under the creative powers of decay. Cans scuttled down paths. Caught by the fervour of it, the Snowcem had fallen off the brick, leaving a leprous dwelling, blowing like dandruff round the porch. And she looked up from the lovely cactus – he had admired it so much, bless him, a good husband – just in time to see the lorry sliding across the road towards her. And then, from behind, the glittering missile of the northbound car. . . .

Charteris leant against the porch, covering his eyes to escape the repetitive image. It had been, was ever coming in the repetitive web.

'It was a conflux of alternatives in which I was trapped, all anti-flowered. I so love the British – you don't understand! I wouldn't hurt anyone. . . . I'm going to show the world how –'

'You won't bring him back by being sorry.'

'Her, the woman with the cactus! Her! Her! Who was she?'

The Escalation had taken over an old Army Recruiting Office in Ashby Road. These surroundings with their old english wood and gymnast smells had influenced two of their most successful songs, 'The Intermittent Tattooed Tattered Prepuce' and 'A Platoon of One' in the Dead Sea Sound days. There were four of them, four shabby young men, sensational and smelly, called, for professional purposes, Phil, Bill, Ruby and Featherstone-Haugh; also Barnaby, who worked the background tapes to make supplementary noise or chorus.

They were doing the new one. They could hear the ambulances still squealing in the distance, and improvised a number embodying the noise called 'Lost My Ring In the Ring Road'. Bill thought they should play it below, or preferably on top of, 'Sanctions, Sanctions'; they decided to keep it for a flip side if they ever made the old circuit of recording.

They began to rehearse the new one.

> Bank all my money in slot machines
> These new coins are strictly for spending
> Old sun goes on its rounds
> Now since we got the metric currency
> I do my personal thinking in pounds
> We haven't associated
> Since twelve and a half new pence of money
> Took over from the half-a-crowns
> Life's supposed to be negotiable, ain't it?
> But I do my personal thinking in pounds

Greta and Flo came in, with Robbins and the Burtons following. Army Burton had lost his lovely new tie, first one he ever had. He was arguing that Charteris should speak publicly as soon as possible – with the group at Nottingham on the following night; Robbins was arguing that there had been a girl at the art college called Hyperthermia; Banjo was telling about London. Greta was saying she was going home.

'Great, boys, great, break it up! You've escalated, like I mean you are now a choir, not just a group, okay, this secular stint? At Nottingham tomorrow night, you're a choir, see? So we hitch our fortunes to Colin Charteris, tomorrow's saint, the author of Fuzzy Sets.'

'Oh, he's on about sex again! I'm going home,' said Greta, and went. Her mum lived only just down the road in a little house on the Inner Relief; Greta didn't live there any more, but they had not quarrelled, just drifted gently apart on the life-death stream. Greta liked squalor and the arabesque decline. What she could not take were the rows of indoor plants with which her mother hedged herself.

> Sister, they've decimalised us
> All of the values are new
> Bet you the five-penny piece in my hip
> When I was a child on that old £. s. d.
> There was a picture of a pretty sailing ship
> Sailing on every ha-penny . . .

They were used to Burton's madness. He had got them the crowds, the high voices from the front aisles. They needed the faces there, the noise, the interference, the phalanx of decibels the audience threw back at them in self-defence, needed it all, and the stink and empathy, to give right out and tear a larynx. In the last verse, The goods you buy with this new coinage, they could have talkchant as counterpoint instead of instrument between lines. May be even Saint Charteris would go for that. Saint Loughborough? Some people said he was a Communist, but he could be all the things they needed, even become fodder for song. They looked back too much. The future and its thoughts they needed. Lips close, New pose, Truth lies in static instants. Well, it had possibilities.

With Charteris tranced, labouring at his masterwork, cutting, superimposing, annotating, Angeline wandered about the house. A tramp lived upstairs in the back room, old yellow mouth like an eye-socket. She avoided him. The front room upstairs was empty because it got so damp where the rain poured in. She stood on the bare frothy boards staring out at the sullen dead sea with shores of city rubbish, poor quality rubbish, becalming flocks of gulls, beaks as cynical as the smiles of reptiles from which they had originated. Land so wet, so dark, so brown nearest black, late February and the trains all running half-cocked with the poor acid head drivers forgetting their duties, chasing their private cobwebs, hot for deeper stations. Nobody was human any more. She'd be better advised to take LSD and join the psychotomimjority, forget the old guilt theories, rub of old mother-sores. Charteris gave her hope, seemed he thought the situation was good and could be improved within fuzzy limits, pull all things from wreckage back.

Wait till you read 'Man the Driver', he told Phil Brasher. You will see. No more conflicts once everyone recognises that he always was a hunter, all time. The modern hunter has become a driver. His main efforts do not go towards improving his lot, but complicating ways of travel. It's all in the big pattern of time-space-mind. In his head is a multi-value motorway. Now, after the Kuwait *coup*, he is free to drive down any lane he wants, any way. No external frictions or restrictions any more. Thus spake Charteris. She had felt compelled to listen, thus possibly accomplishing Phil's death. There had been a rival group setting up in the cellars of Loughborough, the Mellow Bellows. They had taken one title out of thin air: There's a fairy with an Areopagitica, No external frictions or restrictions, We don't need law or war or comfort or that bourgeois stuff, No external frictions or restrictions. Of course, they did say he was a communist or something. What we needed was freedom to drive along our life lines where we would, give or take the odd Brasher. More irrational fragments of the future hit her: through him, of course; a weeping girl, a – a baked bean standing like a minute scruple in the way of self-fulfilment.

She wanted him to have her, if she could square her conscience about Phil. He was okay, but – yes, a change was so so welcome. Sex, too, yes, if he didn't want too much of it. The waste always lay outside the window. He was clean-looking; good opening for bright lad – where had she overheard that? Well, it was self-defence. Wow that smash-up, still she trembled.

The gulls rose up from the mounds of rotting refuse, forming lines in the air. A dog down there, running, free, so free, companion of man, sly among the mountains. Perhaps now man was going to be as free as his companion. Trees in their future? Green? Bare?

Tears trickling down her cheek. Tears falling new from her sad speckled dreams. Even if it proved a better way of life, good things would be lost. Always the loss, the seepage. My sepia years. Sorry, Phil, I loved you all I could for six of them, but I'm going to bed with him if he wants me. The big gymnastic sergeant marching marching. It's you I'm going to betray, not him, if I can make it, because he really has something, don't know what. I don't know if he's what he says, but he is a sort of saint. And you did hit him first. You hit him first. You were always free with your fists. You were that.

She went downstairs. Either that running dog wore a tie or she was going acid head like the others.

'It's a bastard work, a mongrel,' he said. He was eating something out of a can; that was now his way, no meals, only snacks, the fuzzy feeder. Kind of impersonal.

'I'm a mongrel, aren't I? Some Gurdjieff, more Ouspenski, time-obsessed passages from here and there, no zen or that – no Englishmen, but it's going to spread from England out, we'll all take it, unite all Europe at last. A gospel. Falling like PCA. America's ready, too. The readiest place, always.'

'If you're happy.' She touched him. He had dropped a baked bean on to the masterwork. It almost covered a word that might be 'self-fulfilment'.

'See those things crawling in the bare trees out there? Elms,

85

are they? Birds as big as turkeys crawling in the trees, and toads, and that new animal. I often see it. There is an intention moving in them, as there is in us. They seem to keep their distance.'

'Darling, you're in ruins, your mind, you should rest!'

'Yes. Happiness is a yesterday phase. Say, think, "tension-release", maintain a sliding scale, and so you do away with sorrow. Get me, you just have a relief from tension, and that's all you need. Nothing so time-consuming as happiness. Nothing personal. If you have sorrow, you are forced to seek its opposite, and vice versa, so you should try to abolish both. Wake, don't live automatic, I'll get it clear. Time . . . I must speak to people, address them. You have some gift I need. Come round with me, Angelina? Take me on, share my sack.'

She put her arms about him. The big gymnastic sergeant. There was some stale bread on the table, crumbs among the books he was breaking up and crayoning. Activity all the time, her windows, wind over the turning mounds. 'When you love me, love, there'll be something personal in it?'

'It's all evolving, angel, stacked with loot.'

When the Escalation came along, the two of them were half-lying on the camp-bed, limbs entangled, not actually copulating.

Greta wept, supported by two of the group. Featherstone-Haugh touched a chord on his balalaika and sang, 'Her mother was killed by a sunlit Ford Cortina, and the road snapped shut.'

Ruby Dymond turned his cheeks into a poor grey.

'Man the Driver,' Chapter Three. Literature of the Future Affecting Feeling of the Future. Ouspenski's concept of mental photographs postulates many photographs of the personality taken at characteristic moments; viewed together, these photographs will form a record by which man sees himself to be different from his common conception of himself – and truer. So, they will suggest the route of life without themselves having motion. The truth is in static instants; it is arrived at through motion. Motion of auto-crash, copulation, kinetic self- awakenings of any kind. There are many alternatives. Fiction to be mental photographs, motion to be supplied purely by reader. Music as harpoon to sleeping entrails, down out the howls of smaller dogs. Action a blemish as already in existence. Truth thus like a pile of photos, self-cancelling for self-fulfilment, multi-valued. Indecision multi-incisive and non-automatic. Impurity of decision one of the drives towards such truth-piles; the Ouspenskian event of a multiple crash on a modern motorway an extreme example of such impurities.

Wish for truth involved here. Man and landscape interfuse, science presides. Machines predominate.

Charteris stood at the window listening to the noise of the group, looking out at the highly carved landscape. Hedges and trees had no hint of green, were cut from iron, their edges jagged, ungleaming with the brown nearest black, although the winds drove rain shining across the panorama. Middays reduced job-lots from Coventry. Vehicles scouring down the roads trailed spume. Roads like seas like fossilised thought, coproliths of ancestral loinage, father-frigger. The earlier nonsense about the terrors of the population explosion; one learned to live with it. But mistakes still being made. The unemployed were occupied, black midland figures of animated sacks, inplanting young trees along the grand synclines and barrows of the embankments and cuttings and underpasses, thereby destroying their geometry, mistakenly interfusing an abstract of nature back into the grand equation. Got to banish that dark pandemic nature. But the monstrous sky, squelching light out of its darkest corners, counteracted this regressive step towards out-dated reality moulds. The PCA bombs had squirted from the skies; it was their region. Science presided.

There was a picture of a pretty sailing ship
Sailing every ha'penny.

The goods you buy with this new coinage
Weren't made any place I heard of
They give out the meagerest sounds
But I don't hear a thing any longer
Since I do my personal thinking in pounds

I had a good family life and a loving girl
But I had to trade them in for pounds

The damned birds were coming back, too, booking their saplings, grotesques from the pre-psychedelic twilife, ready to squirt eggs into the first nests at the first opportunity. They moved in squadrons, heavy as lead, settled over the mounds of rubbish, picking out the gaudy Omo packets. They had something planned, they were motion without truth, fugitive, to be hated. He had heard them calling to each other in nervous excitement, 'Omo, Omo'. Down by the shores of the dead sea, down by the iron sunset, they were learning to read, a hostile

87

art. And the new animal was among them by the dead elms.

Angeline was comforting Greta, Ruby watching her every fingertip, Burton was turning the pages of 'Man the Driver', thinking of a black and red tie he had worn, his only tie. Words conveyed truth, he had to admit, but that damned tie had really sent him. He thought he had tied it round the neck of a black dog proceeding down Ashby Road. Spread the message.

'Greet, you didn't hear of a dog involved in this pile-up?'

'Leave her alone,' Angeline said. 'Let her cry it out. It's like a tide.'

'There's been a dislocation,' Burton said.

'He did it, you know,' Greta wept. 'You can't have secrets in this city any more. Well, it's more of an urban aggregation than a city, really, I suppose. He pushed the whole chain of events into being, piled up all them lorries, killed by mum and everything.'

'I know,' Angeline said. The heart always so laden, the gulls always so malignant.

In the old kitchen among gash-cans where a single brass tap poured a thin melody out of one note, Ruby had her alone at last clasping her thin wrists by each tapering tendon her face still with youth in its whole imprint.

'Don't start anything, Ruby, get back to play your piece with the boys.'

'You know how I feel about your continued days, how you always play my piece, and now I see you lay with Charteris.'

She pulled from him and he caught her again, a slight look of ox under his eyebrushes. 'I mind mine, you mind yours, you hip me Ruby though I know you mean well!'

'Look, the rumour is he killed Phil – '

Frantic, and a churning mound of rubbish at the sill, 'Ruby, if you are trying to make me – '

'I won't kid, I never liked Phil, you know that, but to go round with the guy who did it – '

She was as thin from her lethargy as stretched teeth could make her. 'He has something that's all I know, and hope I need among you scenemakers, I don't have to trust him. . . . '

In the next room they were calling and formationed birds dipped like sleet across her vision. 'Remember me? I was around before you met Brasher, I knew you when you were a little lanky girl I used to come and play with your brothers, gave you your first kiss – '

'It's looking back, Ruby, looking back,' despairing.

'I thought you loved me, you used to ride on my cycle.'

'It's past, Ruby.' She was afraid of her own tears the very nature of her grottoed self. Leaning back over the choked draining board, she saw the face of him move across her visage like a lantern burning impatience, mutter, turn under its hair-bush and leave her there with the one-note melody unlistened to but ever-piercing.

Creaming crowds in Nottingham to greet the Escalation, teenagers blurry in the streets, hardly whispering, the middle-aged, the old, the crippled and the halt, all those who had not starved, all those who had not died from falling into fires or ditches on roads, all those who had not wandered away after the aerosols drifted down, all those who had not fallen down dead laughing, all those who had not opened their spongy skulls with can-openers to let out the ghosts and the rats. All were hot for the Escalation under the seams of their grey clouts.

After two numbers, the boys, sensational and smelly, had the crowds throwing noise back at them. Burton stood up, announced Saint Charteris, asked if anyone had seen a stray dog wearing a red and black tie. The Escalation howled their new anthem.

> Obdolescent Loughborough
> With slumthing to live through
> Charteris we cry
> Is something to live by
> Try a multi-valued slant
> On the instant instant

He had scarcely thought out what he was going to say. The pattern was there, misty or clear. It seemed so apparent he felt it did not need uttering, except they should wake and know what they knew. The slav dreamers, Ouspenski and the rest, sent him travelling with his message through to his outpost of Europe. If the message had validity, it was shaped by journey and arrival. He couldn't always stand helpless across the river. In Metz, he had realised the world was a web of forces. Their minds, their special Midland minds had to become repositories of thinking also web-like, clear but indefinite, instant but infinite.

If they wanted exterior models, the space-time pattern of

communicationways with which their landscape was riddled functioned as a master plan, monster plan of mind-pattern. Al the incoherent repirations that filled their lives would then fall into place. The empty old nineteenth-century houses built by new classes which now stood rotting in ginger stone on hillsides, carriageways either approached or receded like levels of old lakes, they were not wasted; they functioned as landmarks. No more eggless waters. Nothing should be discarded; everything would re-orient, as the ginger stone mansions or the green stone churches were re-oriented by the changing landscape dynamic, and the crash-ups escalated to a love-in. He was lead of the New Thought. The Fourth World System, Man the Driver, would appear soon, all would wake.

So the words sprang up like bolted birds.

Greta stood and screamed, 'He killed Our Mum! Poor old girl with her flowers! He caused the multi-maxident on the Inner Relief. Kill him! Kill him!'

'Kill him!' also cried Ruby.

White-faced Angeline said from the platform for all to hear, 'And he killed my husband, Phil, you all knew him.' It was sin to her whether she spoke or not; she worked by old moralities, where someone was always betrayed.

Their troubled eyes all turned to his eyes, seeking meaning, like stars in the firment.

'I thought they were going to crucify you,' said Featherstone-Haugh after offering the Serb a glance through perspectives later to be of more transfixion over the desiccated lustrums of western worships, crowns of thorns, crosses of scorn, the love-kill. You couldn't tell the bits of wreckage from the bits of victims. He couldn't stop his heart beating.

'It's true! The lorry was sweeping along the great artery from Glasgow down to Naples, In Naples, they will also mourn. We are all one people now, Europeople, and although this massive region of yours is as special as the Adriatic Coast or the Dutch Lowlands, or the steppes of central Asia, the similarity is also in the differences. It's the impact, as you must feel. You know of my life, that I was Communist like my father, coming from Serbia in Jugoslavia, that I lived long in Italy, dreamed all my while of England and the wide cliffs of Dover. Now I arrive here after the dislocation and fatal events begin, spreading back along my trail. It's a sign. See how in this context even death is multi-valued, the black nearest brown. Brasher falling back into the traffic was a complex impulse-node from which

90

effects still multiplicate along all tension lines. We shall all follow that impulse to the last fracture and serial of recorded time. The Escalation and I are now setting out on a motor-crusade down through our Europe, the autobahns, the war, dislocation, to ultimate unity. All of you come too, a moving event to seize the static instant of truth! Come too! Wake! There are many alternatives!'

They were crying and cheering, discarding I's. It would take on truth, be a new legend, a new communication in the ceaseless dialogue, the ground complexes given younger significance. Even Angeline thought. Perhaps he will really give us something to live by, more than the old fun grind. It surely can't really matter, can it, whether there was a dog with a tie or not; the essential thing was that I saw it and stand by that. A phenomenon's only itself, eh? So it doesn't matter whether he is right or not; just stay in the Banshee with him. Pray the warmth's there, the loot.

You couldn't tell wreckage from victim in the fast-turning shade-shapes of obliquity.

He was talking again, the audience were cheering, the group were improvising a driving song about a Midland-minded girl at the wheel of a sunlit automobile. An ambiguity about whether they meant the steering or the driving wheel.

Plugging the night's orifices with solid sound.

The moonlight of a June night
Casts shadows of crashing airliners
Onto the orthostrada of gaunt erections
Moonlight moonlight
Filling empty patios

And the big gymnastic sergeant's marching marching
And the intermittent tattooed tattered prepuce
Does bayonet practice on a sweet civilian girl

Oh love's a crash a parade-ground bash
An auto-immune disorder from which issues
A pair of bodies destroying their own tissues

Left right left right left
In out in out on guard
Lovers of the world unite
You've nothing to lose but appetite
If winter comes can the following one
Be more than a year away

Could this be loot because I feel
The flying human parts and the bits of steel
In an auto-concussion are the modern way
The military way
Of committing love

And the big gymnastic sergeant's marching marching
And the intermittent tattooed tattered prepuce
Does bayonet practice on a syphilitic civilian girl

Oh love's a smash a uniform cash
Negotiable when the moving parts peeling
Can autocade feeling anti-flowered healing speedily stealing
And the big gymnastic leather-cheeked sergeant's marching
        marching marching

And the intermittent inter-continental tattered tattooed
    prepuce prepuce
Does bayonet practice on a civilised civilian sybaritic syphilitic
Bayonet practice on a civilised civilian sybaritic syphilitic
                  Civilised civilian sybaritic syphilitic
                  Civilised civilian sybaritic syphilitic
                                  Supergirl

Left right left right
Moonlight moonlight
Up the motorways of love

           Phil, Bill, Ruby and Featherstone-Haugh

SMALL DOGS HOWLING

When you sank on my knee in the buggy
You forked your loving tongue in my mouth
And you worked me and made me come

Though your hair didn't fit you properly
I still resemble the blur of your fingers
When the small dogs are howling

    Tray Blanche and Sweetheart on the hem
    Oh throw your acidhead at them

Lives deprived and broken
Bottles empty by dawn
While we were crotching together
Did you mind my shoes was torn

Some place like a magic garden
My friends all call me Rajah
And I'm a demon on the cello

Don't ask me what we're doing on the heath love
Because the estate has become divided
And we're one with the ones who won

This place well the car broke down
But the street lamps were your tall wild lilies
And I couldn't hear the small dogs howling

    Tray Blanche and Sweetheart on the hem
    Oh throw your acidhead at them

THE MELLOW BELLOW

DREAMING

Swept under sleep's terminator
We send out blindfold signals
To a listener in dim Andromeda
We send out our folded signals
To the listeners in all Andromedas
Hoping dreading response

Beyond the lighted alleyways
The multi-motorways of time
Yesterday's day regurgitates
Itself back through the limbic brain
Backwards rattling through orifices
Of ancient bugging systems

Alpha rhythms delta rhythms
Dark transmissions old as sandstone
Wild as pop
     Between communiques
Another sleep-form new-invented
Topiaries upwards outwards
       Through our
Dull planetary bodies other
Messages secreted in the pores
Are also played out backwards
On an unknown waveband

 These thin signals
Pipe from us in automated
Bursts
    To be picked up on stars
      White dwarfs
Monitored in nebulae
Identified
In other galaxies as
     'Dark
Bodies hitherto quite unsuspected'

And still between all human noises
Our figures with their own intent
Run daylight and silence backwards

When you target in to my
                        Perceptions
Am I reading you?
My fullness is a part
Of your thin signals
My visions
            Wreckage of your orbit

From 'The Threepenny Space Opera'

Another Dreaming Poem

My letters delay in their personal boxes
Uncertainty is on the whole my element
And the astrabahns bifurcate steeply

Low temperatures
Curtains drawn tight
A blur on the papered walls
And the night branches drooping
On the furred paths of grass

What you might call my pessimism
Is merely a long dedication
Of involved enquiry
Passionate and still deepening
Into the lost events of everybody's

Days those past and those to come
And those standing on end unsorted
In the night's post orifices

The great well of personal stuff
I don't know or wish to know
Floods me with messages

Is it myself
I walk with or happiness
Found in the low night street
Footsteps on the pavement
Echoing in more than one house

PATTERN MORE THAN CITY MIND

The city has built-in pattern
    city
    city   pattern
    city
         built-in pattern

Mind is more than city
    more than city
Mind   more
    more than
Mind   city

Roads run like fossil thought
    run
        fossil
        fossil
     like fossil

Mind   more
   city
     roads
       fossil
Built-in   thought

Cities
Cities have   patterns
    built-in
Cities
Cities have built-in patterns

     more
Minds are more
Minds
Minds
Minds are more than cities
98

```
    road                    thoughts
A road          fossilised
    road runs
    road runs
A road runs like fossilised thoughts

Roads                    patterns
        runs
            cities
                    fossilised
Thoughts                minds
```

WE'RE ALL FOR THE DARK!
Or, Life's Never Been Better

If you've ever sailed on the ocean
Or cheered when a port hove in sight
There's one thing you'll know – that emotion
Is better indulged in at night!

Since the time when old Noah
Spent those nights in the Ark
With the animals pairing –
It's best after dark!

CHORUS: Life's never been better!
Each night lasts a year –
Stuffed with women and music
And piss-ups and beer!

The girls that by daylight
Would blush to be stark,
Decide that their blushes
Won't show in the dark!

CHORUS: Life's never been better, etc.

Just yesterday breakfast,
We got lit in the park –
And the fire went on burning
Till long after dark.

CHORUS: Life's never been better, etc.

Next morning so early,
We were up with the lark.
We shot it down dead and –
Crawled back in the dark!

CHORUS: Life's never been better, etc.

If you lose your way travelling
And the small dogs do bark,
All the signposts will tell you –
'This way to **the** dark!'

CHORUS: Life's never been better, etc.

As Jesus remarked once
To Matthew and Mark,
'To Hell with Big Daddy –
We're all for the dark!'

CHORUS: Life's never been better!
Each night lasts a year –
Stuffed with women and music
And piss-ups and beer!
Stuffed with women and music
And piss-ups and beer!

ANONYMOUS

THROUGH THE NEW ARCADE

My sweet sweet Phil so often brutal
My bloody Phil so sometimes gentle
The trouble was you didn't love enough
You didn't have to hit him

Those years
I'm too sentimental

You were always too bloody sodding rough
You were too much like my mother
Completely misreading universal patterns
Thinking you could always have your way

Oh Christ my sweet damned Phil
You burst apart
Bits of body wreckage
I never knew I never knew another
Human being was that frail I always hated
All that ranting made me ill

Deep in my heart
You tired me

Even before my sticky-fingered schooldays
I'd learned to sweat it out and all about
But I'm too sentimental
Hanging on to any hand that waited
Well you inspired me
You burst apart
Once and so I stuck by you

The fool I was
                    When you've been crated

You'll see you'll see I saw
The way he looked at me I liked it
And he took your blows so gentle
And he spoke as if he knew
Of universal patterns far beyond me

Perhaps he recognised I could be true

Angline
Anjline
Angelea
Agelea
Aglina
Agline
Can I miss-spell your attitudes
Speech is silver silence earns no interest
Angeline think of me in your own coin
Angline
Gelina
Jellybeana
Agile Geline
In the timescapes of your countenance
My hopes stand paralysed
Paraphrased in flesh and pore
O Ingeline
Itchelino
Age Old Ina
One day I'll get it right

BOOK TWO

Southwards

STILL TRAJECTORIES

THE juke box played a number called 'Low Point X'. It was pub favourite the night that Speed Supervisor Jan Koninkrijk was forced to stay in the second floor back room on his way home from Cologne. He looked out over small cluttered muttering roofs and heard the record, heard it again in his sleep, dreaming of speed and life's intermittent fulfilments as the melancholy tug boats hooted outside the hotel where the Meuse became the Maars.

The girl in the bar, so fair, good North Dutch stock in that dull south Dutch town, hair almost milk-coloured, face so pale and sharp, interested in the sports end of the paper. The fountain sparkled.

She tried to be nice to me last night, to smile with warmth Koninkrijk, speeding into Belgium, said to himself. I'm not interested much in stray women any more, but her life has a mystery. . . . The pathos, having to serve five percent alcoholic drinks and watch night after night games of cards played always by the same men, listening to the tugs and 'Low Point X'. The numbskill acid famine snorting outside in the alleys. Was she signalling for help? I snooped on dialogues of the blood, Only silence there except for Low Point X Giving its coronary thud. . . . I'd better get back to Marta, no signals from her prison. A wife of shutters. Maybe this time she will be improved, so weary.

His Mercedes burned over the highway and hardly touched it, licking at one-sixty kilometres an hour along the autobahn from Cologne and Aachen through Brussels to Ostend and so across to England. All now Arab-squirted. Piercing his mazed thoughts, Koninkrijk kept a sharp eye for madmen: the highway's crash record was bad – his switched-on cops called it Hotpants Highway since the days of the Acid Head War. But this overcast afternoon brought little opposition, so he plunged forward, whistled to himself, joy, boy, joy, hoy jug-a-jig, hug a little pig, follow the band.

She would be slowing, fewer admirers, maybe one faithful one, coming to the bar every evening. Days paid out in hurried washing-lines. Her good will under strain. She smiled and smiled and was a victim. If he pitied, he must still love. It was the possibilities she represented that he thirsted for. Her hand as she stretched out for his guilders. A fine line, ah, that marvellous mystery of the female, something so much finer than just sex. Streamlined. Her little nails like teeth. With an un-Dutch gesture, he had kissed her hand; they were alone; they had looked at each other, he not much the older. The room round them colouring. Had put ten cents in the juke box for her to hear 'Low Point X' again as he walked out. Just to please her.

Had he really looked at her? Had she ever really seen herself? Had she something to reveal, hidden and sweet, to the man who went seeking properly for it? But that was his old romantic idea. No one went seeking others any more; under the psyche-delic rains, they mainlined only after themselves – and never hit true heights.

He lived at Aalter, just off the Highway, in a thin house. 'My life is an art object,' he said jokingly, heaving shoulders under shirt. There were the alternatives; his wife's presence, that girl's presence, his job, his possible new appointment in Cologne, his office, that mad Messiah in England; all were different nodes of his mind, all were substantiated by different nodes of the planetary surface; neither of which could be reached without the other; it was possible that one was the diagram of the other; all that was certain was that the linking medium was speed. It was the mixer, the mixen, cultural midden. Certainly there was speed, as the dial said, 175 kilometres, registering also in the coronary thud.

For some miles, Koninkrijk had been neglecting his thoughts as his eyes took in familiar territory, divesting itself of former naturalistic implications. He was beyond Brussels now, the sound of its cold kitchens. Here the enlargements to the Highway were on a grand scale. Two more lanes were being laid in either direction, thus doubling the previous number. But the new lanes were all twice the width of the previous ones, to allow for the fuzzy-set driving of speedsters under spell. Lips of senile earth had been piled back, cement towers erected; long low huts; immense credit boards with complicated foreign names; lamps, searchlights for night work; gigantic square things on wheels and tracks, yellow-bellied cranes; scaffolding, tips. mounds, ponds, mountains of gravel; old battered cars, new ones gaudy as Kandinskis and Kettels; mofettes like the fudged vents of corpses; and between everything chunky toy figures of men in striped scarlet luminescent work-coats. Into the furrows he saw the new animal go. These men were creating the whole chaos only for speed, the new super fuzzy speed, the catagasm of snared minds.

He slowed at the Aalter turn. It was impossible to say how much he had been affected personally by the sprays, but Koninkrijk recognised that his viewpoint had altered since they fell. although he was working in France at the time of Arablitz; France had remained neutral and the old lie that Tenenti TV *protège les yeux*. Piedboeuf. He slowed as he began the long curve off, its direction confused by impedimenta of construction on either side. Aalter was already being eaten into under the road-widening scheme, the old Timmermans farmhouse obliterated, its fields gone, the footpath under trees destroyed.

The grim thin house occupied by the Koninkrijks was the only one left inhabited in the street, owing to the improvements. Seismological eruptions of the European psyche had thrown up a mass of agglomerate that half-buried nearby terraces. A bulldozer laboured along the top of the ridge like a dung beetle, level with the old chimneys where smoke had once risen from a neighbourly hearth. That was over now. There was no past or future, only the division between known and unknown, sweeping on, terminator of a phantom Earth. The daffodils stood stiff in the Koninkrijk drive against just such a contingency, keeping the devouring detritus at bay, narcotic in their precision.

A thin rain, after moving across the North German Plain for hours, enveloped Aalter as Koninkrijk climbed from his Mercedes. The bellowing machines against my silent house so featureless and she in there, and the new animal with its wet eyes watching. He was not sure about the new animal; but he was slow now, on his feet and no longer stretched at speed, consequently vulnerable. Unpeeled. He bowed his head to the drizzle and made for the closed opaque glass porch. *She* would have no such refuge of privacy; only a back room behind the bar, all too accessible to the landlord when he rose at last, stale from his final cigar and five-per-center, to try and fumble from her person that missing combination of success he had failed to find in the hands of knock-out whist. Marta, as the unknown crept closer, at least had privilege of her devious privacy.

Marta Koninkrijk awaited in this minute and all the other buried minutes a secret someone to crush her up into life; or so she hoped or feared. She sat away all the sterile hours of her husband's absence as if the bright spinning coin would never tarnish or the miser forget his hoard. Time never went by. The bombs had blessed her half into a long-threatened madness, though she was not so insane that she did not try to conceal from her husband how far she lived away from him among the everfalling motes, or to conceal from herself how cherished was the perfection of immobility. She sat with her hands on her lap, sometimes reaching out with a finger to trace a hair-fine crack on the wall. Daring, this, for the day was nearing when the cracks would open and the forces of the earth pour in while the new machines rode triumphantly above the sprouting chimney-tops, bucking in like mnemonics of her deep-boring paralysis.

Koninkrijk had installed omnivision in the thin house for her. She could sit and comfort her barren self by leaving the outer world switched off while the inner world was switched on. From the living-room, with its frail furniture, glistening surfaces, and brilliant bevelled-edge mirrors, she could watch intently the row of screens that showed the other rooms of the house; the screens extended her senses, always so etiolated, palely over the unfrequented mansion, giving her unwinking eyes in the upper corners of five other rooms. Faintly mauve and maureen, nothing moved in them all day except the stealthy play of light and shade trapped there; nothing made a sound, until the receptors picked up the buzz of an early fly, and then Marta leant forward, listening to it, puzzled to think of life assailing the fudged vents of her life. No bicycle wheel turns in the unpedalled mind. The omnivision itself made a faint noise like a fly, fainter than her breathing, conducted so tidily under her unmoving little bust. The stuffy rooms had their walls hung with gleaming mirrors of many shapes and pictures of small children in cornfields which she had brought here from her childhood; they could be viewed in the omnivision screens. Sometimes, she flicked a switch and spoke with a tremor into an empty room.

'Jan!' 'Father!'

The rooms were full of incident from her immobile bastion in a wooden-armed chair. Nothing moved, but in the very immobility was the intense vibration of life she knew, so intense that, like a girlhood delight, it must be kept covert. The very intensity almost betrayed the secrecy for, when the key intruded downstairs into the elaborate orifice of the lock, there appeared to be a universe of time before he would appear at the stair top and discover that long-tranced inactivity of hers. Only after several millennia had passed and the radiations of undigested thought subsided somewhat, and the rasp of the key registered in each room's audio-recepter, did she steal quickly up, dodging the slender image of herself transfixed in every looking-glass, and creep on to the landing to pull the lever in the toilet, assuring him of her activity, her normality, her earthy ordinariness. Into the lavatory bowl rattled a fall of earth. One day it would flood the house and blank out the last mauve image.

Always when he mounted the narrow stairs it was to this sound of rushing water. He put his wet one-piece neatly on its hook before he turned and embraced his wife, her fudged vents of concussion. Dry compressed inflexible orifices tangentially met. When he moved restlessly round the room, disrupting all the eons of stillness, the furniture shook; and from without, the obscene grunts of a dirt-machine, pigging in to clay layers. Life had lost all its loot, as they said.

'Any news?'

'I haven't been out. The machines. I didn't really feel. . . . '

'You ought to get out.'

'It's menacing. Even the daffodils. . . . '

He crossed to the omnivision, switched over to Brussels. Momentary warming images. Bursting latticework, phantom casements. Some confused scenes as if settling into deep water, in some sort of a stadium. The cameraman could be on a perpetual trip judging by his random hand. Unlike Germany, here a government of sorts still held. Perhaps it was some kind of a beauty contest; girls in bikinis strutted, rakish of breast and mons, and many older women had turned up too – some at least in their seventies, flesh grouty and wrinkled, all foxed pudding. One of them was shouting, angry perhaps at getting no prize. Crowds in tight macks, looking all ways, and the stripped shots of a grandstand roof. A band played – not 'Low Point X'. He left it, looked at her, smiled, crossed to a narrow table and picked up the paper, neatly folded. The noise romping across her unwakened room.

'You haven't opened the paper.'

'I didn't have time. Jan – '

'What?'

'Nothing. How was Aachen?'

'We've got this British saint, Charteris, coming through Aalter tomorrow, big crusade and fun you ought to take in.'

'Who's he?'

'I'll have to be on duty early.'

'Do you think he'll – you know – '

'He's a great man,' spoken not looking up as he searched the muddled columns. Renewed piracy in the Adriatic. The Adriatic. New ocean, unknown to pre-psychedelic man. Many such hideous discoveries made every day. Of what degree of reality? 'A saint, at least.'

On page four he found it, a brief mention. New Crusade. Thousands rallying to support new prophet of multi-complex event. From Loughborough in the heart of England's stormy industrial midlands may emerge new movement for washing at least ten times brighter smiled Mr Voon and eventually embrace all of war-torn Europe says our London correspondent. Prophet of multi-complex event, soap powder with new secret psychotomimetic ingredient Jugoslav-born Colin Charteris is rallying take place in absolute darkness and Flemish observers agree that no thousands to his inspirational thinking. His first crusade motorcade through Europe is refrigerators at Ostend at four p.m. today and leaves tomorrow for what one commentator describes as several hundred incinerators automobiles pouring down here past Aalter at full speed, I'm bound to have more than one crash to deal with; better ring area squads now. Permanent alert from five tomorrow. Inform all hospital services too. Show eager. The tumbling bodies doing their impossible catagasms among ricochetting metals the dirty private things too beautifully ugly to be anything but a hoke. Oh in my loins oh Lord disperse do they have the orange tip butterfly in England these killing years?

Both in their frail beds, a gulf of fifty-seven point oh nine centimetres between them. Darkness and the omnivision switched off but that connection nevertheless merely dormant: there would be another time when the currents would flow and the impulses reestablish that which ancestrally was where the glades of the forest stood like wallpaper all round in murmurous shade when the murderous mermaid pulls aside her jalousie and letting in the whispering brands of braided hair stretching to the closed clothed pillows. Koninkrijk he, suddenly rousing, felt the vibrations welling up through him. It was true, one was the diagram of the other, and nobody could decide which. Either vast machines were passing a hundred yards away on the arterial toad, shaking the house minutely in its mortared darkness; or else accumulated fats and silts were building up in the arteries about his heart, stirring his whole anatomy with the premonitions of coronary thrombosis. If he woke Marta, he could presumably decide which was happening; yet even then there was the growing ambiguity about what a happening actually constituted. He could now recognise only areas in which the functionvectors of events radiated either inwards or outwards, so that the old habit of being precise was misleading where not downright irrelevant. And he added to himself, before falling again into trembling sleep, that the Loughborough gospel of multi-complex was already spreading, ahead of its prophet, like disease outrunning its symptoms.

Angeline was crying in the arms of Charteris on the long damp beaches of Ostend, timescape all awash. The Escalation dirged by a dying fire: Her mother married a sunlit Ford Cortina. All the cars, most of them oparted, many stolen, clustered about the red Banshee along the promenade where Belgians loitered and sang, switched on by the rousing words of Charteris, goaded by music's grind.

Take pictures of yourselves, he had said, pictures every moment of the day. That's what you should do, that's what you do do. You drop them and they lie around and other people get into them and turn them into art. Every second take a picture and so you will see that the lives we lead consist of still moments and nothing but. There are many still moments, all different. Be awake but inwards sleeping. You have all these alternatives. Think that way and you will discover still more. Cast out serpents. I am here but equally I am elsewhere. I don't need so much economy – it's the pot-training of the child where the limitation starts. Forget it, live in all regions, part, split wide, be fuzzy, try all places at the same time, indecisivise time itself, shower out your photographs to the benefit of all. Make yourself a million and so you achieve a great still trajectory, not longwise in life but sideways, a unilateral immortality. Try it, friends, try it with me, join me, join me in the great merry multicade!

All Angeline said after was, 'But you aren't indestructible any more than I really saw a dog in a red tie that time.'

He hugged her, half-hugged her, one arm round her while with the free hand he forked in beans to his mouth, at once feeding but not quite feeding as he said, 'There's more than being just organical, like translaterated with the varied images all photopiled. You'll soon begin to see how fuzzy-set-thinking abolishes the old sub-divisions which Ouspenski calls functional defects in the receiving apparatus let go on too personal a closure. Be anti-breasted in a prefrontal sense. As I told the people, self-observation, the taking of soul photographs, brings self-change, developing the real I.'

'Oh, stop it, Colin, you aren't fun to be with any more when you talk like that! How do you think I can hang on as I do, not without my own traits unappeased anyway. Did you or did you not kill my husband, besides, I don't see how you can get away with this multiple thing; I mean, some things are either-or, aren't they?'

With Angelina hanging crossly on his arm, he got up from the voluptuous sand and, moving to the water's edge surrounded by midnight followers, flung the bean tin into the galilean dark.

'What things?'

'Well, either I'm going to have your child or I'm not, isn't that right. I suppose a pretty straight answer.'

'Are you going to have a child?'

'I'm not sure.'

'Then there's a third possibility.' The chill thing flew to her.

Some of them had lights and ran clothed into the water to retrieve his tin, sacred floggable relic, unmindful of drowning, their beads floating about them. And the bean can moved over the face of the waters, out of reach, oiling up and down with orange teeth, beyond the Sabine music. Beyond that, the ambiguity of lunar decline and terrestrial rotation filtering into the dischance of blank night powder with new secret psychotomimetic ingredient.

A dirty boy there called Robbins, once been acclaimed a saint in Nottingham, ran into the water calling to Charteris 'You are greater than me! You contain all cross-references! So stop me drowning myself!'

Charteris stood by the margin of the sea ignoring Robbins as he floundered, reading momentarily the pinched timescapes of her countance. Then he turned towards Ostend and said, 'Friends, we must defy the great either-orness of the crass life that lived us like automata, howl like dogs if needed! Hunt! Hunt! Among the many futures scattled about like pebbles on his beach are a certain finite number of deaths and lives. Hunt them! I see us speeding into a great prongessional future which every blind moment is an eight-lane highway. Beside our catceleration rides splinternity, because the bone comes where the meat is sweetest. Hunt me, hunt the true me, the true you. Tomorrow, I precog that death will swallow me and throw me back to you again, and you will then see I have achieved the farther shore of either-orness. I will discard the dislocation!'

'A miracle!' cried the pop group and the hepos and motor-caders and all weirdies adjacent to the night. Angeline hugged him close, aware that he had to say nothing she could understand and still be wonderful. Near him was happening and the general stamnation broached. Behind them, clutching the holy relic of the bean tin, struggling and evacuating, Robbins went down into an unlit road beyond all terrestrial trajectory.

The promenade like a grey ridge of firn in early dawnlight, life, lootless.

Beyond the post-glacial shelf, where lights burned between night and day, stood derelict projects of hotels, petrified by the coming of French-built Arab aircraft; some half-made, blueprints in girder form, some half-demolished, all blank-eyed, broken-doored, with weeds in the foundations and leprous remains of human habitation. Here from their cattlepsy crawled the crusaders, scratching themselves in the ambiguous morning and blowing acid breath.

Knee-deep in his groins, thin in his increasing thicket, cult-figurc Colin Charteris the Simon Temple of himself makes his own mark in the greylight, emerging like a lion from his lair, his mange of hair all about him. Some of his larger jackals call a greeting, the Burtons, Featherstone-Haugh, little Gloria, thin dark Cass, Rubinstein with an early reefer glowing. The hero half-coughs in answer, scans craftily the stoned reigns of the beach, checks to see no great sweet jail trees sprang up there in the constabulary of the night, im-poisoning them among writhing branches and the rough un-shaven cyanightmarine light in a cellout.

The old church in the Šumadija rags sweet hum of rotten fallen flesh and flowers and a buzzing bee where the old fellow on his last stone bed of all. Going with his so respected father and not a word spoken. The very scent of the grass and walls and a fine checker of stone. The prone face of shagged hair and gristle-vaulted nostril and his father lifting up a mottled hand detached from the slab. Words droning like a bee. The same sick false light in the cell. His own fear and comfort like key-in-lock and then the sick man heaving himself onto a spike of greaseflesh to reach – don't flinch Duśan! – and pat the budding coconut of Colin's mange of harum –

Angeline wondered if her period would not come again today and boiled coffee for her lord and master on a fold-up stove; she was uncertain whether or not she felt sick and, if she did feel sick, whether it was because she was pregnant or because she dreaded the prospect of another day's crazy part-automatic driving. Well, it was a fuzzy set world like her shaman said and she of and with it.

Some of them were already revving their cars or driving them over the ice-rim onto the sand as being the quickest way to extricate from the muddle of beached beasts crouched like whales with beetle wings. Maintenance was going on to a limited extent, mainly in the sphere of bits of rope tying on bits of machine. The sparky thing currently was to fill blown egg-shells with paint and then stick them on to the bonnet with adhesive plaster; when you got moving, the paint peed out in crazy trickles or blew across the windscreen and roof of the automobile or, under sudden acceleration, the egg burst like a duff ventricle. Only Charteris's Banshee was unadorned by such whims. Like France, it was neutral. And Red.

'Where we going today, Col?'

'You know.' In the background, flutes and gritars.

'Brussels?'

'Some name like that.'

'Then where? Tomorrow? The day after, where?'

'That's it. You hit the mood exactly. The question marks the antidope for auto-motion. More coffee there?'

'Drink the first lot, darling, then you get some more; didn't you learn any such thing when you were a boy? Didn't your father tell you? You know, this isn't a crusade – it's a migration! Animals not spirits, revolt of youth you make me laugh!'

The coffee ran down his chin, he was only half-drinking, as he nodded his head and said, 'Sheer inspiration, yes! Crusade has only one object. What you think's deported but the old-time? Migratory is more instinctive, more options open.'

He expanded the theme as they climbed into the car, talking not only to her but to big mottled machine-face Banjo and other people who impinged, Burton now nagging for favours. The Serb had ceased to think what he was saying. It was the migratory converse; the result was that he astonished himself and this elation fed back into his system, rephotographed a thousand times, each time enlarged in a conflagration of spongation in idation or inundation of conflation, so that he could pursue more than one thought simultaneously down into its deep loughburrows, snooper-trooper fashion.

Burton was bellowing something at the top of his voice, but the engines drowned out what he said as they began to roll along the grey deserted front, away from littoral meanings, between echoing shutters and sea. The new autorace, born and bred on motorways; on these great one-dimensional roads rolling they mobius-stripped themselves naked to all sensation, beaded, bearded, belted, busted, bepileptic, tearing across the synthetic twen-cen landskip, seaming all the way across Urp, Aish, Chine, leaving them under their reefer-smoke, to the Archangels, godding it across the skidways in creasingack selleration bitch you'm in us all in catagusts of living.

Great flood of tatterdemalion vehicles in multicolour flooded out onto the Hotpants Highway, rushing swerving' grinding, bumping, bucking, rupting, south towards Aalter and the infinite, travelling up to one-fifty photographs per minute, creasing axle aeration.

He lumbered up from the vast brown inaccessible other-world of sleep and went hurriedly to shave. In the second bed, the wilting leaf of his wife still silent among her own shades.

As he looked at his motionless face, Koninkrijk thought of the good North Dutch girl back in the little hotel in Maastricht. Baby you won't get no sex Off of me in low point X. The last crash, driving with the cop fast to the scene of the accident maybe the same today my form of gratification just a vampire. It was a little Renault nose deep in a cliff of lorry, as if snuggling there. The terrible anticipation as he jumped out of the still-moving car and ran towards it; in a year of life, maybe one moment of truth; in a hundred miles of speedtrack, this one node. The crossover roads like ganglia of an aborted space-time. A tractor-driver hurrying forward, explaining in thick Flemish accident. I saw un I saw un, he swerve out to overtake me, this lorry pull up to let him by, see, this other chap don't pull up in time the first chap get clear away, ought to be a bloody law against it.

There is a law against it, out my way.

Voilà! All the luggage in the back of the car a jerry-built shrine tumbled forward over the shoulders of the driver. He wears no safety belt of harness, is utterly smashed, yet he lives and groans, seems to be begging for something in – German?

The ambulance arriving almost at once, hostile pedestrians also staring in through the now-public car windows. The uniformed men ease the crushed driver out bit by bit; the lorry-driver and the tractor-driver stand by, masking their helplessness with explanations and repeated phrases. He swerve out to overtake me. Koninkrijk with this dirty curiosity, recalling it again now obsessively with self-hate, mauls over the blood-gobbed contents of the car after the ambulance men have teased most of the victim clear.

His cold little distorted image of the man-run world held only this driving and crashing, nothing else; everything else led to climatic moments of driving and crashing, the sparky technological fulfilment offered by the first flint arrowhead, the schizophrenic clash of man's divided nature since he conjured good and bad out of meshing phenomena – to all that, crashung and drivung were the climax, a geared aggression beyond sexuality or indeed any moment's action.

The chemicals could merely mask basics.

Eating and defecating and the rest were just preparatory processes, getting the body tuned for the next cyborg down the roads. His wife-defective. Things other people did were just substitutes for speed death. Chinese peasants, grovelling up to their kneecaps in paddy longing for the day when they too could enjoy speed death. Congenitally deaf, hearing only engines.

He looked at his eyes in horror. His mind was sucked to the constant subject. Profession had become obsession. There would be another call today; he must get down to the station, fearing and hoping. The Charteris crusade was invented for his particular philosophy Charteris is rallying take place in absolute darkness. He heard Marta switch the omnivision on as he unplugged his razor. Tremors still churned at his core.

The immense cliff of earth loomed even higher above his neat red tiles this morning: chugging things like match boxes laboured up there, black against sky. New clay tumbling among daffodils. It was better in the station of the Speed Police – more like being in a liner, less like drowning in a sea.

'Good morning, Jan.'

'Morning, Erik.'

Koninkrijk went up to the tower, where two uniformed men lounged, chatting, smoking cheroots. He could look down through the glass roof of the duty room just below, see the current shift relaxed with their feet up, snuggled in wicker chairs, reading paperbacks and magazines. When the warning sirened, the room would be suddenly untidily empty, the paperbacks curly with open pages rubbed in the floor.

Most of these guys had the acid but kept on. Down in Brussels it was worse. As for Germany, Frankfurt and München were burning, they said.

Scanning the information panel, he took a reading of traffic states from other stations along the Highway. Building up from Ostend.

Already, the first throes of the crusade were bursting through the arteries of the Aalter stretch. From the station tower, a fine view; nobody saw it but Koninkrijk, as he read his own keynotes from the vast maimed spread; the remainder of the dutyites grazed their minds among tales of big-breasted whores, affrays with Nazis in occupied Scandinavia, shoot-ups in Fort Knox, double-crossings in Macao, or the litter of the previous night's activities; two officers going off-duty exchange dirty stories over a concession-price Stella Artois in the canteen; reality had a poor attendance, and I'm really the only one but even my eye's half ahead to the time when the English messiah Banshee jets past here in the saddle of the speed death king and half back to the thought of that Maastricht girl maybe with her I would at last find that certain thing O Lord God I know I don't often but what am I to do about Marta is schizophrenia catching her paralysis my fever meshing causes.

Do you think the emergency government can carry on eh they say it's the food shortage but the Walloons are at the bottom of this you can bet Yeah food shortage they call it a world famine but we know who's at the bottom yeah we know who's at the bottom of it yeah Walloons.

What does she do in there all day long and I'll have to move her at the week-end or they bury the house tombs doleful voices but how will I persuade her Christ O Lord Jesus get out there move man move leave it all behind since her confounded father interfering old.

The warning sounded and he was down into the front park as the men milled. He climbed into N-Car Five; the slam of his door was echoed by others. News coming over the car-radio of a multi-vehicle pile-up on the south lane of the Highway two kilometres north of Aalter. Low Point X. All predicted. Let's go and they roared under the underpass and bucketted out on the feed and from the feed on to the Highway proper, yellow barrier barrels and red warning lights slicing by the hubs. Saliva dying like a tide. Yacketter yacketter speedbeaches of the freeworld man-madman intersurface.

The speedometer his thermometer, creeping up and familiar dirty excitement creaming in him. For someone the moment of truth had come big grind the necessary whiteout the shuttling metal death 3-Ding fast before the windscreen and still many marvellous microseconds safety before impact and the rictus of smiling fracture as the latent forces of acceleration actualised. Koninkrijk hated himself for this greedimaginative vampact of his highflown. Already the cathartos were barking beyond the ditched town, the PILE WONDER sign, the pasty dungheap at the Voeynants house shuttered, and beyond the road-widening the crashfences started on either side, cambered outwards and curved at the top to catch escaping metal. Fast shallow breathing. The acute angle subtended by impacted heart-bleats on mobility.

The accident heralded itself ahead. Bloodstream flowing south faltered, slowed, dribbled. Koninkrijk's vagus nerve fluttered with empathy. Somewhere ahead was the actual thrombus, all but entirely blocking the artery. The police car swung into the nearest emergency lane. Koninkrijk was out before it stopped and unlocking the barrier between lanes, hoiking a walkie-talkie with him. Sun warm on his shoulders grass too long against the chain link got to keep nature out of this the weedicides this bloody war that Arabian spray.

It was a typical nose-to-tail job, ten cars involved, some pig-a-back on others like rough parody of animal or coleoptera copulating, sheaths split. Some still filtering through, all passenger heads craned to see desperately want to know if man still stuffed with red blood, ichor, water, what.

'Koch, Schachter, Deslormes, proceed to the rear, get the barriers up and blinker signals ten kilometres back so that there's no further escalation.'

Moving forward as he spoke. Discipline the cover for lyric lymph-chug.

'Mittels and Arameche, keep a northward lane free for ambulances.'

But they knew. They all needed shouting and excitement

and the roar of engines. Everything was just a pattern, culled may be from the raped paperbacks on the station floor.

So like last time and maybe next time. Verisimilitude eroded. A lumbering Swiss truck with Berne numberplates slewed half-off the verge. Into it rear, nose crumpled, a red Banshee. Man wrapped round the steering wheel, head against shattered screen, piled luggage in back spewed forwards over body and shoulders, some broken open, passenger door broken open, oparted ancient Wolseley piled into rear of Banshee, then terrible cluster of vehicles, British registration mostly, patterned crazily. One shot free, burning steadily against outside barrier, lying on its side. People running limping crawling still in trampled grass shouting and crowding and curiosity reality loose among the psychos. The police helicopter clattering up overhead, photographing it all, fanning smoke flat across the wreckage.

Climax of many dreams. Spilt seed of blood.

Loudspeakers barking farther along the road as Koch got to work.

Ambulances arriving, men at the double with float-stretchers, doing their instant archaeology, digging down through the thin metallic strata to where life had pulsed a few tiny eons ago, surfacing with primitive and unformed artifacts of flesh. Someone saying, 'The Banshee was Charteris's car.' Time converting entirely into activity as matter converted into energy. Lost races dredged here bit by bit from their cumbrous armour.

Two hours' work later, Koninkrijk sitting exhausted jacket off on the muddied verge, listening in a daze to Charteris speaking to the elect.

'You know I half-foretold this would happen as we multicaded south. You heard the word. Here's a sort of semi-miracle as more-or-less predicted yesterday or whenever it was when we were at that place. The only places we really need are the in-between places that aren't places for they are trajectories of maximum possibility – you see how forced stoppage in this place here created maximum non-possibility for many of us which we call death, the low point where all avenues end.

'All our avenues take a discard but we must play to our most multiplicity in the pack-up. Banjo my agent his avenue is right at a dead breakage. All his phantoms nailed down under a shutter. He Burton who hailed from the Midland carmaker city of Coventry stopped me as we churned out of that place begging to be allowed to ride my Banshee. He had no sounds as to why but the whim so for that reason my thrush Angelina and I took to his heap while he in triumph rode the Banshee. Impulses are there for usage. So it can be all explained away that he had some suicidal wish or that he as a good agent stage-managed it to look like a miracle that I was spared from death as predicted or that if I had instead driven no pile-up would have occurred, or that either this accident was already pre-performed in any of its guises or that it was in some way willed by me or us all photoed corporately from some messianic drive in our hidden minds like the serpent of our bosoms. If you all seek dutifully for the certainty of this occasion in its eternal recurrence, each of you will find a different solution more satisfying than others to you, which clips a speciality into the ego-bracket, and so that will be regarded by you as the most "probable" solution alongside all possibles: so like renegade compasses you will each point to a different pole of truth, where on this ribbon all will indicate a personal mean. That's what we side for isn't it, the difference? Don't get automatic! That I beg you to treasure, relish ʾhe uncertainty, shun certainty, search the fuzzy set, for when you find accepted probability, it must surely be a conspiracy not to be free between two or more of you, like the old pre-psychedelic ideologies of non-permissive non-multi-society. All this I shall say less certainly in my book Man the Driver, but never more inspiredly than now in this sparked-out moment by the org-up of buddies where this loss so belts us in.'

He pitched forward on his face as Angeline ran forward to break his fall. The uniformed police, the tatty audience, sun-specked, entropised again. The day hinged forward with mobility-gain.

Koninkrijk saw his chance. Running forward to two police, he said lowly, 'Get him into my car and let's take him back to H.Q. The coming prophet!'

He was sitting up on the hard white bunk picking with a fork at police hamandbeans on a hard white police plate in the hard grey migrainey room, with Angeline hard by him, and Konin-krijk respectful standing.

'Another miracle? I'm only moving on the big web. But I will see your wife, yes, bombardment of images tells me. It all floats us nearer to the lithocarp Brussels and her alternatives to transpelt for Burton's. Also I intuit she could have a need for me. Or a sort of need for which we could substitute a fulfilment.' He half-smiled, sipping at a tumbler of water, sifting the water across his palate, seeing the plastic glass was made in France: Duraplex.

'He has a sort of impersonal thing helps people,' Angeline said.

'I think she is schizophrenic, sir. She flushes the what's-it when I come in.'

'We all do, most of us. The wish to live more than one life – natural now, as the brain complexifies from generation. The world will soon tolerate only multi-livers. All pedestrians are at their exits. You too? No dream world or semi-realised thing aborting in the mental motorways?'

Slight bricky flush concealed under Koninkrijk's jowls. All the joys and sorrows really aborted into a secret drain-life of autoplexy none shared except for her blue eyes, the tired willowy hand stretched over the sports page of a Maastricht paper.

'They do clash sometimes. I'll drive you to my house. She'll be there.'

The girl Angeline came too. So he did not live entirely inside himself, or else found there echoes from those about in her head of weeping black hair. So he could be a genuine messiah – but what nonsense when he himself claimed but semi-messiahhood, and after all Europe wasn't the Levant, was it? In under a kilometre, small space to burn the gas and the thin house present.

Wondering where he was he recalled all past confidence and frenzy and signed to them that he would enter the thin coffin door alone.

'Very well. I warn you, you'll find her reserved.' Nervous glance at the woman Angeline. 'Not pretty, my wife. Very thin, I think the spring disagrees with her, she can't unwind.' Who was without these failures in their stationary time?

And father had said that she should have a new bicycle
On her birthday at the end of May, as summer
Began; but they had been too poor when her birthday arrived
And he had given her instead a carton of crayons –
The very best Swiss crayons –
But she had never used them just to show her displeasure
Because she had wanted to rove the Ardennes countryside;
And perhaps it was since then that her father had been cold
To her and ceased to show his love. Sometimes it almost seemed

That if she kept rigid still he might appear stern
In one of the other noiseless rooms, dark
And showing his slight and characteristically lop-sided smile,
Saying, Marta, my child, come to your old Papa!
She had arranged the mirrors differently in the rooms,
Stacking them so that she could also observe the landing
Via one of the violet-tinted screens
The maureen-coloured mirrors
With a side glance down along
The melancholy perspective
Of the stair -
Case.
Later, she would have to move herself
To clean the house; but she so much preferred the sight of her
Lair in abstraction through mirror and screen
That first she must be permitted
The vigil of watching and listening the morning through,
Of watching and listening all mornings through.
All her private rooms were unused by other
Persons; nobody was allowed
To come and go in them; their silence was the sanctity
Like even unto the sanctity
Yea of St Barnabas Church
Yea wherein she had visited, visited every Sunday
As a child with her parents every Sunday stiffly
Dressed in Sabbath clothes;
But this secret silence was of a different quality;
Each room she surveyed possessed individual silences:
One, a more ricketty silence,
Another a more rumpled one;
Another a veined silence;
Another like a cross-section through calf's meat,
With a young-patterned texture;
Another with a domineering glassy silence;
These deserted quiets were more balmful and constricting
To her viscera than April's flowers.
A starker shape of silence ruled the stairwell.
Stealthily she moved her attention to it and
Came upon her father standing
There waiting amid the shade.
In his attitude of great attention she knew him. 'Marta!'
    'Father, I
Am here!' 'Don't be alarmed!' 'Oh, Father,

You have come at last!' She could not understand but
Delight grew high and flowered in the stalks of her confusion
Telling itself as always in a burst of penitence
And self-reproach, till her lips grew younger. He
Attempted no answer to her flow, advanced
Towards her through the mirrored rooms, walking
Delicate as if he saw
The ancient barbs she still cultivated sharp
About his path. She flung herself at him, all she had to give
As she gave her self-denigration, closing her eyes, clutching
Him. He half-leaned, half-stood, half-understanding
The scent of trauma in the scene, glancingly taking
In the fetishistic idols of emptiness on the bare walls, seeing
Again the clever duplication of life she had contrived
Imaged in the bottom of his French plastic tumbler: Duraplex:
She has her alternatives. 'Live
In both worlds, Marta, come with me!' 'Father, you give
Me your blessing once again?' 'I give
You my new blessing – fuzzy though you may find it, you must
Learn to live by it, you understand? My wish is this,
That you sojourn with nobody who desires to force you to live
On one plane at a time all the time: time must be divisible
And allowed gordian complexities. You must be
At once the erring child as we all are
And the reasoning adult as we all try to be
No strain placed on either
The two together tending towards
The greatly hopeful state we half-call godliness
Is that semi-understood?'
'And Jan, Papa?'
'For a while you come to live with me and Angelina
And let your man go free, for he has been more cut
By your trammels than you. You must learn to bide
Outside
Where constriction binds less, so one later spring you may
Come together again to find water flushing in the earth
Closet.' 'I see father.' Now she looked at him and realised
Like a trump turned up
He was not entirely her father, but the revelation had no
Poison: beneath the last moment's hand of mighty truth
Another shuffled: that in truth Marta did not want her father
And would now sprout free of him and his mirroring
Eyes that saw her only with disfavour: so her lips

Growing younger a mask cracked and fluttered
To the carpet unnoticed. 'Jan
And I will meet again, Father? After I have duped him so
  badly
With my hateful secret passion all these over-furnished
Years? There is no final parting?' 'Well,
There's really no final meeting.
It's your own collusions that conspire or not towards
Another person – but you'll see directly. . . . Come along
There's a daffodil or two left outside in the wet and soon
Sweet rocket will flower in your secret garden, Marta.' She
Looked at his eyes. They went down the stairs, undusted
That and every following morning, leaving the omnivision
  working
Still. The cracks rioted on the walls like bindweed, flowering
in peeled distemper; and as they grew more open-lipped,
the rumbling town-destroying machines clowned over the
roof-tree and clay pouted through the fissures. The mirroring
screens showed how the earth soiled in through every whispering room, bringing familiar despoliation; but by then the
sweet rocket flowered for Marta.

Jan also, as the reformed crusade turned south, turned east,
burning his tyres and singing the song whose words he had
forgotten and never known, towards freer arms whose meaning
he had never known, where the Meuse became the Maars.

AUTO-ANCESTRAL
FRACTURE

FOR Charteris fingering a domestic thing, the shadowy city Brussels was no harbour but a straight of beach along the endless litterals of his season. The towsers on the skyline lingering spelled a cast on his persistence of vision. He had no interest in privateering among those knuckled spoils. So his multi-motorcade pitched on a paved grind and tried to prefigure the variable geometry of event.

But on that stainey patch grounded among the fossil walls and brickoliths his myth grew and the story went over big what if each ear made him its own epic? The small dogs howled underground bells rang on semi-suits and song got its undertongue heating and the well-thumbed string. Though he himself was anchored deep in the rut of a two-girl problem forgetting other fervours.

Charteris they sang to many resonances and the spring's illwinds sprang it back in a real raddle of uncanned beat and a laughter not heard the year before.

Some of the crusaders' cars were burning in the camp as if it was auto-da-fé day, where the drivniks with cheerful shuck had forgotten that the golden juice they poured down the auto-throats would burn. Like precognitive mass-images of the nearing future, the reek of inflammation brought its early pain and redness to the fatidical flare. Tyres smouldered, sending a black stink lurching across the waste ground where they all shacked.

You coughed and didn't care or snow was peddled in deeper gulches to the vein's distraction. The little fugitive shaggy figures were a new tribe, high after the miracle when the Master Charteris had died and risen again in a sparky way after only three minutes following the multi-man speed death up at Aalter. Tribally, they mucked in making legends. Bead groups flowered and ceded, lyrics became old history before the turning night wheeled in drawn. Some of the girls rinsed underclothes and hung them on lines between the kerouacs while others high-jinxed the boys or got autoerotic in the dicky seats. A level thousand drivniks locusted in the stony patch, mostly British, and the word spread inspired to the spired city.

There lifespendulum ticked upside down and the time was rape for legendermoan: for the hard heads and the business hearts found that their rhythms now worked only to a less punctilious clock and speculation had another tone. War had turned the metrognome off chime in general pixilation to a whole new countryslide upbraided.

What raised the threshold a bit was the Brussels haze. The bombing here had been heavy as the millionaire Kuwaiti pilots themselves flipped in a gone thing and the psycho-chemicals rained down. Life was newly neolithic, weird, and drab or glittering as the hypo-glossal towers staggered. Appalling shawls of illusion draped across the people where the grey mattered. Occult lights still veiled the rooftops and aurora borealis clouded the corner of the eye. Jamming their stations signals of new bodies scarcely suspected before or different birds of intent. It was a place for the news of New Saviour Charteris to nest.

Many came, some remained; many heard, some retained. Food was short and disease plentiful, plague grunted in the backstreets of the mind, and cholera in the capital. but the goodfolk had thrown off the tiresome shacks of Wesciv and unhoused cults of microbes and bacteria; this was the spontaneous generation and neutral Pasteur had been wrong. These circadian days, you could whistle along your own bones and the empty plate held roses. In Flanders field, the suckling poppies rose poppy-high, puppying all along in the dugged days of war's aftermyth. Gristle though the breast was all were at it. So it was gregarious and who cared.

Of these the Escalation was foremost. Among the petering cars they made their music, Bill, black Phil, Ruby Dymond with his consolations and Featherstone-Haugh, plus Army and their technicians who saw that the more sparky sounds reached tape. This day they had escalated to a new format and a new name. They now hit the note as the Tonic Traffic and had infrasound, ground from Banjo's grinder machine worked by Greta and Flo, who shacked with them and other musicniks.

Through mirror-sunglasses they peered at the oneway world, frisking it for telling dislocations in which to savour most possibility. The flat wind-smoke covered them part-coloured. They had a new number going needling into the new stations to really pierce wax called Famine Starting at the Head. Sometimes they talked round the lyric or with laughter sent it up.

On the Golden Coast cymbals start to sound some place like a magic garden I'm just a demon on the cello. Play the clarinet pretty good too man!

In his tent-cave Charteris with two women heard the noise and distant other flutes in flower-powdered falsetto, but had his own anguish to blow through the stops of strained relationship.

Stranding his pearl underseers to glaub the timeskip of Ange Old's farce its tragictory of otherwhens and all plausticities made flesh in the mating. Like him fashioned from parental lobotomy truncated by the mainspring glories of a rain shower slanting through the coral trees where greened the glowing white of landscape. Figures moving dragging dropping enduring in her glowworm eyes the candlesphere of hallucidity she's the mouth and cheekbox of my hope's facial tissurc to come back like soft evening's curtains. It's what I see in her all all the peonies the blackbirds the white-thighs all and if not her all all I see of any voyaging.

Yet Marta has her own unopened chambers of possibility the locked door calling to my quay my coast Bohemian coast my reefs that decimate steamships. On the piston of this later Drake lost in spume rankest alternature.

'Do me a fervour! I try to work on this document of human destiny and you want to know whether or not I took in the slack with Marta last night. Why not trip out of needling my alternatives? Get from me!' The ceiling was only canvas billowing, standing in for plaster in a ruinous convent later old people's home, which the autobahn-builders had half-nudged out of the way as they drove their wedges into the city-heart. Undemolished now almost self-demolished this wing flew the Charteris flag; here his disciples clustered elbows brick-coloured as plaster peppered down like the dust of crunched hourglasses. As starving Brussels besieged itself for a miracle domestic drama flourinched.

'Oh entropise human detestiny!' Angeline was washed and white like concentrate campallour, still calculating against the aftermaths of warcalculus, still by the chemicals not too treblinkered. 'I don't want to know if you slacked because I know if you slacked you slackered Marta tonight last night every night and I just damned won't stand it, so you just damned fuzzy-settle for her or me! None of your either-whoring here!'

'All that old anti-life stuff snuffed it with your wesciv world – from now it's a multi-vulval state and the office blocks off.'

'Your big pronounce! Hotair your views to others, stay off top of Marta, you grotnik!'

'Meat injection and the life she needs, Angel, pumped in, like the big gymnastic sergeant you sing. She has no impact with frozen actions like long disuse now quickened with the fleetsin for her. If I poke some import all's love in fair unwar and the sailor home from the seizure! Be pacific!'

'Sea my Azov! And you messiah on a shemensplash as and when is it, eh? A matlottery! Over my bedboddy! Don't you kindermarken me mate why how you can come it I don't know – look at the consolation! Prize her legs a part you'd be licky! Caspian kid! – All dribbled-rabble and emuctory!'

'I'll baltic where my thighs thew my honey, I the upand-coming!'

'You subserbiant Dalmatian! From now on you go adriantic up some mother tree – just don't profligainst me! Didn't I the one who moist you most with nakidity remembrane to mem-brainfever pudentically, or if not twot hot hand gambidexter pulping lipscrew bailing boat in prepucepeeling arbor of every obscene stance?'

She now had the big bosombeating act, buckaneering in the dusty half-room before his ambiguity, riding to master and be mastered, knowing he punched her husband in the traffic, gesturing with scatologic to the greyer girl, Marta on the master's corner couch cuckoobird unsinging. Phantom nets of mauve and maureen joined them like three captured parrot fish, web of twain, chain of time.

'Did I ever say you were not the sparkiest? Or the bell-ringing belle-blottomed? Sap out of it angelfish and don't parrot membrain there's suck a thing as polygam.'

Among the dark hair the branches of her face in tempest.

'Bombastard it's to be she or me and now's your morment of incision. Cut it out or cut your rigging!'

But he broadsided advanced grasping her by the united fronter so that when she tugged away the blouse torn buttons falling like broken teeth and one escampaigning teeter. He laughed in lust and shrouds of anger. She slapped him across his molar plex he a quick one to her companion way and they cavorted in a tanglewords the nettingroll.

For first time Marta brought her unbending mind and body to attention scudded to his rescue from the bedspace where they had seemed and tuckered and with a dexterritory he landed them both judies with squirming gust for keel-whoring and his digit rigid as he had voided mannymoon to squire their accunts and cummerbendle in their scrubberies dualigned by real and pseudoprod tongs and clappers circumjascentedly. In out in out moonlight moonlight.

They lay repanting. Marta said, 'Oh forgive me, Father, but you gnaw my need to bring me back where the circulation stammers.'

He said nothing in a fluid state. Around lay the pages and quires of the ream of his destinotionary tract Man the Driver in which he tried by shortcuttings from the sparky philisopher to prime mankindly on the better way of awareness.

Angelina said, 'To think that all your thinking comes to this and you so big in the mind can't see the world's slippered across the plimsoll line with you just some damned wandering bump swelling with the warfallout's megabreath doing two defeated dames in a dungy belgunmaden bad! What's there of metavision ask?'

Momentarily the roseplink lining parted and he saw with her eyes lavatory life going downheeled all the way as he fledabout of madness and hiveless ones begged him to be for them and be for them the big beatal and endal to some bitter end. Scrambling back, he said to spark himself, 'I am the grate I am where fools burn for greater light and from me shall come a new order beyond your comprehandling.'

Chance in that room sat also while the ceiling billowed the dark man Cass. He now managed as Charteris agent from the dark English Midlands all his life a self-punitive in a narrow way pinned behind a counterpain in drapershop where having broken out he now netted his advantages at fifty-nine eleven three a yard all right and gaudy as the smiling tout of Saviour Charteris flower-breasted plus other sidelines.

Many-monkeyed in his head he rose now saying, 'Hail the great I am! Hail chaptered Charteris! All burn for greater light from you. You fisher us a greater net of possibilities and what you photograph is multi-photographed with all possible value.' He sprawled at Charteris's pedestal for his idol to claim him; but Charteris cooled: 'You better go and fix the cascade down to the main Frankfurt route. Under my lid the sign still burns there in a precog frame.'

'Sure, we'll skim the menu of possibilities but first you have to speak in Brussels where life's real looty for us and people know you miracled death's aaltercation where the carcentinas buckled.'

Sweat dry on a skin of eagerness.

'No growth that way, Cass, believe! In every in every no line no loot on Brussels my bombardment of images dries me out. Famine starting at the head tells me we take our bellies away from the emptiness of a Bristles brushoff.'

Still he had no confidence in the meat of his glazed tongue.

From the corner of his eyes, the females under a flapping lid swung like two monkeys. Trees grew on beaches. New animals lurked. Wall angles hinged.

'You call the dance! You are the skipper of the new Ouspenski order beyond our compension and I ship with you the greatest.' Thus Cass's little horn piping.

So saying but Cass rode on the motorcade a prey to more than piety and thus in the cholera courts of the capital. The pitted music of the back streets was his quarry. These thousand rocketting disciples gathering quantity as they moved had a needle for some supply and just a cosy cosa nostra to keep them smoking along towards the profitable reefs in a parasitical pass. He came out from the ruined building gathering air and dragging in a sort of awareness before jetting off for the centre.

Waves of reality came and went, breaking over him, drenching him. Wall angles hinged. He was aware where he was going yet at moments the streets appeared a transparent rues; he imaged that this was just another mock-up of the quest he had follyed all his life, looking for some final authority perhaps: the central point of the quest never revealed itself, so that he was driving on the B route. He sang a line of Ouspenski's: Men may torture themselves but these tortures will not make them awake. Also Charteris so worked in him that he said to himself: You see how I released more potentialities in you, Cass – you carry on several lives at once!

Men may torture themselves. He could write it for the Tonic Traffic or the Genosides or the Snowbeams to sing. Their numbers had taken over the nine-to-fives. They must make themselves awake. The magician hypnotised his sheep and they turned to mutton believing they were immortal. All flocks there to be preyed on, and this new kind no exemption. Soon to be cassoulet. He always drove at more than one wheel, whoever took lead car.

In the centre of the city, people whistled along their own bones though the empty bowl held roses. The European dislocation had harvested no fields and canned no fish. In hospitals, nurses with prodromic eyes dreamed islands, doctors smiled in lunar orbits whistling down syringes or snubbed their scalpels abscessmindedly on submerged patient bones. Although it's true the bakers ritually baked in massive factories, the formulas were scrambled and even what was edible did not all reach mouths, for the distributors so hot for truth drove their loads into amnesiac fields of wheat and lay there till they fecundated in the calendar of decay. The parliament still took its conclave but all the ceremony these last two months had brought were these laws passed: a law to stop the drinking of the good earth; a law to prohabit hats from becoming unseen when the sun set; a law to make Belgian hounds sing the night away like nightingales, with an amendment asking cats to try their best in that melodious direction too; a law to permit redness in traffic lights; a law to abolish the plague; a law against Arab invasion; a law to extend the hours of sunshine in cloudy winter months; and a far-sighted law to encourage all members of parliament to be more industrious by the granting of six months leave to them per annum.

Cass had the secret contacts. A drink in a bar, a ritual holding of the glass, a certain stance, a procedure of guarded phrases, and there was help for him and he smoking secretly with seven men. Who said to him at the end of an hour or so: 'Sure, it's for trade the maximum goodness that Charteris gets billed big and comes into town. Come he must. You go and see Nicholas Boreas the film director and put to him what we say.'

And Cass was given certain assurances and pay and moved along to see the mighty and highly-sung Boreas.

Under the tawning in the semi-house time buckled and they were still saddled by the sporadic barney with Him downtrodden in a multi-positional stance on a chaircase and Marta racked on the bunk-up while Angeline barn-stormed about the gesticulating room, rehorsing her old nightmares.

'Face it, Colin, you're now stuck on an escalation okay ride along but just don't forget the old human loot like what you did to my husband or maybe that's all gone overhead in your reeling skullways maybe maybe not?'

'It was the christmas cactus there blinding as the lorry

133

swerved and I could never make you understand. Don't go through all that again. It's the velocity, girl – '

'Verocity nothing you killed him and why should I pull down my knickers and open up my pealy gapes for you to come in beefs me oh the sheer sheer tears of every diving day and now I shape and rave at you and who knows through the encephallic centre you have shot some of that steamin' acid so I'm hipping too and like to flip oh meanin' Christ Colin what and where the dung day dirt is done and you know how I itch I never dote a damned desire without my shift and all my upbringing undone!'

And Marta said, 'You're chattering your passion into threads Angel cause isn't there enough I mean he can the carnal both twomescence and I don't mound no moral membrane in a threesome and we sort of sisterly! Isn't the organ-grinding the big thing?'

So she seemed to flip and like a seafouling man embarked on culling Marta for a frigid and bustless chick while egging her on with premaritimely oaths to reveal what a poultry little shrubby hen-penned canal awaited bushwanking or the semenship of motiongoing loiner under her counterplain and how those specious sulcal locks were just the antartickled coups of man's ambit or if more trapical then merely multi-locked the vaginisthmus of panamama!

Thus spurred slim Marta unbuckled and pulled enragged away her entire and nylonvestments to kneel up flagrantly tightitted the slander ovals with an undividual stare took them like young imporktunny pigscheeks in lividinous palmystry squeezing to pot them smoothly at all rivels cried the heir erect command insprict the gawds meanwhile thirsting out her chubby plumdendumdum with its hennaed thatch of un-own feelds and throaty labyrings of kutch with cinnamons di-splayed.

The other sneered but he to her cheeky pasture lured advanced to graze and on her stirry eyepitch clove his spiced regarb as if his universion centered there his mace approaching friggerhuddle. She now as never evoluptuary bloomed in her showy exinbintion outward easily spread her cunative flower by rolling sternbawd rumpflexed to make him see the fissile smole of spicery fragiloquent of tongue almoist articulpate well-coming with spine archipelavis and her hands abreasted eagerly. He snared his bait engorged in cleft vessalage like a landlopped fissureman on the foreshawm groined.

'So that's the little spat that catches the bawdy muckerel the

briney abasement where we scomber at our libertined gaol!'
So far all jackular but now a saltier infection. 'I teened tined
without embarkration down that slitway my jolly tarjack
yearning for the fretdown of this narrow fineconment swished-
for incunceration ounspeaking O where noughtical men wisely
feast in silence a coop or lock-up maybe Angel but for the
brightest cockalorys no lighthouse but a folderoloflesh es-
pressionless no landmast certainly no buoy yet more than
polestar to the marinader the milky wet itself the yin-and-yank
by which life orients the loadstir that aweights all tonninch on
the populocean incontinents awash the very auto-incestral
fracturn between generoceans mother of emoceans gulf where
the seacunning sextant steers and never more gladly flock we to
that flocculent in carcerationen like sheep incult cumbency on
the long combers O so furly I will my rompant chuck of gristle
uncanvas to cell and serve as croptive to her in the shuckling
socket and set soul for dungeoness!'
He launched himself to the briney swell with merry horn-
poop in her focsle and cox'nd every vibrant strokc till her un-
fathom ablepuddle deigned and drained his saloot but her
aglued mutions rollocked on.

Angeline walked impotiently outside and some of the tribe
noted or did not note – caught in their own variable relation-
ships – how her face was fleshcrumbled with folded eyes. So it
was these days and no one had too much in mind of others
though the mood was good – too wrapped in selfhood and even
selfishness to aggress, no matter who aggrised, on alcohol or the
needle. She was thrown to a sexual nadir and would not bed,
not with Charteris, not with Ruby Dymond even when he
folked up the blues for her, backed by infrasound and its
bowelchurning effects. Even for her it was getting not for-real,
as the war-showers still lingering acidly in the old alleyways,
curled into her and she too dug the spectrums of thought made
visible, leaping up exclaiming from a lonely blanket to see herself sometimes surrounded by the wavering igneous racks of
baleful colour: or at gentle moments able to watch bushes and
elms erupt in crusty outline singed by the glow of cerebral
sundowns, in which climbed and chuckled a fresh unbeaten
generation of mammalphibians, toads with sprightly wings and
birds of lead and new animals generally that with feral stealth
stayed always out of focus.
So it was also with Nicholas Boreas but more splendidly

trumpets with icing on. He too had more inhabitants than reached consciousness and drank news of the motorcade miracle from Cass in his palatial bath. A mighty figure he was, bare without a hair, though with a poet's eye he had schillered his breasts and pate by dint of a bronze lacquer to lend a sort of piebald distinction. His flower was water hyacinth and in the foetid warmth of his apartment the tuberous plants multiplied and festered. Having heard Cass's spiel, he pushed his current nymph aside and slid under water, neptunelike, snorkel between crowned teeth. There submerged, he lay as in a trance, letting the feathery floating roots caress him, tickle his lax flesh, gazing up between the stiff fleshy leaves, nibbled by snails, nudged by carp and orfe bursting past his eyelids like coronary spasms.

Finally, he rose again, hyacinth-laurelled.

'I'm in full agreement with your suggestion as long as I can make it my way. Pour all my genius in! It should be a great film: Charteris Auto-Trip or some such title. Maybe High Point Y? The first panorama of post-psychedelic man with the climax the emergence of this messiah-guy after the colossal smash-up on the motorway when he was killed then risen again unscathed. Ring my casting director on this number and we'll start auditioning straight away for someone to play Charters. Also we'll want smashees.'

Whitewhale-like he rose, brushing black ramshorns from his knotted sheepshanks and the band began to play. In his veined eye gleamed the real madness; again he could explore – now on the grandest mafiabacked scale – the fissured continent of death. His best-known film was The Unaimed Deadman, in which a white man wearing suitable garments slowly killed a negro on a deserted heliport. He had been inspired to find a negro willing to volunteer to give a real death to art; now his messianic power would transfix on a large scale the problem of the vigour-mortis intersurface.

Attended by the plushy nymph, Boreas began to issue his orders.

His organisation staggered into action.

The idea was that the film should be made with all speed to take advantage of topicality. Archives could be plundered for effective passages. Except for the climax, little footage need be newly shot. Episodes from The Unaimed Deadman could be used again. In particular, there was a sequence showing the Optimistic Man doing his topological topology act which seemed applicable. The Optimistic Man walked along a wide white line with hands outstretched, his hands and head and the white line filling the whole screen against the ground. The camera slowly disengaged itself from his shoulder as the line became more intricate, rising upwards like a billowing roof, revealing that more made less sense for the Man now seemed to be doing the impossible and walking on the rim of a gigantic eye; but, with increase of altitude, the eye is seen as the eye of a horse carved from the flank of an enormous mountain. Slowly the whole horse comes into view and the Man is lost in distance; but as this anomaly clarifies another obtrudes itself for we see that the great downland on which the cabbalistic horse is etched is itself astir like a flank and itself cabaline. This mystery is never clarified, there is only the nervous indecision of the whole hill's glimpsed movement – we cut back to the Man who now, in a white suit, stretches himself out wider and wider until he can saddle the horse. He has shed all humanity but bones; skeletally, he rides the charger, which is given motion by the rippling flank on which it is engraved.

There are sequences from old-fashioned wars, when the processes of corruption sometimes had a presynchronicity to moribundity, and a shot of a nuclear bomb detonated underground, with a whole sparse country rumpling upward into a gigantic ulcerated blister and rolling outwards at predatorial speed towards the fluttering camera. There are sequences in shuttered streets, where the dust lies heavy and onions rot in gutters; not a soul moves, though a kite flutters from an overhead wire; somewhere distantly, a radio utters old-fashioned dance music interspersed with static; sunshine burns down into the engraved street; finally a shutter opens, a window opens; an iguana pants out into the roadway, its golden gullet wide.

After this came the Gurdjieff Episode, taken from a coloured Ukrainian TV musical based on the life of Ouspenski and entitled Different Levels of the Centres.

A is a busy Moscow newspaper man, bustling here, bustling there, speaking publicly on this and that. A man of affairs whom people turn to; his opinion is worth having, his help worth seeking. Enter shabby old Ouspenski with an oriental smile, manages to buttonhole A, invites him along to meet the great philosopher Gurdjieff. A is interested, tells O he will certainly spare the time. G reclines on a sunny bedstead, derelict from the mundane world; he has a flowering moustache, already turning white. He holds on to one slippered foot. In his shabby room, it is not possible to lie: nonsense is talked but not lies – the very lines of the old dresser and the plaid cloth over the table and the empty bowl standing on the deep window sill declare it.

The window has double casements with a lever-fastener in the centre. The two halves of the window swing outwards. There are shutters, latched back to the wall outside. The woodwork has not been painted for many years; it rests comfortable in morning sunlight, faded but not rotten, seamed but not too sear. It wears an expression like G's.

G gives what is a grand feast for this poor time of war. Fifteen of his disciples come, and some have an almost Indian unworldliness. They sit about the room and do not speak. With lying out of the way, presumably there is less to say. One of the disciples bears a resemblance to the actor who will play Colin Charteris.

In comes O, arm-in-arm with A, and introduces him with something of a flourish to G. G is very kind and with flowing gestures invites A to sit near him. The meal begins. There are *zakuski*, pies, *shashlik*, *palachinke*. It is a Caucasian feast, beginning on the stroke of noon and continuing until the evening. G smiles and does not speak. None of his people speak. A politely talks. Poor O is dismayed. We see that he realises that G has set this meal up as a test of A.

Under the spell of hospitality, soothed by the warm Khagetia wine, A sets himself out to be the public and entertaining man who can enliven even the dullest company. The chorus takes the words from his moving lips and tells us what A talks about.

He spoke about the war; he was not vague at all; he knew what was happening on the Western Front.

He gave us word of all our allies, those we could trust, those we couldn't, and had a bit of innocent fun about the Belgians.

He gave us word of Germany and how already there were signs of crumbling: but of course the real enemy was the Dual Monarchy.

And here he took more wine and smiled.

He communicated all the opinions of the public men in Moscow and St Petersburg upon all possible public subjects.

Then he talked about the desiccation of green vegetables for the Army: a cause with which he was involved, he said: and in particular the desiccation of onions, which did not keep as well as cabbages.

This led him on to discuss artificial manures and fertilisers, and agricultural chemistry, chemistry in general, and the great strides made by Russian industry.

And here he took more wine and smiled.

He then showed how well he was informed upon philosophy, perhaps in deference to his host.

He spoke of melioration and told us all about spiritism, and went pretty thoroughly into what he called the material-isation of hands.

What else he said we don't remember, save that once he touched on cosmogony, a subject he had somewhat studied.

He was the jolliest and certainly the happiest man in the room. And then he took more wine and smiled and said he must be off.

Poor O had tried to interrupt this monologue but G had looked at him fiercely. Now O hung his head while A heartily shook hands with G and thanked him for a pleasant meal and a very interesting conversation. Glancing at the camera, G laughed slyly. His trap had worked.

Afterwards, G jumps up and sings his song, and the disciples join in. Gradually, the whole screen is choked with whirling bodies.

While the film was being pieced together, a French actor called Minstral was engaged to play Charteris. Because France had been neutral in the war, Minstral was one of the few pre-psychedelic men left in Brussels. He played tough roles. When not filming, he kept himself apart, ate tinned food sent from Toulouse, meditated in a Sufic way, occasionally visited two young Greek sisters in the suburbs, and looked at volumes of beautiful photographs published by Gallimard.

Boreas's script director, Jacques de Grand, made his way out to the motorcamp on the lunatic fringes of the city with a haircut full of gentian hairoil. He wanted to get some background for the messiah's life, him and his success-drive both.

When de Grand arrived at the smokescream, the messiah was sitting on an old bedstead, picking his toes; from his two women he had only bad images; they would not yield to his healing power and he was feeling several things at once, that nothing could be done on any level unless women were involved in creative roles, that they were trapped in a history jelly, that he was a discarded I, and that the world was on the whole perched on the back of a radioactive tortoise.

'We're very fortunate to have you here at the early stages of your career, Mr Master, and witnessing the first miracles. How you like Belgium? Planning to stay long? Planning to resurrect anyone in the near future? My card!'

The card held a hand in it on a detachable body materialising in rubber smokelp.

'It was the vision I had in Metz. That's what betrayed me on my adjourney north up the web of photofailures, fleeing that Italian camp.'

'I see.' Quick application of more refreshing hairoil, head chest mouth. *Nom,* but the PCA was thick here and all hair growing whispers on it. 'You say photofailures, I gather from reports you enlarge Ouspavski's thought?'

'Well like Ouspavski I dig the west got too hairy with everyone and so the Arabian nightmare was just a justice and on the ill-painted poser the near-nordic blonde grew a moustache like a shadow across her force. . . .

'And so how about some more erections in the near future? Please speak clearly into the visiting card.'

The whole mesozoic mess-up of the best west pretensions going themselves with the buns turning to gutter and silence is golden but a Diners Club card gets you anywhere. It was the whole city of a ruined version I had, he told de Grand. 'Now Europe's bracken up from a basic oil-need-greed and beggars can ride so even Gelina and Marta and me can't get along in a harness and all clapped out of the big ambushes of Westciv, eh?'

'I see. You think the bill's at last been paid?'

'Yes, the treadbill, trodden back to low point X and the city open to the noman. My friend, that was a short round we trod, less than two hundred degenerations the flintnapping cavesleepers first opened stareyes and we break down again with twentieth sensory perception of the circuit. . . .

'I see. More hairoil quick, and you think we're back where we squirted?'

'. . . which bust be the time for real awakening from machinality and jump off the treads into a new race that I will lead.' And the new animals falling out of new trees on the old beaches of stone.

'Yes, I see, Master. So you have no definite pains to insurrect anyone in the near future?'

'Angelina sees if she's not by now hyacinth-hipped the waters of sickness wrys and where we might have been balsam only balsa on the flord but me urgenus impatiens spends on merely the unhealing womenwound that helotrope witch tows me with its bloodstone balmy fragrance unaveiling nector's womenwound me my ackilleaseheal.'

'You motion the waters of sickness, so you don't entirely rile out the possibility of insufflation in the near-flowering fuchsia?'

Taking back the visiting cod he filed his nail-dropping in a filing *gabinetto*.

'I am a fugitive from that perfumarole yet all beneath our feet the quakeline blows and vulcanows which runway lies firm aground for all this ilyushine is a flight merely from other ilyushins and not from anything called real.' The broken wind of his sail lay under the tall shrouds of offices.

'I see. I see what you're goating at. Like there's been a disulcation. Hair owl? No? Tell me couldn't you practise on a dead child if we brought you one?'

Charteris coughed his eyeblink a world gone then back in its imposture. Lies he could take, not disfigurements.

'Perfect sample of what I'm trying to gut over with the prolapse of old stricture of christchen moralcold all pisserbill it is are phornographable smirch as childermastication to be hung by the necrophage until strange phagocyte of the crowd.'

'So you deignt insufect anyone in the puncture?'

'Lonly Angina and the flowerhip-syrup girls.'

He coughed. When world came back steadied, in the big carred-up arena, tyres were still burning. The smoke crawled and capered a black nearest brown; up the side of a ruinous housewall where wallpaper hung montaged, its shadow grew like wisteria in the palid sun. Over one side, some disciples in gaudy hats and ruby beards were making a sing-in on the torture song. Another, a guy stoked an old auto with its upholstery in flames by flinging on petrol arcing from a can. The flames flowered at him and he rolled over yelling. Several people looked across him and the unbelievable patterning of it all, life's gaudy grey riches richer richness. The world of motion-in-stillness. All rested here today from the speed death but a migratory word and they would be away again, switched on to the signal the Master would unzip from his banana-brain. Right now, even as he proclaimed, all possibilities were open to them and under the crawling black tyresmog lay no menace that did not also swerve for poetry, so the tribe let all burn.

A strip of the motorway south of Brussels to Namur and Luxembourg had been closed to traffic. Boreas's men worked and sweated, hundreds of them, many skilled in electronics, to fake up the big smash-in.

Some got through their work by being cowboys. Yipping and yelping, they thundered down upon the frightened cars, which stampeded like mad steers along the course, tossing their horns and snorting and backfiring in the canyon of their cavalcade. Branding irons transfixed hot red figures.

Other men from Battersea treated the steeds as underwater wrecks. In mask and flippers, down they sank through the turbid air, securing limpet cameras to cabins and bows and battered sterns which would record the moment of the mighty metal storm, rigging their mikes unfathomably, helter-scootering.

Other men with mottled cheeks worked as if they were charge nurses in an old people's home. Their patients were as smooth as they were stiff of limb, dummies with nude sexless faces, dummies without female fractures or male mizzenmasts, non-naval dummies, dummies lacking meatmuscle or temperature who pretended to be men, dummies with plaster hair and amenorrhoea who pretended to be women, dwarf dummies with a semblance to children, all staring ahead with blue eyes impevious, upholders all of the couth past wesciv world that could afford to buy its saudistruction, all terribly brave before their oncoming death, all as unspeaking O as G desired.

Rudely, the charge nurses pressed their patients into place, the backseat-drivers and the frontseat-sitters, twisted their heads to look ahead, to stare sideways out of the windows, to enjoy their speed deathride, to be mute and unhairy and non-drivnik.

It was an all-day labour, and to wire the cars. The crews revelled that night in Namur, shacking in an old hotel or sleeping in a big marquee tent pitched on the banks of the Meuse, with a beat trobbing like a temple. Boreas went belting back to Brussels and with a shivering sight stripped virgin bare, gripped tight the snorkel in his crowned teeth and sank beneath the feathery roots of his water hyacinths. The plants were spreading like a nylon nile, growing in the steamy atmosphere over the floor and up the black-tiled walls.

'Escrape from these lootless psychedelics showing their barbed crutches round the eyes,' he gruntled wallowing, 'as if I don't own all my own univorce!'

'Don't you believe in Charteris as new Christ, darling?' the nymph asked, floating pasturised cowslips on the sumper surface. She was delicious to his sight and taste, good Flemish stock.

'I believe in my film,' he said and grasping her alligator-like in his jaws he looted her down into her depths.

Next day refreshed and bellyrolled, Boreas drove down towards the scene of the faked authentic speed death with his script director de Grand who gave golden speech about the Master between cranial embrocations.

'Okay, so he was kinky about children and gone on flowers and didn't seem to have plans about bringing anyone back from the deadly nightshade. Similar to thousand of people I know or don't know as the case. Did you get a glimpse of his life story?'

'You know those ruins out by Sacré Coeur, boss? They had a five gallow saturation bomb on them when the Arab air strike came down! You can't hardly see out there. I was switched on myself and it seemed to me his logic was all logogriph and missing every fourth syllable of recorded time. That fabled bird, the logogrip, took wing, was really hippocrene in all his gutterance, where I way-did but could never plum.'

'Cut out that jar-jargon, de Grand! A hell of a help you are! What about his bird?' Chin belly and balls are jetting promontories.

'I tell you the logogriph, the new pterospondee, roasts on his burning shoulder!'

'His bird, his judy! Did you get to speak to her?'

'He mentioned a part of her with some circumlocution.'

'*Godverdomme!* Get her and bring her to me in my pallase tonight. Ask her to dinner! She'll give me the low-down of this Master Man! Have you sot that straight in your adderplate?'

'Is registered.' And bennies quickly swigged down in oil.

'Okay. And get some more snow delivered to Cass – some of the motorcaders need a harder ticket in the arterial lane. *Comprenez?*'

They march from each other together in the web.

His unit was already setting up the crash-in. Technicians swarmed about the location with cowherd and keelhaul cries. By somebody's noon, the cars were all linked umbiliously with cables to the power control and the dummies sitting tight. They ran through the whole operation over and over, checking and rechecking acidulously to see if in their hippie state they had overlooked a technicolor time error. The four-lane motorway was transfilmed into a great racetrick where the outgoing species could stunt-in for its one and only one-way parade, a great tracerack in tombtime where sterile generations would last for many milliseconds and great progress appear to be made as at ever-accelerating speed they hurtled on, further from shiftless and forgotten origins the unknown target. This species on the vergin of extinction bore its role with detachment, waxed unsentimentality, was collected, chaste, impeccable, punctual, stiff upper lip, unwinking gaze. Remembered its offices and bungalows of iron sunset. Its lean servants, ragged even, not so; excitement raced among them; they all believed in this authentic moment of film-life, cared not for a fake-up, slaved for Boreas's belief, harboured their dimensions.

And to Boreas when all was ready came his chief prop man, Ranceville, with shoulder-gestures and slime in his mouth's corners.

'We can't just let them gadarine like this! It's sadism! They are as human as you or me, in our different way. Couldn't there be thought inside those china skulls – china thought? China feelings? China love and sincerity!'

'Out my way, Ranceville!'

'It isn't right! Spare them, Nicholas, spare them! They got china hearts like you and me! Death will only make them realer! Real china death-in!'

'*Miljardenondedjuu!* We want them to look real, be real. What's real for if you can't use it, I ask? Now, out my way!'

'What have they ever done to you?' The mouth all slaving lotion. 'What have they ever done?'

Boreas gestured, brushing away a fly or snail from his barricaves.

'I'll tell you something deep deep down, Ranceville . . . I've always hated dummies ever since china shop-rows of them stared in contempt at me as a poor small boy in the ruptured alleys off Place Roup. That's how I began you know! Me a dirty slum boy, son of a Flemish peasant! Weren't they the privileged, I thought, all beautifully dresden every day by lackeys, growing no baggy genitals, working or spinning clean out the question, glazed with superiority behind glass, made in god's image more than we? Dimmies I called them to belittle them, dimmies, prissy inhibitionists! Now these shop-haunting horrors shall die for the benefit of mankind.'

'Your box-official verdict, so!' Gesture of a gaudy cross.

'Okay, Nicholas, then I ask to ride with them, to belt in boldly in the red Banshee beside these innocent chinahands. They're sinless, guiltless, cool – I'll bleed to death with them, that's all I ask!'

Open mouths gathered all round turned their stained suspicious teeth to ogle gleaning Boreas, who waited only the splittest second before he bayed from his mountain top

'Get looted, Ranceville! You're hipped! You think you can't die – you're like a drunkard sleeping in the ditch, drowning for ever because he didn't realise there was a stream running over his pillow!'

'So what, if the drinking water has drunks in it, okay, that proves its proof. How can I die the death if those dimmies are not alive?'

'You'll see how real a phoney death is!'

Now on the waiting road was silence while they chewed on it. Like workers who joined a continent's coasts by forging a new railway, the unit stood frozen by their finished work, awaiting perhaps a cascade of photographs to commemorate their achievement of new possibilities: while behind them fashionably the unlined pink faces ignored them from the cars. The mouths came forward now, to see what Boreas would say, to hear out the logic, to try once again to puzzle out how death differed from sleep and sleep from waking, or how the spring sunlight felt when you weren't there to dig it and flesh and china all one to me.

Boreas again was sweating on the heliport, in his blood the hard ticket of harm as he filmed the climax of The Unaimed Deadman, had the negro, Cassius Clay Robertson, fight to start up the engine of his little glass-windowed invalid carriage. And then the longshot of the white man in his suitable garb running impossibly fast with big gloved hands from behind the far deserted sheds, the black sheds with tarred asphalt sides, running over for the kill with mirth on his mouth. Now he could have real death again, had it offered, because the occasional man was hepped enough on art to die for it.

'Okay, Ranceville, as long as you see this is the big oneway ride, we'll draw up a waiver contract.'

Ranceville drew himself up thin. 'I shan't waver! As the Master says, we have abolished the one-ways. I believe in all alternatives. If you massacre innocents, you massacre me! Long live Charteris!'

The watching mouths drew apart from him. One pair of lips

patted him on the shoulder and then stared at the hand. Some sighed, some whispered. Boreas stood alone, bronze of his bare head shining. The invalid car had fired at last and was slowly lurching on the move. The white man with the terrible anger had reached it and was hammering on the glass, rocking it with his blows. They'd had a hovercamera in the cab with Robertson then, with another leeched outside the misting glass, and used for the final print shots from these two cameras alternately, giving a rocking rhythm, bursting in and out of Robertson's terror-trance.

'Get yourself in focus of the cameras!' Boreas called huskily.

With a sign to show he had heard, Ranceville climbed into the old Banshee, a scrapped blue model they found in a yard by the Gare du Nord and had hurriedly repainted. Ranceville had red on clothes and hands as he squeezed in with the dummies. Their heads nodded graciously like British royalty in an arctic wind.

'Okay, then we're ready to go!' Boreas said. 'Stations, everyone!'

He watched all his mouths like a hawk, the only one sane, whistling under his breath the theme from The Unaimed Deadman. Things would fall apart this time from the dead centre.

Marta was sprawling on the bed practically in tears and said, 'You don't understand, Angelina, I'd no wish to pot your joint out, but my loaf was nothing, not the leanest slice, and I was just a baby doldrums until the Father came along and woke all my other I's and freeked me from my awful husband and my awful prixon home and all the non-looty things I try now to put outside the windrums.'

Angelina sat on the side of the bed without touching Marta. Her head hung down. Beyond, Charteris was holding a starve-in.

'Fine, I sympathise with you when you stop whining. We've all had subsistence-living lives in rich places. But the way things are, he belongs to me you've got to get yourself another mankind. There'll be a group-grope tonight – any grotesque grot they grapple – now that's for you instead of all this ruin-haunting here!'

'And supposing I pick on your Ruby you so despise! My life's a ruin and the light dwindles on the loving couple. The Master said to me Arise – '

'Rupture all that, daisy! You just don't spark! Look, I know how you feel, the big love-feelings heart-high, but it wasn't like that so don't try to hipple out of it. All he did was walk in and make an offer as you sat single in your little house! That doesn't mean he's yours!'

'You don't understand. . . . It's a religious thing and mauve and maureen webworks come from him binding me! With his sweet rocket it's a sacrament.'

The ceiling simmering like a saucepan lid and Angelina hit her with a welp of rage and called her all mangey mother-suppurating things. 'You Early Christian whore! Go throw yoursylph to other loins! He's my man and stays that way!'

In anger, she drove the Marta from this ruined arena out, and then herself collapsed on to the single bed. There she still was when de Grand riled in, slipping a little packet to Case before he sought her out. She lay and let time set over her not unpleasure-ably, idly listening as the raucous noise of a song and plucked strings filtered in the shadow, wondering if anything mattered. That was the crux of it; they were all escaping from a state where the wrong things had mattered; but they were now in a state where nothing matters to us. At least if I can still thing this way I'm sane – but how to put it over to them and that they should be building. . . . The possibility exists, and some days he does build: almost by accident like a weaver bird adding an extra room for teenage chicks to creep up at the back where it stark and on the stares a big woman all all naked bottoms and beasts. . . . Bum weaver yes Colin he still has the glimpse. . . . A sort of genius and might stage a build-on. . . . Pull this lot together must make him listen maybe if I put it in a song for the Tonic all get the message. The table you use the table you take immense suck cess likely me running naked through loveburrow. . . . Old Mumma Goostale. . . .

As she dozed he entered, not uncivil with untrimmed moustache, de Grand, of secret history in plenty parishes.

'Excuse you saw me interviewing for the film the Master. Second time I'm pleasure of drivnik-visiting.'

'I'm thinking. I know it's extinct. Blow!'

'What intelligence! I'm full of aspiration. I left my own child to come on this quest to film the lootest Masterpiece.'

'Bloody typical. Go back to your child, Paddy, marry her, bear lots of lovely morechild, marry them off, live humble, avoid oil-shares, stay away from the excitements of master-peace, rumpling upwards and rolling at speed towards the fluttering artnik.'

'The director needs your prosfessional guy dance routine to insight the Master to him. Has a dinner cooking wed local indelicacies and you tenderly invited.'

She sat up and tugged down the flower-blue shirt and bongo beads she was wearing, her modernity unfit, forgot arrested flow, with an effort focused on him.

'The director you say?'

'Nick Boreas of The Overtaker and The Unaimed Dead now moving to High Point Y to film your husband's life in compaint colour. The great Nick Boreas you must have heard.'

'He wants the truth about Charteris? Is that what you are saying? My god, these stinking runes are so high I'm almost indechypreable – Boreas wants the truth?' She fanned herself, he also, gasping like fishes in a mean lake.

'You have me defused a moment. Excuse – some pomaid! We're making a movie not a gospel we must want material like a sort of biogriffin job, right?'

'The mythic bird what else is struth! A movie you say! You my opportunity I zip on my head boy and you take me to your leader now?' With nails she tries to calm her wild dark hair.

'My fiat awaits delighted.' He with a byzantine bow.

She paused. 'You driving? You're so high, no?'

But he was in a studio car with hired driver and they yawed towards the fossil-pattern centre with moderate risk to life.

On the brittlements of the town auroras flattered in a proud mindflagging and old phantasms took trilobites at her. She was a guttered target for their technicolon pinctuated in a single frame as the assassin went home, feeling her face flatten and balloon as if centred in a whirling telescopular site. Tumultaneously, the broad Leopold II sloughed its pavements for grey sand and cliffs cascaded up where buildings were, unpocked by window or stratum. Turning her tormented head, she saw the ocean weakly flail the macadam margins of shore bearing in change, long, resounding, raw – and knew again as some tiresome visiting professor of microscopic sanity made clear to her that hear again repetitively iron mankind zinc was on the slide between two elements, beaten back to seawrack while he prepared to digest another evolutionary change and none the less stranded because motors roared for him up the hell and highwatershed.

Such sounds seemed sexplicable, nexplicable, inexplicable,

plicable, lickable, ickable, able, sickable. She was able to differentiate the roar into eight different noises, all flittering towards her under the cover of each other. Things that slid and fused let out a particularly evil gargle, so that she grasped de Grand's moustached arm and cried, 'They won't allow me to be the only one left sane, they won't allow me!'

Wrapping a moist hand about her, the scar of his lips unhealing on the face pustule its genetic slide screaching, he said, 'Baby, we all swing on the same astral plane and there's a new thing now.'

And in the variable geometry of her mind, great wings retracted and the thin whine let in stratosfear.

Boreas rose black, deadly-electric, face masked and goggled, hyacinthine from his bathpool, beetling baldbright, not unmanly, a eunuch but with fullgorged appendages. A palatial meal was being prepared in the next room.

'Let me feel you first.'

'I'm in no feeling mood.' Age-old Angeline. He invited her to swim; when she refused, he reluctantly came from the green water and swaddled himself in towels, quite prepared to wreck her.

'After the meal, the rushes!'

'I don't swim, thanks.'

'You'll have a breast stroke when you see the dimmies caroom into their smash-in!' Full of tittering good humour, he led her through, a heliogabbic figure eight of a man and she bedraggled with a little brave chin, saying, 'I want to talk seriously with you about the lying-in-state of our old world.'

He paraded with her slowly round the grand room, already partly hyacinth-invaded as they foliaged intricoarsely across the wallpagan, he speaking here and there to the chattering mass of his invitees, all to Angeline maroonly macabre and flowing from the head as part of the mythology of the palapse and from their infested breath and words crawled the crystalagmites she dreamed of dreading in the coral city trees without window or stratum.

A speech was made by one of the gaudier figmies in a tapestry, beginning by praising Boreas, ascending on a brief description of the steel industry of a nearby un-named state, and working through references to Van Gogh and a woman called Marie Brashendorf or Bratzendorf who had brought forth live puppies after a nine-day confinement up the scales of madness

149

to a high sea reference to Atlantic grails and the difficulty of making salami from same. Then the company sat or sprawled down, Boreas taking a firm hold of Angelina to guide her next to him, one great hand under her shirt grappling the life out of her left breast into multi-variable contour.

The first course of the banquet was presented, consisting only of hot water tainted by a shredded leaf, and all following courses and intercases showed similar liquididity in these hoard times, except for warm slices of *bodding*, and no silence settled like at the G mealtime he led us all a merry dance.

'All the known world,' she said sliding in, 'loses its old staples and in only a few months everything will drop apart for lack of care. People who can must save the old order for better times before we're all psychedelic salvages and you in your film can show them how to keep a grip until the bombeffect wears thin, do a preachment of the value of pre-acidity and the need to rebuild wesciv.'

'No no no, *cherie*, concoursely, my High Point Y is an improachmen of the old technological odour, which was only built up by reprunsion and maintained by everyone's anxiety, or dummied into inhabition. Okay, so it all go and no worries. You husbind is a saviour man who lead us to a greater dustance away from old steerotypes and a new belief in the immaterial. So I picture him.'

'Okay, I agree as everyone must that there were many greedy faults but put at its lowest wesciv maimtamed in reasonable comfort a high population which now must die badly by plague and starve off to its last wither.'

'You talk to wrong guy, girlie, because I enormously like to see those ferretty technilogy people die off with all the maimtamed burrgeoisie and black in the ground slump in bulldozing massgraves in Mechelen and Manchester.'

'You shock me, Boreas. And who then will watch your epix?'

Slices of Christmas cactus succulent and inedible were placed before them.

He took her with his roystering gaze she so thin and succulenten.

'I will eye my films! To the ego egofruit. For me only is they made and to enjoy! For long since the sixties have I and many lesser I's pouring clout our decompositional fluid medium preparing for this dessintegration of sorciety and now you want again the tripewaiters and oilgushers and the offices clattering?' He sipped shallowly at the long sour *gueuze-lambic* as it came round. 'Balls to the late phase we've been through.'

'Some of the old evils maybe die but worse still live on. 'She would not sup. Her eyelids low.

'We live authentic now and the new way which your husbond cries!'

Under her waif-thin lids she gauzed at the continuum mumbling guests all butterflies or hot rock without rest and each in an amber clockdrill of our mechanissmus that to new born retinal grasp showed in ever moo and ghestune.

'And are these the authenticks as you mountain?' Scorning.

Grinding his heavensgravelstone teeth, resting predirty ham on her pecked muscle, 'Don't perspine for the judge's tone when you're jabbed in the witless blox woman!'

So for the first time she muddled into revelation and the silent goose grass was again in motion that Colin grasped society went in autosleep his ennemas enemy and wanever jungle he battled in it lay only a March day's march from her own plot. In even his sickmares might be more health than this fat man's articles.

'Why did you invite me here?' And vonnegutsy whines in her visceration.

'Not for the size of your bobbies mine are bigger you slim spratlady! Listen, I want the word on your man we know you have a thing or true against him and that's for revelation.'

'If I damned well don't?'

Butterflies and hot rock flowed up the hyacynth panels to the bright openings of numerous beetel mouths of the tracery.

'If you don't theres multi-ways of setting an entire squeeze-in round the motorcave and such I warn you solo voce here and never!'

'Are you threatening me?' All round her the artichokers were unheard as her head's mainline flowed more regularly in this duress and she viewed with clarity his mantled cheeks and eyes of menace.

'If you don't want your motorcod tempered with you'll peach me the laydown with all loot on how your saviourboy committed a murder in the British traffic, didn't he?'

And the whole sparse countryside unrolling to her camera, dodging – 'Who'll temper with us – you? Our little motorcade tries to ride in innosense but always an evil parashitting grip strangles it you know you know know what I mean the Mafia with their hard relief are maffiking?'

His jelly flesh was suddenly hard contracted and the mouth

gash sealed and done. 'Don't say that name in here or you'll be in a sidealley lying with the lovely lubrication gone and nothing swinging babe be warn!'

Now all jungular noises cease and the dusky rook hovers.

She was standing again in the ruined garden where sweet rocket sent its sprays among the grass and thistle and her mother screamed I'll murder you if you come in again before you're told! No flowers or fruit ever on the old entangled damson trees except the dripping mildew where their leaves curdled in brown knots perhaps she had seen them among the branches the new animal the fey dog with red tie and been inoculated with the wildered beauty of despair against this future moment's recurrence.

Music now played and the vegetattles chattered on as two flower-decked seamen sang of black sheds down a runway. One last stormblown look, Boreas had dislocated and was seen away on the otherside where the mob was most like a market marakeshed with hippie hordes and de Grand in oil-welled mirth. Moving forward, this throng swept up Angeline and broke her into a adjoining private theatre. 'What's the rush?'

'You don't swing! They're coming!'

The ceiling flew away the nightbox closed and glaring careyes filled the screen with coloured rattle 5 4 3 2 One buildings surged and broke along the autobahn at troglo-daybreak in grey unconvincing weather, autostrata punctuated by windows, their boxrooms stuffed with the comic strip of family bedroomdress as all rose crying 'Master! Charteris!' in braces and curling clips. Now paper familias folds and rises from his breakfast serially lifts the kids into the roaring garage monsters gentle monsters gentile masters one by one gliding and choking carring their human scarifice out along the dangerous beaches flashing in variable geography oriented against accident of the urban switchbank.

The film is as yet unedited. Again and a second time the mechanical riptide roars along the breach discontinuity of time and space armoured armoured green and grey and blue and red a race indeed and carried helpless in them the wheel born ones from their brickhills.

The dummies register percognitive impulses of the coming crash. Scenes of the resurrention flash like traffic controls in clarkeian universe, they view themselves disjointed in the rough joinery of impact amortised in the outstretchered am-bulanes and finally in the sexton's sinkingfung drowned by stink and stone in their own neutrifaction beneath the wave freeze. With unwinking blueness they view unwivering blackness and with waxen calm survey the chinalined vacuums in their dollyskulls of this annulity their last civil divorce.

Now from far above ravening like the aerosoiling arabs the eye takes in a checkerboard black-and-white of roads marked like a deserted heliport with the far black sheds of Brussels lying low plunges like a hypodetic to disgorge the main artery of shittlecock. It's plain lanes erupt into prefognotive shock as force lines fault lines seismographic lines demarcation lines lines of variable geolatry and least resistance lines of cronology besom out from the future impact point. Towards this webpoint scudding come the motordollies. They still have several age-long microseconds before point of intersex and times abolition.

In the leading car from Namur rides fashionable cool Mrs Crack dressed to the nines for high point in a teetotal expatriate sun-and-fun commando suit in well-tailored casual style of almond green nylon gaberdine of a knockout simplicity deep patch pockets and ample vaginal versatility trimmed in petunia piping planned to contrast with a snazzy safari hat of saffron acrylan especially designed for crunch-occasions and scarlet patent slingback shoes in nubile moygashel. Her house is always cool and free from hairy guests of the nonconformist world because she uses new immaculate Plastic with the exciting new impeach-coloured plastic coating and a truculent egg-timer free with every canister so get in the egg-time today! Interviewed just before her death, Mrs Crack explained, 'It's fuzzy man. I so admire my lack of vitality.' Laid her head back unspeaking on surrealistic pillow, applied Sun in the new egregious shade.

The interviewer riding bareback on the bonnet thrust the mike at her superbly tailored husband Mr Servo Crack sitting exstatically back not driving in the driving seat with no facial or racial hair painted bronze head and lips to match who said, 'We both moddle many dapper uncreased outfits often in public windows of shops and such places where the elite meet to be neat this we enjoy very much on account of antiseptic lack of any form of marital relations you understand this is not my son in the back just a prefect smaller dummy and a real growing human called Ranceville because as you know my wife Mrs Crack Mrs Historecta Crack that is actually has no capillaceous growth upon her addendum in fact frankly no addendum so of course no capillary attraction since happily I have no gentians or testaments, in the manner of pre-psyche-delic mankind so we are just goodly friends and able to consti-pate on the old middle-class virtues like dressing properly which escalated Europe since hanseatic times of course to the glory of god and his gentleman's gentleman the pope of be-loved memory.'

He was preparing to say more and the gonaddicts were chuckling and fumbling each other in the darkroom for counter-evidence of non-dummiehood when the lemanster encasing Mr Crack flung itself armoured against a monster raving in the apposite direction. Mr and Mrs Crack suffered extinction. Their perfect boy also impeccably crunched. Unfortunately the camera focusing on Ranceville failed to work so that his final blood-letting gestures were not revealed to the celebrating eyes.

Now the whole cock-up took on the slobber-slob motion-rhythm of orgasm sowards the climax of the film and the wet-mouthed awedience watched expectorately. More terrible than humans, the dummies caroomed stiffly forward in the slow frames pressing towards point of impact in tethered flight stretching their belts as over towards the scarring windshields they bucketed eyes of blueness still and all around them gloves and maps and michelins and scattering chocolate boxes parabolaed like pigeons startled at the buckling of the sides and still the honest eggshell eyes and spumeless lips started into nanoseconds of futurity. Gravitidal waving limp arms swinging stiff shoulders unshrugging make-up staying put them swam their butterfly in the only saline solution to the deceleration problem.

All the other armoured lemmings rushed to be in on the destruction. Expressions blank of dismay the dummies had their heads cracked and chipped and knocked and shattered and ground and mashed and eggshelled and blown away with new miracle Crump aiming their last ricocheting nanocheek towards the impactpoint of speedeath the ipaccint of speeeth ipint seeth inteeth ih i i i.

Time and again the cameras peeped on the unbleeding victims and on the cracking tin carcases that with rumptured wings in courtship dragging ground tupped one aonther beetle-bowed in the giddyup of the randabout, till the toms built up an audiction and their cheers were heard above the hubcab of metallurging grinderbiles. But Boreas wept because his film had frightened and to the mainshaft struck him.

His tears scattered. Once they had had a goose to fatten and in the long blight of summer where the damsons festered it made some company with its simple ways not unapproachable. Once her mother brought it out a bucket of water in the heat for it to duck over and over its long head and flail its pruned wings with pleasure scattering the drops across small Angeline. She heard the wings flail now as out she crept nostalgic for the gormless bird they later ate.

At last she came back wearily to where a broken Stella Art sign buzzed and burned in the desolation of their parking lot. She stood there in a wet shift breathing. Under the mauve and maureen flash her face showed like a shuttered street from which might crawl iguaneous things. But just a mental block away where she only blindly knew directions a lane stood in old summer green some place like a magic garden where a young barefoot girl might drive her would-be swans and never think of harsher either-ors.

A small rain filled the incommense thoroughfares of night but still among the guttering buggies stilled tangents of smoke and rib-roofed skeletombs a guitar string or flute fought loneliness with loneliness and a poppied light or naked carbulb gave the flowerdpeople nightpower. Oh Phil the small dogs howl don't ask me what I'm doing on the health Col. She plashes the raddlepuddles in a dim blue fermentation. A round of vestal voices plays noughts and crosses her subterranean path with a whole sparse countryside rumpling the stone-trees. Such shadows in her way she brushes off knowing the nets that await her in the shallows of a nightsunk city. She crounches and pees by old brickhaps. Oh don't be pregnant in this tupturned world!

Sickly still bedummied by the ill winds she staggered through her own grotesquely shatteredporch to find the blanket cold and stiff and Charteris not in. Groping with all menaces she unsandaled herself and beneath crawled heavily. Charteris not in not in the starve-in still? Small sound not rain not dogs reached her and immediate anxieties peopled the grotto with haggard dimmies half in flight with speed as closing in on her she propped and stared. Even hoping-fearing it might be Ruby Dymond?

In the corner Marta only sniffing on a broken chair, lumpkin in the fluttered darklight with her crushed appeal.

'Get to bed girl!'

'The toad is going to get me pushing up my thinghs.'

'Go to sleep stop worrying till tomorrow. The holed world's had enough tonight.'

'But throbbing toadspower! It's trying to force my skull up and climb into my barn my grain and then motor me away to some awful slimy pool of toadstales!'

'You're dreaming! Pack it in!'

Laying down her tawdry head she tucked her motherless eyelids on her cheeks and took herself far away from drivniks a goosegirl in an old summer lane drove her would-be-swans barefoot. And cellos hit a seldom chord.

Every day Charteris like a bird of prayer spoke to new crowds finding new things to say giving outwards and never sleeping never tired sustained by his overiding fantasy. Two three days passed so at the big starve-in for Belgium's famine or Germany's bad news. He sat with a can of beans that Cass and Cass's buddy Buddy Docre had brought him half-forking them into his mouth and smilingly half-listening to some disciples who parrited back at him a loose interpretation of what they had gleaned in all enthusiasm.

When he had filled his crop enough he rose slowly and began to walk slowly so as not to disturb the ripples of the talk from which he slowly wove his own designs half-hearing of the fishernet of feeling. In these famine days they all grew gaunt he especially captain on his scoured bridge his face clawed by multi-colour beard to startling angles and all of them in their walk angular stylised as if they viewed themselves from a crow's nest distanced. Partly this walk was designed to keep their flapping shoes on their feet and to avoid the litter in the lands stirred by thin breezes breaking: for they had now camped here three unmoving days or weeks and were a circus for the citizens who brought them wine and clothes and sometimes cake.

Charteris kept his gaze steady as hair hid his eyes in the wind hover.

Cass said gently to him almost singing, 'This evening is our great triumphal entry, Master, when we break at last from this poor rookery and the lights of Brussels will welcome you and show your film and turn the prized town over to you. We have prepared the ground well and your followers flock in by hundreds. There is no need to motor farther for here we have a fine feathered jerusalem where you will be welcome for ever.'

Sometimes he did not say all that he thought. Privately he

said to himself, 'While under the lid the finger is still to Frankfurt how shall we do more than park overnight in Belgium? How can Cass be so blind he does not see that if there is no trip there is nothing? He must be eyeless with purpose.'

So he swooped down upon the field of truth that Cass and Buddy pushed and that Cass like Angeline had no habit in his dark draper suit. Behind his shutters he saw bright-lit Cro-Magnons fearful in feathers and brutally flowered hunt the ponderous Neanderthal through fleet bush and drive them off and decimate them: not for hatred or violence but because it was the natural order and he uttered, 'Predelic man must leave our caves as we reach each valley.'

'Caves! Here's a whole hogging city ours for the carve-in!' said blind Cass. But there were those present who dug the Master and soon this casually important word of His went round and new attitudes were born in the bombsites and a solitary zither taking up this hunting song was joined by other instruments. And the world sailed too amid the Master's brainwaves.

Leaving the others aside, he stylised himself back to his ruined roost where Angeline sat with her back curved to the light unspeaking.

'After the film tonight all possibilities say we flit,' he told her.

She did not look up.

'Leave the will open to all winds and the right one blows. This is the multi-valued choice that we should snarl on and no more middle here.' Echoing his words the first engine broke air as crude maintenance started for the farther trek; soon blue smoke ripped farting across the acid perimeters as more and more switched on.

Still she had no face for him.

'You're escaping, Colin, why don't you face the truth about yourself? It's not a positive decision – you're leaving because you know that what I say about Cass and the others is a whole sparky truth and you hope to shake them off, don't you?'

'After this film and the adulation we flit on a head-start. Maybe a preach-in.' He fumbled and half-lit a half-smoked cigar with an old fouled furcoat over his shoulder.

She stood up facing him more haggard than he. 'He pushes but you don't care, Col! You have the word about the Mafia but you don't care. It was through him Marta died but you don't care. Whatever happens you don't care if we all fall dead in our trips!'

He was looking through the cracked pane. Mostly now they

sat around with a trance-in going even among the rolling cars. But the beer brigade could caper – one of their plump girls danced now in the steel engraving air of a jew's harp slow but sturdy.

'This place has lost all its loot so we'll take in my film and then we'll give it a scan and we'll blow. Open up another city. Why don't you dance, Angelpants?'

'Phil. Robbins, now Marta – oh, you really have lost all loot yourself, man! You wouldn't care if you got cut dead yourself and to think I stood up for you!'

The cigar wasn't working. His hand twitched it into a corner, he moved to the door's gape.

'You use the old fleshioned terms and feelings, Angle, all extinct with no potentiality. There's a new thing you aren't with but I begin to gravel. Somewhere Marta got a wrong drug, somewhere she caught hipatitis or pushed herself over. So? It's down-trip and she had a thing we'll never know in her mind, a latent death. She was destined and that's bad. We did the best and can't bind too much if she freaks out.'

Lying with the lovely lubrication gone and nothing swinging.

'Well I bind, for God's sake! I could have helped her when she mewed to me about a toad levering up her skull or whatever it was and instead I sogged back like the rest of them! It was the night of the filmrush and now tonight they let the complete epic roll – I see more death tonight – right here in the toadstool I see it!' She rapped her brow as if for answer.

'Flame,' he said. 'A light to see us off by I see but I don't see you dance like that chubby girl her cheeks. Angey, you can't motorcade – I want you to stay and shack in with the golden Boreas in Bruxelles who'll care for you and is not wholly gone.'

She threw herself at him and clutched him, holding round his neck with one hand stroking his beard his hair his ears his pileum with the other. 'No, no, I can't stay a moment in this stone vortex. Besides, my place is with you. I give you loot, I need you! You know your seed is sealed in me! Have pity!'

'Woman, you won't stay silent at Ouspenski's spread!'

'I'll switch on, I will, and be like you and all the others. I'll dance!'

He side-stepped and the vague promises of a mind-closure near engine stutter.

'You don't take one pinch of loot to my sainthood!'

'Darling, we don't have to take that come-on straight!'

Half to one side he pushed her peering through his own murk

and the broken-down air, muttering, 'So let's get powered!'

'Colin, – you need me! You need someone near you who isn't – you know – hippie!' Her eyes were soft again the wild goose-girl.

'That was yesterday. Listen!' He pointed among the buck-ling roadsters. Ruby Dymond's voice – Ruby always so turned-on to a new vibration – lifted against a Tonic rhythm singing.

> Fearsome in our feathers brutally flowered
> We warn the predelics we're powered
> We warn the predelics we're powered
> We warn the predelics we're powered
> Fearsome in our feathers and brutally flowered

The Word gathered loot as gears kicked in.

And another voice came in shouting 'There are strangers over the hill, wow wow, strangers over the hill.' In the back-ground noise of backfiring and general revving and the tooth-aching zither sound. More plump girls dancing.

'I need only the many now,' he said.

They required little to eat, clothes mattered not much to them, in the strengthening air was the gossamer and hard tack of webwork. What they were given they traded for the precious fluid and this stored in tanks or hidden in saucepans under car seats so that when they had to go they had plenty of go – those who ran out of golden gas got left behind sans loot sans end.

By evening, a rackety carqucuc moved towards the blistered dome of Sacré Coeur and citycentre where every pinnacle concealed its iguana of night. First came the Master in the new red Banshee his Brussels disciples had brought him as tribute, saluting with Angelina huddled despairing in the back seat. Then his tribe in all gay tarnation.

From one shuttered day to the next his mindpower fluctuated and now wheelborn again he, finding the images came fast, tried to order them but what truth they looted seemed to lie in their random complexity. He radiated the net or web to all ends and to cut away strands was not to differentiate the holes. Clearly as the patterns turned in slow mindsbreeze he saw among them an upturned invalid car with wheels still spinning and by it lying a crippled negro on his back lashing out with metal crutches at a strangely dressed whiteman with machine qualities. Near at hand stood in separate frame a fat bare man with painted skull shouting encouragement by megavoice.

Simultaneously this fat bare man lay floating in a lake of flame.

Simultaneously this fat bare man lay in the throes of love with a bare bald female dolly of human scale.

Simultaneously this bare bald dolly was Angeline with her suffering shoulders.

Simultaneously the face was cracked. China griefs seeped from wounds.

Startled, he turned and looked back at her on the back seat. Catching his glance, she lifted her hand and took his reassuringly, mother to child.

She said, 'This good moment is an interim in our long deline.'

He said, 'Wear this moment then with it all *baraka* as if you had it comfortable on your feet for ever in the timeflow,' and at the prompt unprompted words his whole ornate idea of reincarnation in endless cycles flooded his hindusty horizons with eternal recurrence.

Outside their moving windows faces clystered with hunger and hope.

She said, 'They acclaim you in the streets as if you did not come with downfall for them,' gazing at the action.

Cass said to him looking angrily at her, 'They salute you and would keep you here for all the evers, *bapu,* as the wheel turns.'

Thin-cheeked children of Brussels ran like wolves uniting in a pack packing and howling about the car – not all acclaiming, many jeering and attempting to stop the progress. Scuffles broke out. Fights kindled near the slowcade and spread like a bush fire among the stone forests. Half a mile from the Grand Place, the cars piled to a stop and crowds swarmed over them. Some of the drivniks in the cars wept but there was no help for them, the police force having dissolved to rustle cattle on the ignoble German border.

At last the Tonic Traffic managed to climb free and with other helping hands set the infrasound machine with its husky rasped throat extended towards the bobbing heads. Its low vibrations sent a grey shudder across the crowd and a vision of the sick daybreak across untilled land where an old canal dragged straight over the landscape for a hundred versts. With many hands raised to steady the terrible machine, it progressed and the crowds fell back and the other autos moved forward so they grated gradually to Grand Place, with the group bellowing song and all present taking it up as far as able, detonated underground with a whole sparse country rumpling upwards and rolling at predatorial speed towards the fluttering heart with every kind of looted image.

In the Grand Place, a huge screen structured of plastic cubes had been set up on the front of some of the old Guild houses. From the Hotel de Ville oposite, a platform was built perilously out. High resplendent equinoctial on this platform sat the golden Boreas with shadowy men behind him and amid cheering the Master also ascended to sit here among the hatcheteers.

Thus met the two great men and the Bapu knew this was the fat bare ego of megavoice who could radiate powerful drama-dreams and later a song was sung telling that they exchanged views on exitsence with particular reference to what was to be considered inside and what outside or where deautomation lay: but the truth was that the huobub in the square below was so great that both were forced to play Gurdjieff at their own feast and even the offering of Angeline as a dolly substitute which the Master intended had to be forgotten she shrinking nevertheless from him.

Chilled wind rose, petals sweetly scattering. The square had been given rough nautical ceiling by immense canvas sails stretched over it and secured to the stone pinnacles of the guilds encrusting the titled place like stalagmites. This ceiling kept off the seasonal rain that fell as well as supporting strings of multi-coloured lights that glowed in a square way. Now it all became more sparky as the bulbs swung and fluttered where the whole sky was one big switchedonstellation with Cassiopeia dancing and ton-weights of conserved water off-loaded with grotesque effect to the Tonic Traffic dirges. Then the circuits failed and all milling place swung unlit except by torches and one randy probing searchlight until unknown warriors funeral-pyred a bright-burning black motor-hearse.

The night was maniac over self-sold Europe.

Fighting broke out again and counter-singing, a car was overturned converted into variable geometry and set alight to predatory slogans. It was a big loot-in with action all round.

A colour slide show beginning, the crowd settled slightly to watch and smells of reefers densed the choleric air. Glaring colours such as delft blue ornamental red dead grey tabby amber persian turquoise eyeball blue cunt pink avocado green bile yellow prepuce puce donkey topaz urine primrose body lichen man cream arctic white puss copper jasmine thatch chinese black pekinese lavender jazz tangerine moss green gangrene green spitoon green slut green horsy olive bum blue erotic silver peyote pale and a faint civilised wedgwood mushroom that got the bird were squirted direct onto the projector lens and radiated across the place where the pinnacle cliffs of buildings ran spurted and squidged amazing hues until they came like great organic things pumping out spermatorrhoeic rainbows in some last vast chthonic spectral orgamashem of brute creogulation while the small-dogging sky howled downfalls and shattered coloured lightbulbs.

The junketing eferetted into every nanosecond, not all in many sparky spirits for those who wished to leave the square for illness or emergency unable to exculpate a limb in the milling mass. Some weaker and fainter Bruxellois fell beneath beating feet to be beaujolaised under the press. Cholera had to loot its victims standing as their bursting sweats ransacked to fertilise itself all round the strinkled garmen but bulging eyes not making much extinction in exprulsion between agony and ecstasy of a stockstill stampede sparked the harm beneath the harmony and many perished gaily unaware they burst at the gland and vein and head and vent and died swinging in the choke of its choleric fellation.

Only when morning slutted at its lucid shutters the last crazed chords and colours writhed away did the paint-spattered herd gather what their rituals had wrought. From the cattle-pensioners rattled a great and terrible exclamor! Several who had in delurium clambered to the prismatic pinnacles to lick the suppurating hues now cast themselves for a final fling down to the fast-varying-geometry of the groundwave. The rest with remourning strength dancers horsevoiced singers drugees gaunt thieves true believers boozers and paletooled lovers crept away into clogged side alleys to coven their despair.

Only then as Boreas crawled off the platform to lie again in peace under the caressing feathers of his heated pond did the Master speak to him.

'You are an artist – come with us along the multi-value mazes of our mission. Your film caught all the spirit of our cause my life my thought the unspeaking nature of spontagnous living in mystic state!'

Then Boreas turning his great bare head and naked tear-lined cheeks like udders grey with dawn: 'You stupid *godver-domme* acidheads and junkies all the same you live inside your crazy nuts and never see a thing beyond! So you mastered my masterpiece, was it? Pah! My fool man de Grand was supposed to bring the cans of film but in his stinking state forgot – and once caught here impossible to leave again the cattlepen. And so my masterpiece my High Point Y unseen and unshown this golden importunity!'

'We saw it all! It sparked right over with total lootage!'

Sick with disgust salivating.

'God knows what you thought you saw! God knows, I swear I'll drown myself, shoot myself, harpoon myself to death, never film again! Not only is my masterpiece unshown but not one of your armada knows it or misses it. This is the nadirene anti-death of art!'

Bitter and acid, Angeline's rank morning laughter bit them.

Charteris took in breezy semi-grasp Boreas's coat and pointed at the emptying square of stood squampede grey in washed-out light but ambered by flames that now consumed the pinnacles recently putrescent in other taints.

'You have no faith in transmutation or my well of the miraculous! Your oldtime art has caught a light at last! Everything you Boreas tried for broke fire materially and burns into our sounding chambers! You are my second blazer henchforth, Boreas, a black wind blowing off the old alternatives and hurricaning those who cling to what was, electric, electric, see the sign! What you making here in newchanced happens! Stellar art!' He laughed and cried tired dregs leaping leaping.

Through his blandering tears stared electric Boreas, clutching at his bare brow, screaming, 'You gurglingodfool – your rainbowheaded randyears have set fire to the place! It's the last loot! My poor beloved city burning! *Bruxelles, Bruxelles!*'

The poison that powered their inner scrutinies seeped into beetling baldbright Boreas so he saw himself tumultaneously making the cripple still upon the cabbalistic asphalt making couch among a lake of flames making love to a dummivulva making Age old Ina suffer him. His face cracked its banks china thoughts depiggied. Boreas saw more of boreased self than he could dare or wish to see. He rocked with unreason on the staggered balcony of outsight.

Manifolding with discardment he cheek in hand into the dull inner chambers of shade past old banners toothed with black lions collided with the birdlike nervous drapery-deportment figure of a human cassowary to his shoulder lept unmoving and instantly with locking blubber arm seized him groaning and yowling for accompaniment.

'I am ill – magisterially ill!' Hollowly to his lackneed squir.

Thus the blind bleeding the blind and dankring leech to leech upon romaining leechions highways where this wesciv sinbiote first took its blindwheeling veinhold with the cohorts tormenta in hurling knowhow to the punchy vein and murk the scenariover evermorgue till savvy was a scavengers filiure of which this sciatic scattering long kuwaited just the last blood-strained curtain. After the legendary coherets among the dark-falling walls of oh my westering world the venomilk of progross gains its bright eclipse and suppurages from the drawbridge-heads of cleverknowing Charteris gold-pated Nicholas Boreas and black jack cass.

Nothing for Cass but this supporting role uneasy-eyed or never rubicond to shuffer with the ruined borean bulk out down a lamenting grand stair and by tenuous tenebrous betelgrained deathsquared slipways to Boreas' luxconapt.

There with continuing cunning whines for succour, Boreas almost hauled him to his pool edge. But at the sight of those bulbous hyacinths the castaway squealed like a lifted root seeking too in the convex gilt eyes twin unaimed deadmen of himself!

'Yes, die-by-drowning, Cass, you undreaming schemer of your hire-oglyphed runways! Wasn't it you who brought this pyromanichee circus into city just for hope of trade, Cass, for hope of trade? You neo-Nero para-promethean primp, they've sacked our silver-breasted capital, haven't they? Haven't they? Under the gargling lilies with your scant scruballs!'

He wrenched and tugged in buttacking flapping angony but Cass was nimble and falling took the epicurer man off balance with one tricky twisting cast of leg. Together they struck and smacked among showering orfe and weed and tame piranhas glimpsing for a nanoment undersea eyes of each with sibyling hatred widely divinited beneath the parting roots. Then Cass was sourfacing and outkelping himself, evading Boreas's doctopurulent grasp to snatch from his stocking nestling a slender beak of knife.

So they confronted, Boreas half-submanged with foliaged

morses dotting his sunken suit. Then he recalled his anger with
flecked lungs, leaped up brandishing his arm and in megavoice
again on set bellowed in long bursting vein the terrors of his
repudation!

Wilting Cass turned his tail before the wind and like a
deflayded animal ran away somewhere into the smoking cityhive to hide.

That cityhive and what its singeing symbolled did cosmic
Charteris survey from the shaking platform.

Angeline shook the Master's arm. 'Come on. Masterpiece,
let's shake this unaimed scenario before the whole action goes
Vesuvius! Come on! Uncoil the Kundalini!'

He stood enwrapped staring as the centuries fevered to
the edges and breathed and blew themselves to heat again and
their stones ran in showers kill slate cracked down the long
glacier of mansard roofs and hurtled into the extinct square
below to be devoured with its old common order in the long
morain of alienation.

He pushed her away.

'Colin! Colin! I'm not flame-proof if you are! It's the last
loot-in else!'

Rich curtains at the windows of an old embroidery now released a noise like cheering and whistling swept the blaze and the
crushed bodies in the square below burst into conflagration
with amazing joy. One or two cars were still careening madly
about to lie with black bellies uppermost lewdly burning tyres
still rotating as their votaries dragged themselves away. The
emptying bowls held ashes and a lascivious flute held court.

Angelina was having a mild hysteric fit, crying this was
London burning and slapping Charteris wildly on the face.
He in his eyes scribbled on the retinal wall saw the graffiti
of her blazing hate and all behind her flames like christmas
cacti flowering with a lorry coming fast recalled her husband
the white land as it rushes up but no impact and his blows and
knew among the microseconds lay a terminal alternative to
silence her and have no more inspector at his feast for she as
much as any of the predelic enemies among the Neanders
dream her speckled wake.

She in her turn was not too wild to see a redder shade of
crimson leap up his retaining wall and with a lesser scream now
our valleys fall echoing before them now in our shattered towns

the smoke clings still as the ulcerated countryside rumpled outwards at predatorial speed to her fluttering chimera she did the sleight-of-hand and dodged him as he once more sprang and pushed clutching at his ancient blue coat of Inner Relief but now no Christmas innocence. Slipping he fell and at the rickety platform edge hung down to see bloodied cobbles under surflare. With instinct she on top of him flung her bony trunk loading him back and cosseted him and goosed and mewed and sat him up and like a mother made all kindliness but milk there though the sun novaed.

Half-stunned he sighed, 'You are my all-ternatives,' and she half-wept upon him at such grudged sign.

Their hair singed and Buddy Docre came in an illusory moment with Ruby who fancied her and Bill and Greta yelling murder. They together all but not in unison climbed tumbled down the foul inner chimney stair and ran among the flailing lava of another Eurape to the battered cavalcade jarring to take off in another street with the nervewreck d bangwaggon.

'Boreas!' cast the whiteface Master. 'We must save Boreas!'

And she glowed him amazed still in his headwound he had some human part that plugged for the schillerskulled director. But she was learning now and now stayed silent at his murderous feast with inward tremor knowing she would not break a single crust if Boreas loafed or died as maybe the Master minded: a gulf of more than language lay between them.

Vanquished she tottered against Ruby his face moonstrous in the setglow and he grasped to the smouldering pompous columns gasping 'Change gear Ange your way doesn't have to be his or my car in the Chartercade you know that you know how I skid for you even since before Phil's day two rotten no good bums –'

But he gave up as through her frantic goosetears she began on tearawy note that she was not good enough for him was no good to any man deserved to die or could render to no man the true grips of loves clutchment till the others turned back calling and Charteris took her failing wrist abraptly.

For him the self was once again in its throne called back from the purged night's exile and he commanded no more as he faced the lack of his own divinity in all its anarchic alternative. His pyre grew behind him as they barged off across the ruby pavements for as Buddy passed a reefer he flipped the photograph that he had godded himself because they had to crown some earthly king then had forgotten that he was their moulding not his make so tunnelling upwards through the sparce countryside the mole-truth set up its tiny hill that all was counterfate in a counterfeit kingdoom.

He had cried for Boreas because that artifacer could help blow blazes from his parky wavering nature with the bellows of his counterfaking craft.

Before real miracles he had to dislocate the miraculous in himself. New dogs shagged along alleyways with ties of flame. A man ran blazing down a side street. Dischorded impages of choleranis sang along the bars of his perplextives. All were infected from him and in that pandemetic lay his power to make or sicken till nature itself couched underground.

A smoke pall canopiled overhead the new angrimals swimming powerfully in it or hopping along the crestfallen buildings. Shops stood plagened open entrailed on the echoing gravements as men noised abroad and struck at each other with fansticks more than one fire was buckling up its lootage as they acidheaded out towards the oceanic piracy of their motorways.

FAMINE STARTING AT THE HEAD

She clad herself in nylon
Walked the flagstones by my side
The feathered eagle
To the skies
No more uprises
Instead a palm of dust grows
You know that earthly tree now bears no bread
A hand outstretched is trembling
The flagstaff has an ensign
Only madmen see
With famine starting at the head

Some judy delivers a punchline
In the breadbasket today
No fond embraces
Are afoot
Death puts a boot
Where the bounce was once
In among the listening lilies a silent tread
Bite the fruit to taste the stone
Throughout the Gobi seed awaits
The rain to stalk
Famine starting at the head

He only has to say one word
Roses grow from an empty bowl
In our shuttered streets
The cars roam
Don't need a home
Or volume control
Wandering sizeless with the unaimed dead
We hear his voice cry 'Paradise!'
On the Golden Coast the cymbals
Start to sound
Salvation starting at the head

TORTURES

There's no answer from the old exchange
I want to push inside you
The sensations you find in yourself
May just be within my range

Grimly sitting round a table
Fifteen men with life at stake
They may torture themselves but those tortures
Will not make them awake

The cards were somehow different
The board I had not seen before
Their iron maiden gleamed dimly cherry-red with sex
Down in the basement I reached Low Point X

Last year they stopped their playing
Phone just ceased to buzz
But if you find them there tomorrow
Better start in there praying

Reincarnation where the cobwebs
Are comes daily from your keep
We may torture ourselves but those tortures
Cannot break our sleep

POOR A!
(Gurdjieff's Mocking Song)

Poor A! Poor A! Now there's a clever man!
He only wants to talk and he is happy!
I could have pulled his trousers off
   Un-noticed, silly chappie!

Poor A! Poor A! What sort of man is it
Who only wants to talk and he's okay?
I tell you everyone's like that –
   They fill the world today.

I might say poor old A is rather better
Then some wild talkniks I have met, a
Chap who in his way knows what is what –
On military onions he knows quite a lot.
In a superficial public way he tries to find out Why:
And he'd hate to think he ever told a lie.

Poor A! Poor A! He is no longer young!
He said so much I think and was uncouth
To guard against an awful chance
To listen to the truth –
He led himself a merry dance –
He hid his head in circumstance –
To fight against the truth!

Disciples: Poor us! Poor us! We really felt his tongue!
He drank Khagetia and chattered without ruth
To guard against his only chance
To hear G give out truth –
He led us all a merry dance –
He leads himself a dreary prance –
To smite against the truth!
To fight against the truth!

THE UNAIMED DEADMAN THEME

Foreign familiar filthy fastidious forgotten forbidden
Suicide's revelation its sunnyside hidden
Death's black-and-white checker is down on the table
Fugitive fustian funebral infinite formidable

Far down the runway the black sheds are standing
My love talks to me with a delicate air
I am the victim the assassin the wounder
Her face looks no larger as I stand close than
It simultaneously does in my telescope sights
But pleasant is walking where elmtrees paint shadow
If I fire I might as well hit me

I walked with her once where her elms brought their
shadows
The dogrose dies now while the invalid car
Barks vainly and I the assassin the wounder
On the runways the markings are no longer valid
Hieroglyphs of a system now long obsolete
No this button first love yes that's the idea
If I fire I might as well hit me

Foreign familiar filthy fastidious forbidden forgotten
I sprinted a dozen times over where rotten
Things grew and she cried for a sweet-flavoured minute
Fugitive fustian funebral formidable infinite

LAMENT OF THE REPRESENTATIVES
OF THE OLD ORDER
(A silent dummy dirge)

We kept up our facade
The unworld showed the third world how
And prized its pretty inhibitions
   They undressed us
   And possessed us

And now that times are hard
The unworld holds its outward show
Too late for us to change positions
   They have dressed us
   And confessed us

THE SHUTTERED STREET GIRL
(Love song for flutes)

Her face showed like a shuttered street
    Under the mauve and maureen flash
From which iguanas might crawl
    Golden gullets wide

She stood there in a wet shift breathing
    And just a mental block away
A lane lay in old summer green
    Behind her pregnant eyes

Where a young barefoot girl might drive
    Her would-be-swans all day
Or night for night and day are both
    They don't apply

There's always summer in the dreaming elms
    Till your last shuttered white year
And while the small rain fills
    The thoroughfares of love

So her face in blue fermentation
    When she crouches seems
Like an ever-visiting miracle
    As she pees by old brickheaps

There's whole sparse countryside
    Buckling up from far
Underground as she stoops there
    And our small rain raining

THE INFRASOUND SONG

Where the goose drinks wait the wildmen
Wait the wildmen watching their reflections
When the damson fruits the wildmen
Wild Neanders dream their speckled sleep

They have their dances ochre-limbed to a stone's tune
And their heavy hymns for the solstice dawn
Their dead go down into their offices berobed
With ceremony. Their virgins paint
Their cinnamon lips with juice of berry
They owned the world before us

Now their valleys fall echoing our footfall
In their shattered towns the smoke clings still
Down the autobahn arrows in the afternoon
As we drive them convert them or ride them

We are the strangers over the hilltop
Peace on our brows but our dreams are armoured
Fearsome in our feathers brutally flowered
Pushing the trip-time up faster and faster
Pre-psychedelic men know that extinction
Sits on their hilltops all drearily towered
As we cavalry in with the master
Cavalry in with the master
With the master

AT THE STARVE-IN

Met this girl at the starve-in
I met this girl at the starve-in
I said I met today's girl at the starve-in
Protein deficiency's good for the loins

She said there's bad news from Deutschland
Yes she said there's bad news from Deutschland
She lay there and said there's bad news from Deutschland
Can you hear those little states marching

I raised my self kingly in the stony playsquare
Ground my elbow like a sapling in dirt
Looked through the stilled plantangents of smoke
Proclaimed that even the bad news was good

We've marched under banner headlines
Closed down the stone-aged universities
See ally fall upon ally
Oh Prague don't dismember me please
It was all in the Wesciv work-out
Now we got some other disease

Met my fate in the work-out
Man, I met my fate in the work-out
No denying I met my fate in the work-out
And no one knows what's clobbered me

Rainbows at starvation corner
There's rainbows at starvation corner
I keep seeing rainbows at starvation corner
Like they're the spectrums at the feast

Met this girl at the starve-in
Yeah met this girl at the starve-in
Oh yeah I met this pussy at the starve-in
And we dreamed that we ruled Germany
We dreamed we ruled all Germany

It's One of Those Times

It's   sim   ply
  One of those times
    when you're going to pot
  one of those crimes
    when you really should rot
one of those times you do not

It's   sim   ply
  one of those mornings
    they've all got you taped
  one of those dawnings
    you hoped you'd escaped
one of those mornings you're raped

  The cities are falling like rain from the skies
The toadthings are leaving the ground as you watch
  You're laughing and dancing with joy and surprise
It helps with that pain in your crotch

So   it's   just
  one of those rages
    that rupture and burn
  one of those ages
    you get what you earn
  one of those pages
    you wish you could turn
'Cos its none of your bloody concern
No it's none of your bloody concern
        It knocks you sideways
    None of your bloody concern

The Poison that Powered Their Scrutinies

The poison that powered their inner scrutinies
Seeped into beetling baldbright Boreas
So he saw himself tumultaneously
 Making the cripple still
  Upon the cabbalistic asphalt
 Making couch upon a lake of flames
 Making love to a dummy vulva
 Making Age Old Ina suffer him

 His face cracked its banks
China thoughts depiggied
Boreas saw more of his borearsed self
Than he could dare or wish to see

He rocked with unreason on
The staggered balcony of insight
Manifolding in discardment
As his capital lost all loot

THE MIRACULOUS IN SEARCH OF ME

It could all have turned out differently.
Indeed, to other peeled-off I's
The difference is an eternal recurrence:
And the stone trees that erupt along
My beaches, roots washed bone-clever
By the tow and rinse of change –
They shade one instance only of me,
For circumstance is more than character.

At this bare fence I once turned left
And became another person: laughed
Where else I cried and now sit lingering
Looking at Japanese prints;
Or in a restaurant decked with pine
Cones taste in company
Silver carp and damson tart.
          Along the walls
Other I's went, strangers in word and deed,
Alien photocopies, spooks
Closer than blood-brothers, more alarming
Than haggard face spectral in empty room,
Lonelier than stone age campfires, doppelgangers.
They are my possibilities. Their pasts were once
My past, but in the surging wheels
And cogs become distorted. So, this one –
On a far-distant spoke! – danced
All night and had splendid lovers,
Wrote love letters still kept locked
Treasured in a bureau-drawer, knew girls
The world now knows by name and voice.

But this I chose to wander down
My stony beach, my own rejection.
My past is like a fable. Truly,
Circumstance is more than character.
Whatever other peel-offs saw –
My I was on the stranded alien land,

The restlessness of broken cities,
Mute messages that only after years
Open, the crime of vulnerability,
Patched land of people never known to be
Known or knighted, wild bombed world,
World where I taste the flavour on
The tongue, knowing not if my other eyes
Would call it happiness or doom.

   I am, but what I am –
Others may know, others may care. Only
The dear light goes in her hand
Away among the childhood trees.
In the perspectives of my mind
It never dwindles. I always live
With myself; and that's too much.
I need
The overpowering circumstance
The nostalgia of
That eternal return
As if the unstructured hours
My uninstructed hours
Of day are pulped like
Newspaper
And used on us again
With the odd word
Here and there
Locked
Starting up out of context
Treasured
An old ghost
Haunting another
Discardment.
Indeed it is
Always eternally
Turning out

Different.

BOOK THREE

Homewards

OUSPENSKI'S ASTRABAHN

SPARKILY flinging up stones from the tired wheels the gravel-cade towed darkness. Headlights beams of granite bars battering the eternal nowhere signposting the dark. The cuspidaughters of darkness somebody sang play toe with the spittoons of noon the cuspidaughters of darkness play toe with the spittoons of noon the cuspidaughters of darkness play toe with the spittoons of noon. Only some of the blind white eyes of joyride was yellow or others but altirely because the bashing the cars the jostling in the autocayed. And hob with the gobs of season.

In these primitive jalopsides herding their way like sham-peding cattletrap across the last ranges of Frankreich that square squeezing country sang the drivniks. Cluttering through stick-it-up-your-assberg its nasal neutral squares its window-bankage to where the Rhine oiled its gunmottal under the northstar-barrels and a wide bridge warned zoll. Break lights a flutter red I'd ride the rifled engines ricochetting off the tracered flow below.

Cryogenetic winds bourning another spring croaking forth on the tundrugged land doing it all over and bloodcounts low at a small hour with the weep of dream-pressure in the cyclic rebirth-redeath calling for a fast doss all round or heads will roll beyond the tidal rave. RECHTS FAHREN big yellow arrows splitting the roadcrown. Writhing bellies upward large painted arrows letters meaningless distant burriers seducing him to a sighfer in a diaphram.

Clobwebbed Charteris stopped the Banshee. He and Angeline climb out and he wonders if he sees himself lie there annulled, looks up into the blind white cliffs of night cloud to smell the clap of spring break its alternature. About him grind all the autodisciples flipping from their pillions and all shout and yawn make jacketed gestures through their fogstacks.

They all talk and Gloria comes over says to Angeline, 'Feels to me I have bound the hound across this country before.'

183

'It's the flickering of an unextinguished loveplay starting odour at this stale standpoint Glor.'

'So you say? It lies here under night yet? Like some other place! You should say we wanted to come here or was that some place else?'

Hearing distonished by the hour.

'Anyhow, I can cool inspection while we get the kettle on this groggy mote.'

And other yattering earvoices crying to him through the labyrinths set in a concrete head of nightsloth he Charteris Shaman with the painful yellow arrows almost vertical more difficult to negotiate and maybe transfixed his own powers watercoarsed. More than the voices, breathing, ominous movements of bodies inside clothes, writhing of toes inside shoes and sly growth of the corkscrewing curls inside a million pants locutions and dislocations.

Breathing deep to force out his voice drown the sense of drowning he said, 'We hit the present aimed alternative friends. So let's doss down and tear off a new chain tomorrow rate where we stunned.'

Wraithlike in the dying beams, they pulled out sacks or piled together on backseats or a few took pains to boil up coffee or tea with pale flames dazed upon their chained eyelids or fleeting countrysides pillowed on their greasy locks of sleep. So was Angeline's belly mountained with the Drake-Man's seed but she nestled alone under blankets. He harboured to the girl who had joined the motorcad at Luxembourg Elsbeth with her fine young jewish warmth.

Humbly they all had to narrow to the enemy breath of night flood with their closing rhythms lowered body temperature slatted venetian thoughtpulses that all blankets and small fires and pillows could not dam or defer for more than

Deeper limbos other deaths crueller sleeps exist in which the fuzzed alternative Is stand watching peeling off from the spool of probability like negatives that never reach the developer haunting the slumberer click of shutter snicker of rapid eye movement old self-photographs number the data-reducer

Aged amokanisms of comprension guttering

Mending morn he takes delight knowing her juiciness in feeling the tousled dryness of crutch and turning that unseen

smile to mossture Whereon she wrickles and strokes his semi-
erect griston with a thigh giving him mandate pulling plump
arms compulsively about his neck constrictly harsh acid breath
of morn mingled and the high old stinkle of feet and bum and
body in the bag mantling them as he mounts smelsbeth all here
and now be physical like all stubble on the rolling summer
mountains where the skies steam upward over the incredible
brow and motion everywhere in the sapient earth multi-
limbed freedom of the heat –

Breaking in the harsh cries of uniform throats and yells of
drivniks together with some rumpling and footmaching where
the pace is fractured. This Rhine-bridge and engines roaring
all hell out there and my juices seeping unporpelled sort of
semi-ohgasm shit it's just a slimeoff this time Elsbeth honeypit.

Big boots by his nose passing and Charteris emerges to
dianoise the seem. Oh boy the metal camp or mobile scrap-
dump wheeled junkade raddling the end of bridge nose to
nose or tail like they just beetled out the Rhine and disciples
heads among them flowering in cool dazes like they stargazed
an astrobahn.

Bucketing about bigbooted the Deutscher polizei falling
around the bumpers and crying for order.

Charteris laughing and feeling for his jeans propped on one
elbow.

'Hey, dig the inspired popular image of worldorder in this
pure pink faces of authority shining and lovely smarched
uniforms spruce like pressed plants running!' But gathering his
mind to take a closer fix on them he snuffed that the Schwabe
fell apart uniform-wise many without belts or buttons or boots
or Klimpenflashengewurstklumpen to their name and even
the jackets hung upon a bygone hook elsewhere. Still for effect
they scraped traffink jam noises from their throats.

One crusader broke from the autodump with his bedroll
yelping and the big lorries had him down and up and a one-two
round the shaggy side-chops left right left right moonlight
moonlight to the fuzzwagon.

'You try the uncivil disobendiate! God help you!' they
yelled.

'Get this goddamned mobile scrap mobile!' they yelled.

'This is a nice tidy police state not a drosshouse!' they
yelled.

'We'll have you Schrott-makers shot!' they yelled.

'Clear the way for the traffic!' they yelled, though the road flowed as silent as the river straight back to Switzerland like cut cloth and Army jumped up with his flute and piped and others sang, 'Clear the way for the traffic Nice clean autobahns we want to see Leave no human litter lay Clear the traffic for the way' as the cops schwarmereid in among their vehicles.

One looked down at all Elsbeth showed as she sat up, yelled, 'Ach ein Zwolfpersonenausschnitt!' and she snatched her vest about her vocal bubes, crying back abuse at him with a vingor jangled decibels adding to the general racket where one or two cars started up and backed or bucked smokily on the region great dizzy din.

Angeline came hurrying as he bent up and with attention in another part pulled at his jeans saying, 'Colin you see they're going to take our kids off to the nick if you don't do something quick we defied law and odur by settling right down here in the traffic route forgetting it was going to be sunrise soon or something mad or else just tired I don't know but you better do something quick.' On Elsbeth she could not look the dark hair round her shoulders and all entrances slack.

'Only we're traffic the only traffic apart from us there's no another car in slight it don't make a hold-up holed up here.'

'Better go and tell that to the Fuehrer here he comes!'

Pointing to a big white police car like a spaceship a yacht a heinleiner beyond reach of storms opening all ways and spilling most noticeably a mighty man in a white uniform big patched with a thousand medals like over-stamped bundle of laundry and boots and a cap with bright peak while rammed in his bathysphere a monster cigar approaching and two minions round him crying the Kommandant.

Then all the Schwabe crying 'Who in charge here?'

Sawn trees on parade streetside.

Time like a never-rolling steam.

Bridge of nerve-defying metalangles.

Slowly the cries silence the scene and all stock-still except a little morning breeze through which the drivniks are thin and pale with hair that made them in England part of nature growing right down sweet and unswept from hair and head and lips and cheeks and shoulder part of the pubic earth itself but here on this barren not so damned good and analogous. 'Who in charm hair?'

All get a charge or no one. Petrifaction of inner posture though Army pipes.

Heaving still his unzipped hipjeans Charteris he moves

among the carmaze towards the white man Angeline at his side small but big seeing the eternal pattern as the object arrangement makes a readymade more beautiful than planned an emblem of eternity capable of slowing time something he had known before this marvellous he inside the ducks-and-drake man skimming over a deeper ocean of truth in which he wished to dive deeper and deeper away from the times too grave for mere communication on an average plane or old grey steps misleading to old brown building rucked in railings curled to dilate Italian-made and now up he's in a grey-brown room black-and-red tiles of a transcendental patterning oh rest me again for ever in the minds murmuring mysteries where I belong and could walk through and walk through forever the hall the long within withit for ever the pattern where time stalks sideways birds flying backwards reemerge as lizards before the days never-ending.

'You are in charge of this rabble?' The brilliant laundry bundle before his unzipped eyes and what was that place where I was I was there for a minute? eternity? Metzronome tick? In some late time-bracket feasting beyond this schwabian illusion of the present tell them why not.

Did they hand me over old betrayal?

Raising his voice, 'I am in all command and to me time swings back off its hinge mersing the tiny present – no, no, I tell you – I am Charteris. Paradise is in me I feel it I know it!' Now he waved his arms saw them above him making off in the sky this way that seeking the new dimensions or old dimensions seen as fresh alternatives as the birds cryrated into lizards and the new anima instantly back to stone. 'What we have seen is worth all collapse and the old christianity world so rightly in ruins if you forsake all and live where there is most life in the world I offer. There the laternatives flick flock thickly by and again with his hands and hair he conveyed to there the great intellectual system that Man the Driver synthesised relating all phenomena and postulating a new map – a map he said wandering in and out of speech as dropping his jeans entirely he climbed hair-legged onto the heinleiner car and rallied them all – a man deminiating the topography related belaying a sparky relevationship between this Europlexion and the explexion of conventual time the time by which predecyclic man imposed himself against nature by armed marching cross-wise to conceal body-mind apart hide dissillusion.

Cheering and singing only the cops stamped around and

offered dials of non-radiance. He still upbraidcast.

'And to these levels also another pirate transmitter with emissions on the self-life-mitter band for you got to mash your own consciousness into the introwaving road routage and the general timeweb only achieve by the disciplation of my thought the disciplation of proper erectitude like a disciplation of any distinct order and to achieve finally well you need what Ouspenski calls certain luggage and then the true sidereal time can faze with your arcadian rhythms of living.'

'Get off my automobile!' said the big pink white laundry-bundle chief of police.

Two policement hupped Charteris down as he called, 'For all of you also timeflow can hold the orbital radiance of a spyers web if you will follow me. Let your circharacters centrifuse in the spinrads of centricourse! Follow me or you will drown in the flowing timeflow!'

So he comes away kicking as they assimob and fling his pants at him wrapping round the timeflapperture. You are not asleep at this moment. Many things were like sleep many things had no relationship to reality. Truer: reality had no relationship to the true things. They just built these wooden walls with wooden windows to sail on regardless. Many things that I said at that time must have surprised my companions in this strange adventure very much. I was surprised by much myself. I stopped and turned towards G. He was smiling. His old friendly fallible familiar smile. 'Afterwards it was very strange for me to remember the things I had said.' I was walking along the Troitsky street and everyone was asleep.

The Schwabe officers conferred with rapid eye movements and a thin cracked music started from the escampade. Many things that I said at that time. The brilliant laundry bundle made clockwork gestures parabola starting and ending at low point X and two polizei grabbed Ouspenkian I.

Set a speech to clash a speech.

Orated the laundrobund in machine-style 'Fine leadership I have appreciape and the exhaustation but even god almighty must here be circumstrict according to the authority of law and not park his car contrary to stated regalations. Else there's distrumblanches and the crumble-off of state and diction but right here is still my desportment and you hippies are all contraveined. So it's a rest this hairshirted malefracture do his freakout in a cell! Move!'

'Hey, they're going to take away our saviour!' warcried

188

Ruby Dymond running to Angelside. He flung a reality-object of unvariable geometry and metallic origin in semi-lethal parabol and the other sleep-runners started to mill marvellously unstewing from their rancid and autobreasted pluckered in to the uniform defeat. Hit a Kraut for Easter. Then leaped the bold gendarmes also acid-hipped but swinging in the name of Ordentlichkeit to let battle commensurate with duty the PCA bombs when dissembling produced according to each character in its own intensification.

By the perspective transfixed was the police point with its flags and signs and from here gorged more polizei slowly inflating themselves with self-pumping steps as they evolved themselves from the middle distance becoming part of the fore-grind where the mass milled and Herr Polizeikommissar Laundrei clasped enchanted Charteris to his postage stamps.

Ordentlichkeit having boots and truncheons won.

So a march began slowly and with bloody eyes and ripgear and straggling struggle to the lock-up all baretoed hepos while by the cobbles a few wooden pudestrials started at the de-linquents Herr and Frau Krach and little Zeitgeist Krack who when pushed bobbed up again and soberly registered gut show nodding as the procession hobnobbed to the great slapup HQ with many drivniks still plunching.

Now the harsh bones of that great creature were stone and its flesh mortar and plaster painted democrappic yellow lying in feigned fossil sleep and all its viscerca dark and cool with powerfailure or the awful processes of parquet flooring turning corridors reflected dim outside light entrailing from all surfaces constantly interupted returning interupted broken continuous of a special manufacture greylight patent. You are no longer awake many things that I said.

The blundering polizei themselves bemused. Pattern of bars no more italianate where the reverie bursts into the old brown building but industrial north dull parallels to close the mind unblown. Clash of bars and swinging blatterplang with no regard ringing unanswerable. The sittlichkeitsvergehen of German standingrheumonly.

Blundering they grey big honey cops with striding arms dull in the confinement space swing swinging to the repetitive doors themselves trapping on the wrong side and commense hammer-cry which the disciples stand dumbfloundered like a whole new range of unfeeling in a brown nearest black till one judy shrieks that they are merely stacked in the corridor. All begin panicake

panicake round the shattered vision down or up stone steps or mindless groins digested seeking exit. Bars bars false leads dead ends long vistas dim greylight like a broken circuit entrailing from all sourplaces in the harsh bones time's loot-out rings unanswerable. More cops flushtuate in the hide-and-seek. Now bellies the whole building rangorously. Mindfallen new race rapidly cell-dwells and all anti-flowered. Garish alarms zibbernaut into cavities the grot graves. Life down to the low point of textbook level. Lungs hammer limbs scissor feet clatter in the machineage moment.

Clever guards slamslamslam outer doorment. In the maze long vistas slowly the charterisers clobbered and clapped into parallel cells. The harsh bones cease their crunk but from the lesser interstine sounds an invisible flute.

Entranced by Herr Laundrei's door stood his buddyguard Hirst Wechsel who opened to let in the Herr and Charteris followed to pour them both thin schnapps but Charteris stood amazed to find almost tanible reality transformed into this particular figment with a bare rich squareness of hard black forest wood in even the softer things while the Laundrei cordially explained how the State now malfunctioned owing to the temporary emergency following psycho-chemical spraying on which the scientists of the nation were feverishly working to produce an infallible errorproof arabproof antidope that would guarantee to the race that took it a thousand years of sanitary sanity without deviations in any direction such as weakness brought on among even the most favoured of peoples though of course any old racist theories were long discredited.

'I don't need to tell you as an Englishman that.' Laughing and even Hirst Wechsel operating musculature of a broad grin.

However with the joking aside it must be privately confessed that the malfunctioning of government already touched upon causes certain complications of a legislative nature away and beyond the mere dying of six or seven million fellowcountrymen from famine brought on from lack of organisation at the headquarters perhaps stemming from the lack of discipline at the hindquarters any leadership vital to a dynamic nation and one of these legislative failures was that he here ran his little police force as an independent army you might say.

'What do you mean what you going to do with all my friends in the cells we're no invading army only tourists tourists spreading the light?'

Spreading the light was a happy expression was it not of course one knows that light like all basic things such as shall we say sex is made of hydrogen but one can well imagine this sort of hydrogen-compoundcondiment to be spread on ones bread like butter you excuse of I joke and the musculature again mindblowing.

'My friends in the cells?'

All dependent upon Saint Charteris himself. We two would talk it was necessary to establish if you were a genuine leader but if so well here was this modest little army maybe a little barebooted in the shall we say head but knowing well on which side of the condiment their light shone put it together with the crying need for a proper leadership to the country after all you could not be content with genuine messiah to remain head only of those hairy things with people inside a ragged flock of feathered friends like a new animals hopping from instant immobility to instant immobility leaping from the lawn close-clipped to the eaves of the bungalow where the sunset for ever in its ironed mottling how different oh my dear British decline from this a comic white-uniformed A busy Moscow newspaper man so its necessary to test you if you pass of course all pardons all round but when a traffic regulation is violated it is after all violated I mean that is basic philosophy old man eh nicht war.

So comes forth Hirst Wechsel with forms laden for Charteris to fill while Laundrei quits the room. Sitting at a table in unkindly light he stares through the lines and dots and little boxes anweisungen defences against the light take multi-forms of all the forms of dreaming activity is perhaps the deepest passivity is true guise activity lies and this is the landt where the truly eat the lotus suffering is permanent obscure and dark and shares the nature of infinity they even invent the concept of anti-suffering a clever form to conceal real angst and infectious disease if any suppose I pretended to fall in with his idea might the multi-word not be spread his clouted clowns all accidentally aid me oh zbogom the old serpent but my rotten thoughts far from the driving have no wing-ding next of kin my fruitful angeline something still gets through perhaps for your stake.

There he wrestled locked mute in the hard Rhenish light till Wechsel brought him a warm sausage.

'How you love my boss?'

'For me he is just a uniform.'

'Isn't it engorgeous uniform?'

'That's incompatible.'

'I don't think so, I think it suits him a treat. White just sets off his complexion.'

'Off-white.'

'He doesn't exercise enough.' He bent lower so that his labroses were almost in contact with the folded labyrinths of statement. 'He's more of a thinker you see. He's a great thinker he has his own laboratory here I'll show you while he's out come on.'

'This sausage is enough adventure my adversary.'

'Glad you like it but look you see his place here.' It rocked over to another door flinging wide and beyond again the stark geometry and pohlar parade of apparatus old Boreas with his realitoys. He shook his head and commenced resuming the patterplexity of the intraformity Wechsel hovered.

'He wouldn't mind you seeing it not if I let you I don't quite know how he strikes you but he's really a very kind man indeed a thinker and keeps himself very clean insists that I keep myself clean too finds you lot very unhygienic you're not a real prophet are you you don't somehow look the part I reckon my boss will come up with the solution to the world's troubles I do I sincerely do he works all night sometimes goes without sleep I never saw such a saintly man.'

State blood group and whether you have ever been donor or donator of blood or practised acupuncture.

'He's trying to synthesise Hydrogen 12 that's what he's doing in there synthesis says the Rhine river is the main artery of the body corporate analogous to an actual organism which with a chain contraction would convey Hydogen 12 from source to mouth and thus infect the total statement and spread from Germany out into the oceans until the druplets fructify the mondial globule in profit from his inversion and never no more by any deviation from the correctum orderly way of life you ought to concourse him about it oh it's a real privilege to work for such a splendid man and for such a splendid man and for such a splendid uniformed official man he's marching marching marching of which the human race is capable is caperble is cape-er-bull!' All this vocal accompaniment to a sort of sweeping jig about the black-forested room with a lightly pointed jacktoe fluttering and the odd coy pirouette to saint's unheeding back.

Down behind the parallel bars they took some semiphysical jerks at guitars and howled an improvised stave in memory of colour and the wild-headed moment. To the bargemen this music clumped by me over the liquid hydrogen 12 with a fine echoing prison flow as if the great stone creature finally foundered its voice in its tailpiece.

Above all that Meinherr Laundrei revealed himself from under the white parcel and took on oblation in a blackforest-scented bath gristoning with Wechsel to perform the mastaging dry him compulsively and clad him in a flowing white towelling bathrobe with white matching leatherboots erminelined. So came he glowing forth murkless unto his feathery captive now socketted by the deep-eyed window watching natural France gobble off the golden phallus of the sun.

'Before I go to labour all night in my what I jokingly call my private den of stinks – cracklehund Hirst makes with the musculature – you and I Herr Charteris will have a discussion on philosophy and the sexual dynamic for in this little beleagured miniskirt of empire where we repell the frontiers with jockstrips against such penny barbarous tribes as the cascaders penisenvy sagacity as whores hardon to come by.' Coughing clearing throttle wattle and daubed crimson uncontrollable freudian slipway fazing him.

Groping in drawer of desk sitting down heavily letting robe flap bringing out in fist mighty cigars. 'Pardon, we must be good buddies and talk with proper form and usury, nict war. Have a nice big Lungentorpedo.'

'Don't use tobacco.'

'Well, you should. Smoke always smoke keeps me calm in this duration of stress yes yes very good for the nerve scenters and concentrates the mind on the objection – here take one!'

'I don't use the stuff!'

'We will see who uses it and who doesn't. Hirst get the Schnapps!'

'Immediately master.'

'Hurry you fool!' He stood glowering in towelling the boy came and trembling poured two measures from the bottle then adroitly downed the measure through an open throat calling simultaneously for more and shouting for one for Charteris.

'It's just prison poison.' Tipping it on the wood floor.

'Insulting dog!' He swinging a ham in clever textbook demonstration of anatomical leverage connecting with physiognomy of seated opponent with consequential impact subsequential entropyloss carrying victim off chair continuity of energy in previously steady state universe. 'That will teach you when your betters try to show you courtesy men in dirty rags have to be polite and look after their manners in good order now get up!'

He rises against gravity and the giantkiller smokes himself back into better humour behind grey self-made curtain haze finally saying, 'Now we will discuss privately my sex problems in absolute confidence. Hirst kindly make yourself scared. You see for a man like me in the very power of my prime and pink used to violent exercise and and shall we say such constant hobbies as swordplay and horseriding even since extreme infancy for my grandfather and father harsh men and great believers in mortification and also if I say so with all modesty both genitalmen were profound thinkers and unrecognised scientific genius who may yet save the world beginning with our own blessed soil – come I show you about my stinks den as I talk – and these rare gifts also going gland in glove with great administrative qualities and strong gift of leadership – Hirst!'

'Sir!' Anxious nose only round door executing own cute disarming bow and the musculate animate.

'Have I not strong gifts for leadership?'

'The strongest and for what it's worth a really kind man indeed a thinker – '

'Go! You're discharged!' Marching into the laboratory waving his torpedo like a wand at the alchemaic impedimenta lowering voice to his own reverence, 'All these rare qualities Charteris rare qualities and yet how shall I say. Though I am so bushy with all these schemes I am tornamented by the synthesis of the flesh the sins of the flesh and in this as in all things I am outrageous and priapic it is a torment to me for how can I be holy its the one aspect of leadership I perceive immediately that you have and I have not for its the sex centre perpetually overheating and my degenerative organ perpetually tumessing. Naturally once I have mangled to synthesise my Hydrogen 12 and release it in the Rhineflow then all such tortures can be extirpanted and we stump out sex altogether it rolls us with a rod of iron stump it out you hear – ' he tripped over a snaking cable and grasped the workbench. 'In a properly functioning world this random element will not be introduced but till then in my torment I ask you what sort of help you are a seer and prophet can give me that is an order I give for the positive assistance of mankind and in exchange my assistance on future.'

'Would the truth awaken you or your serpent?'

'I am a depraved man though a hero and savant and great leader. You see I confess without jurisprudence! Save me from that snake-in-my-grass I need your truth.'

'It is import to know if you have the Kundalini – '

'Yes yes I admit I have practised that vile sin and fallen into many fellacious ways so how am I to lead if I am led by my unruly part.'

Gurdjieff also that sly old city shaman in his worn slippers smiled under his moustache at similar questions always coming back – eternal recurrence and the nostalgia of constantly repeated for people of lost possibilities who had drawn away into a deeper dust. His truth could be told to Laundrei in such a way as to defeat him and keep him in G & O powerlessness.

'Sex is a normal and natural way to horness energy and create further possibilities in the organisms. Being alpervasive like hydrogen it forms one of the main springs of the multivalued and self-creating fuzziness so we find philosophicantly that everything people do connected with sex – politincs reliction art theatre music is all sex. People go to the theatre or church or sport event not for its own sake but simply because there in the crowds of men and women is the centre of gravity of sex. That's why people go to any meeting or occasion or rally. You are merged each more than you note in a general empathy. So you see sex is the principal motive force of all mechanicalness. Hypnosis depends upon it. So you must ledgerdemise more room for this extralactivity among your other rattributes so become more mechanical.'

'So!' Dragging in a fever on the torpedo sucking down the smoky poison of the GO-warning. 'So! Mechanicalness yes the great modern force all working with the beneficiency of the machination. That is how it will be under hydrogeneration! We'll strop this nonsense of astral bodies then and the whispering anoise of spirituality – only physical bodies aloud .hen. You are right. I will be glad and make myself machinelike.' He strode up and down. 'Hirst!' Hirst. 'Hirst be a good boy take this saint and lock him up in a singlecell then first thing tomorrow we will make one last little testicle and see how the godhead manages miracles.'

As they paced through the dim stonebone maze Wechsel said, 'I don't know what you did to him but I can tell he's going to be a devil tonight I'm half scared to go back there his rod of iron!' Leaving Charteris in a dark locked place returning to his manchine.

Charteris lying back recalled as best he could the immortal conversation and foxy old G saying to his disciples that mechanicalness was the destroyer as he well knew and sex was not mechanicalness when itself and not masquerading – pure when pure evil when self-deceiving – and here he had helped in the disintegration of Laundrei in real G style by getting him on a sterile trackway.

Once recurrent more experience of night in which a planet rounds its imagrained edges and sky blancks like an eyelid or the minds downcast clearing hevens daze echoes playback the dischard progrimm in drems highspield Discofete

But steamputteed kommandant made brief apparition at his bunkside to announce to Charteris half-awaken yar the saints worms of advice will be utilised to tranceform the polizei more mechanical he must also himself become robot-erotic marshalling already phalliscallthenics for daily parage. Drill square all pressure and corrupt piston pulling pushing with electonic force jackoff-booted polizei will present forearms per zent fore ARMS perfect eunision now massturbashing on the march commense updown updown keep the tumessence there you in the rear wank that man links links links reckt links moonlight moonlight stick out your chesticles there prick up the undressing in front no shooting before I give the sommand shoot or there will be someone up on a dishcharge

So the penal square shakes to footdrilling objection of personelity like the sparse wilderness pillowing forth and all the prairie under plough cracking thorowing up fooldrilling objects anjy

old coffins craking ramshack doors grimd open where look grabbling mummies of skeletall desire the nocterning dead hold to themselves weathered wallflowers in sepia phorno-gravure with my lurching steps forced farce-to-farce grim-croaking incumberland heavies waddled I barely foot it down into trumpery old decade church protestine that the sign mis-laid my tread shell of smellarage

furflying estumnal dust all all round all excrusimation of the impalid rose out ostone damp damp sump turannean roomour me my arms outstranked shaden light shaden light makes motet anthemist clearing reviles three of the gravure mumbos jumble fearwards at me futhorks in their scrulls two intently loading on me trumperished rainment with schoden goods hairglooms one whose armoured hanks all sack-wristed one a serafemale in the oldem broildered light and third fligger blackly small in fumireal drapery transponting water before him flauting to transfuse me from this fissure I at his viscage of necromercy cream I with object tennor openjewl before the three am eam rem ream cream scream screaming

He startled up at shaking shoulderhand and there was his penumbral cell and Herr Laundrei amoured in white no colour anywhere from dreams. The oiled daze echoes pluckback of shady freudulence.

'You – creaking out holy man all down the passage don't toll me your nightmars!'

'They were three here – '

'I I have watched and parayed all nightlong now morning climes again and I must make a last taste of you.'

'What do you know of disintegrayment and the night's boil down.'

'Dawn and the test-down for you holy howling man!'

Charteris pushed aside the rancid blanket and stiffly stood at the end of his spare of implements. Nobody spoke or thought of food mindgruel was concentrated on leverage of limb and closed probability.

So clammy-early it was in the great stone creature that men lay bedburied in the gravy of yesterday only the kommandant and Charteris burned two sallow candles of constription. Starextinguishing light here laid its loot aside and stood mourning on stony vigil. As they descended greyshot down stonesteps from the cells no waking sounds splashed. Although my snuffering bids me stay. Out by a small rear door stabbed by foggy chill with brainwitchingday sulking the cobbled stains and gutter round the yellow corner to confront the bleak new year of morning with a wide submersed expanse flat wash of water chimera on which adrift a phlotasm of opalque eddifices.

Black maimed thing rising from the closed front steps bulging towards them gestures and some tone returns.

'Angelune! In disembroidered night you waiting for a skiff on this translucid tide to the far world-weather.'

She ransacked and clung to him her stark touch finding him substantial. 'Colin, darling. Oh Colin, you did come for me I knew you would! They said there was a state law against women having babies in prison – "No women allowed to have babies in state prison" as if it was okay for men – so they locked me out – I've been in some state – '

'It's the crossroads they nail us just this marlarky day.'

'Colin I've been so frightened – '

'Malady love we're all nervended the least of worries in this imposition.'

Herr Laundrei spoke firmly, 'We are busy, lady. Stand back, enjoy your compulsory freedom while it has you or there will be worse trouble we can always eject you back across the rational frontier. Stand back.'

'Wait I'll be retiding.' He turned towards the misty Rhine of low points to avoid her gravied eyes. 'On such a morning like water flowing from everyone's head the old hopeless human thing that made misery humantic.'

'Stand back from him, woman!'

He a thing seen with no direct looking always looming trailing scented metallic dust seizing of joints and the nervending christendoom of the epoch.

'Colin, leave this crimped luniform let's get away – Colin you hear me? What speedy offence are we supposed to?'

'Ploughed up mummies grappling in the density of this nether atmosphere demanding me if I own the upper tributes.' Or with full-bellying sail becalms my prowed course into the lumonstricity.

Kommandant with slicing motion fends her off uttering low counter-revolutionary cyclic sounds designatory of machinery and with his grasp quick leftrightleft motorvates his figurehead forwards through the pall across with every step the verge the lined lanes of astrobahn the marchens of the wide crewcut embanks the ruhig waters of dark-thighed Rhine all veiled by low uncertain mornlight.

Here the phull-dicked imaginings of galaxies lie raped to ashes.

Now I embark with each step on a new voyage these patterned halls know that entranced exits lie cell-to-cell and on these borning ghats ripples ever spreading outwards to the banks of death my personality strikes to every second of time's encompassment with the ouspenskian eye drowsing in light of this multipacity infinite riches of a god one human tread.

Quailed from their male abrogation she as always fell back into her second reposition stood in the vast vacancy of space and her long submission drowned unknowing. To amend her carped deforces she preened the cressfallen hair glaring in a shard of mirror I had this in Phil's day his days my fizzog without the equality of Elsbeth well that's what Mum always used to say I'd never be what my brothers were he doesn't think enough of me I wonder why I hang around like I do honest I did try to break in to prison to reach you Col do my best I'm not a bloody saint you know. . . .

On dark grey muscles Loreldrei mechs to the edge of the shrouded flood and beckons stands ramrigid in the rigmilrole and utters 'I do believe you are a divine leader come again to lead and you shall find me pillar of discipline rather than discussion greater the force the more obedience demanded test myself to the utmost as we gather in intensity and momentum with all inner conflicts canalised and final unification I will be the new man of steel in your crusade but to you saint John beloved disciplin bare to beat about and a whipping boy to all else steelsteel your right hand man march and convert and 'Hydrogen 12 molecularising the regiments of converts and no sex but autosex the machineries' again restore correct government superstricture everywhere under one leader for united world realisation of paradise.'

Thus grandiloquently gesturing he might himself have advanced buoyantly upon the flood so ravelwrapped in the heavy swaddle of futurity or peering into more than mist. But checked himself on the bank and elevated both hands for the pelissed shore.

'Give the last proof I need walk across to neutral Frank shore and back again on the waters! Show me a miracle!'

He Charteris peered into the mist of all precarious passages one perhaps no more than others or bird's flight unmarked through solvent air the golden hind through antipodean mazes seeing self-photographs peel off in fluttering disarray disgorging by hair's gesture from the previous one with he the unknown triggering agantdealer. Which way was forwarmths? In this multi-perceptual cosweb was there still again as in the old maths world a unirection? Or he autostarring across a fresh infirmament? How many discarded duplicants of time how many sparky charges switched their currents truned awry or this big chance mist and he here in obscurity and discard with the sun set for ever its last rays caught in mottled iron further he for ever here in obscurity and discard with the vacant headlights fixed across that flood with something dear going down to cross to cross!

But wet feet? Webbing?

Walking.

And bursting out of the old limits.

Disintegrating and redissembling beyond the old dis-
loccasion.

The assumed world had its own appuisances. From the
dodgy vapours buiterknifed one blunted braid of sun among
the clipped bank trees. Lit the couched vampours. Lit the
nightflushed Rhinebow. Lit a figure striding on the far bank
Charteris in a black mack sly and dry spectral!

Staring double glaze of Laundrei tottering on the brink.

The figure looking back and signalling.

Charteris transfixed in terror. *Jebem te pas mater!* the horrors
still my damned slavonik addled acid head of schizogod!

Optic skull thought pertifozzing up through eystrils and
morifices crapulolsar welkanschauung

end in beginning's mouth serpent tail in serpent's mouth
my cerebelly mindwind blowing it

fling yourself in and drown this false baptistry of self this
tripped pretence.

But Laundrei screaming with a forged belief cried Paradise
closed his eyes

fell two paces to the left

revelation

vision triumphing over event

Gibbering sprawling he fell to the ground spotted the
master's feet clutched his ankles splurged his pedestrian
kisses there crying as if all contractions were miracles and
madness an escape from self. Then reeling up he took to his
own heels and plodded automadly back to Polizei HQ.

Angeline with feathers in her lair moved thinly through
the washout bearing her female burden and kneeling by him
on the cobbles gazing down on man's first disobedience and
the fall-out of our mortal minds lifted his head from the rhine-
stone and cradled it.

'Oh my exile darling how the splashes flecked me from the
down and you too on the very verge my love my lover love.'

'Angela listen what alternatives. . . . Either I walked across
the water or else we are finally ruinous of the mind and gluttony
starting at the head fleshes out my phantasms.'

'There there my love we all must fight our way in and out
the misticuffs remember it's the PSA bombs isn't it we're only
human.'

'Are we any more? Is Serbia sunk? What effects who knows
for sure any more than when the first brain blossomed who

was there to cry for Kossovo. If that effect gives new alternatives I may have walked across the water and be mad the same time.'

'We'll get away we'll go away I'll be good to you. South it's Switzerland and the cooler air less loony-lunged.'

'But perhaps I must counter terms with what I am or else stand starving at my own feast. This polizei man with his sagging wrists and lungentorpedos will escalcade me to the flowerpitching streets of capital cheering and I in blessing ra'sed above the motorcade my hand over all more multivalued in their addleation crying Charteris Paradise and liberating them all their eyelids autolipped with my celestine kiss and my driving words echoed at every diestamped intake.'

'Colin it's not for you just temptation of a family form. You remember how they godded you.'

'My hand in the altobreasted egocade raised in motivalue over every man's addle.'

'Not you not you my love. You still distinguish truth at heart!'

'And spreading my parts foreverywhere Charteris – the only but is but can I go where they have godded me when the green sparkling fuse of belief burns in their mansions not mine! That's my question not yours no one loots me. What happens when the contagion comes from them to me and not from me to them will I tire of its simplicity their cheers merely a form of invalid silence?'

On the old backterial bed his wise big toe wagged to the moultitude.

He sat up bedraggled and round their human shoulders the shawls of mist drew away in sepia although underground the new animals in rotted lead rodded and rutted in obscurity.

'Stay with me privately away from chariots my lovebird keep on our autocade into the cool bewildernesses of the Alps.' I too have my presentiments to express and he could have been stark to the fanaticides of marching menchen a word of leadership the old ambitions gleam its better a ruined mind than the old agonisms they still wait by the reeded bank and that flat white sluggy bastart 'Col'n you take that escalading way into the capital with clouds of cheering fantiks and they'll *crucify* you.'

'I creamed openjewlled at his vision over the water but the chance is just variable. Stop riding me. Woman be more multi!'

'Don't jeer at me who's in the family way by you you'll go the way of all saviours and they'll crucify you. They always

need another crucifixion. There's never enough for them!'
Tears bursting now.

He turned his twilight into her pregnant eyes at the disturbu-
lence there transfixtured by her word. 'Is it another eternal
recurrence then? Series of fake christs on series of faked crosses?
How's the multiplicity figure?'

Her head shook the ragged locks of it like dishabitation.
'Don't ask me Colin my old dad was a methodist. He used to
spout like Christ had a new idea of individual salve instead of
massalve so they killed him because my old dad said we weren't
really individual yet – that sort of spiritual crap.'

'The capitualism of God's son with his loser takes all and
blessed are the earth-grabbing meek. Gogetting what you
have you hold like the world's big dealers but that's all done
now. Wesciv's chunks fall off. The individual's chunks fall off.
Nothing holds.' He looked to the sunken ground in wan con-
templay with cheeks shagged to pick at his appearing toe.

She touched him. 'Even for a faked christ it's real death's
real isn't it so? You didn't want to die – didn't in Brussels.'

The blackmacked figure dry and inspectral in the mindwind.
He glared swift murder at her like a dowsed headlight.

Standing he found which side of the river he stood and
surely never on that neutral shore a trick of light still puzzling
his mindfit miracle. Under the sawn plane trees he coldly said
to her 'Go and sprout by stone dam of dross I want to think.'

You pulverise the mere shadow of cerebral shade she cried
at him but then less bitterly with an clouded smile not to
torture himself or believe she would not wait. Why did she
never give her animal feelings full rein? More and more
what it was he wanted seemed denied or she herself likewise
with no refuge in full psychotomimicry.

The parallel bars still had a whichsidedness and that morning
at wurst-time the mix-up again occurred so that captor and
captive could not determine their roles except by elaborate
reference beyond their bother. They fed well and in the pale
pulped meat anyone could spit out the odd punctueating
fingermail helped on by pepper seasoning and nature's which-
sideness of eater-eaten question.

On the dull air any bruised noses healed and oiled calm
of illusion deadened buttons that otherwise shone spite. The
big heavies had hepos inside which slowly rolled to fuzzier
beats as they warmed to acid freakuency one polizei sang

moonjune songs four hours at a standing.

It was anything time to undergo the elemental rituals of friendship that mystical state where reservations stand their sharp points in the corner and fires blurr in a common grate.

Some of them unbuttoning their tunics revealed amazing feats of tatotemism etched in tomato pink and inkblink blue where one glimpsed disembedded legs pierced hearts tangles of thorns weeping faces famous negroes dripping daggers mercedes battleships obscene inscriptions and butterflutes gothickly growing round breast or gristle so Gloria screamed from underneath 'Ooh this bloke's body's his mindmap!'

All untold the fey atmosfuddle of selforiented libidoting wooze trixfixed the constabulary into poets longhaired boxers instrumentalists vocalists meditationers on a semisyllable card trick-exponents voyeurs of the worlds box word-munchering fellowsophere semi-lovers of course with the greatest pretensions wrackonteurs charmers butchboys frenchmen twokissing mystics like-feathered nestlings vanvogtian autobiographers laughers chucklers starers stargazers villagers and simple heart-burglars all seeing themselves shining in their hip-packet mirrors.

Often they spoke of Charteris he had their licences. The wind blew from his direction but Ruby and the group had their baffles up. Music took on a shield of all blows.

At the same time a dead leaf whisked through the circle of vision over the step and was gone into the darkness that always surrounded the circle of vision. But none of the watchers any longer cared for the old movements.

To these unguarded guards now came packed and stamped Laundrei with his Hirst Wechsel perched on an epaulette squealing he 'Heraus heraus' and Paulette 'Up you tumbling bitches' all over the brothel-mongering assheadquarters to sprinkle them across the parryground.

Soon the ribble-rabble were hearing the glad news of stentorian tone glandruffling immensity Charteris was son of god and would groove a hand in the march on Frankfurt and Bonn and Berlin estabellish a new odour and cheers from the unbelieving believers saying on to Moscow what about Moscow assisted of course by his pop those present and the secret weapong Hydrogenous 12 and and new ornamated selfrepelled Supersex mascodistic marchers but whatever the band played each had his own tune.

'These hyenas no longer have any respect for the state,'

angrily crying Laundrei.

'Nor the individual either' – Wechsel turning into a cockatoo and brightly fluttering into the tropical foliage underhead.

Under the sawn-off planes he passed with a certain tread certain tread certain tread patterning their well-drawn branches spick span spick span how long to pass this one memorise its meaning shape how long to pass this one memorise its meaning shape how long to pass or its internal shape the banal is grotesque
these trees automated in their neat dressing
roots ploughing through eternal metal and asphalt cracking
three old figures cryptic
robing me robbing me
the lights of other daze
grotesque is trees with their winter crewcut
into each second the eternal nanoccurrences of isness and these trees is there just one tree I keep perceiving as I permeate more of the metzian webtime or all particles of myself springing from me on random time trajectories

all the words I have said or spoken were minced of my blood my semen my moan-barrow of weeping tissue in dis-inegation

what is I in truth is in their locality not here

trees ruin me too particular

and the specified woman

anonymous

all anonymous that felty well in the lanquid dark against thighs of unknown speech and every faculty distended to some farther shore like aface with nothing personal in it just the big chemical loot-in of eternal burn-down
in the nerved networks and elastic roadways of me is the traffic passing for thought but this eternal recurrence of trees signals me that no decision is possible that decision is impossible for everything will come again back to the same centre
alternatives must be more multi-valued than that I either go with Kommandant on his hosanno dominotion or speed with Angel south but if one crossed martyranny if the other

another series of eitherors with death always the first choice
somewhere find a new word new animal
transgress
in their heads they have only old words
insisting that history repeats itself
the stale hydrogenes of a previous combustion rolling in
an old river and elder landscape footprinted to the last tree
gnarled landscape of I stamped flat by the limbous brain
its their behaviour and its geared experience is lessening
and cuts me down to sighs morality nostalgia sentiment
closure falsight all I have to drive through their old faded
photograph of life
how that crumbling nightdream thunderclouds round my
orizons
He looked up hand on the trunk of the last tree before the
square opened heavy swaddled and spring held jacknifed in the
winds.
Growing in the Rhine perspective was fumirealdrapery sly
and dry figurative –
the confruction? the momentum of truth?
It grew and in the daggered sublight clearly personed the
familiar was the merely familiar Crass the once-agent ex-
drapist pusher scampfollower lost or fled when Brussels
blurned showing his teeth now in a smile of grating.
'The eternal returns' said Charteris. Up and down the
bare bole spring's first flies crawled across the corse of winter.
Over the supplicatory amputree they hastened towards infinite
points of intersexion and in the top cropped branches thudded
his great blackmacked bird leashing its vulturine feathers
claws beaks calling through its raw red wurst of neck.
'Master forgive me you must have thought my feet were
in the eternal flying dust and the impaled rose from my sump-
turanean stool.'
'I don't want to talk of decay.'
The fustian feathers held a small vibration. 'Who knows
what will talk or decay when all people your paradise of multi-
valour. I have kept under my wigspan and my grations led me
here to you. Your servant still.'
'I don't want to talk Cass so come down from that Judas
tree the looming decision of all direction and to make something new devise from under that old moustache while the
wescivilians of lost possibilities drawn into deeper dusk where
the parallel bars have no in or out.'

So Cass took his arm and said, 'I know of your systemstrain You're hung up on a curve. Earlier when the mists were shipping to the tugladen mouth I saw and signalled you across the flux but you had other directions. I am too poorly without potension to flutter up into your tree of notice but you are as rich as a new Christ in populous and you must not park here by the rivenstribe but autocass on to domination and the world your word.'

'Cass off! Back into the bare branches!'

'No I tell you winging the way to my master your humble serpent boarded with an old widowed impoverished official who in his long-rowed rooms above the Alzette ravines lodges two coachdrivers and a filling station owner he tells me how the continent fills into small strifes for lack of leadership – '

'Cass – '

'Speak at the world's megaphone Master. These small strifes are your larger bartlefield or the states your pulpit. Pay the big taxi fare to a Rome address! Talk out the lungs cancer. Rocket right up the lordly astralbahn. Flush the worlds motions into your own bowl and I'll back you.'

The door of the big square refrigerator burst open as Angeline came in upon her metatarsals her chicken bones and plum eyes and the whole different meaning of sunlit succour sumpt.

'Hello Cass I thought we'd lost you doing the suttee act in sparky Brussels.'

Lips bone-infested – 'You still campfollowing you widowed mite!'

'Colin the fat commander is letting the boys unlocked in a sort of panjandramonica and what are we going to do?'

Flighting off the carrion cross he took her and half-kissed her murmuring nonnegotiably relishing the bold bare bones in her like branches.

'Oh Angeline I see you're among the favoured yet I wish you'd tell the master to unpack his oysterand smash the saviour-part into a real cruscade.'

'That's all nonsense. We're trying to turn into human beings first Cass and don't need your snow-job for aid.'

Beady he preened among his black scales. 'Body's so wo-manish and nothing beyond. You want him all to yourself don't you you selfish bitch but times change and he's got nothing to lose it's not like I mean the Germany's not the Holy Land in any sense – '

But blank. World of total silence. Box off. A last mind-bowing dislocation. He had his fix with the elemental and the deep dischian roots under the etern..l subsurface where they sleepwalked and the elegant connections between love and death. He saw through. Dropped. Turned human.

To them he grew bearded beaded and feathered. Primal. Behind them the old grey square and fineformed town hall of an earlier clockage rich in history sauce now served in bright plumage as it flowered to his wisdom.

'Listen the multi-valued answer. All resolved. I had it in my dream turning down the old clothes.' Then mute in his wonderment so she asked him darling?

'Whatever you all think you think you all think in the old stale repeating masadistrick Judeo-Christian rhythm because its in your bloodshed. Your heritage taken or rejected dormant. Be rich as Christ indeed. But Croesus Christ is to me pauperised an old figment and just another capitalist lackey whose had our heads isn't it? It's the histiric recess over and over a western eternal recurrence of hope and word and blood and sword and Croesus vitimises your thinkstreams.' Continued in this blastheme of Christ Plutocrat schekelgrabbing bled-white christendamn till Cass fluttered.

'I don't believe in him either Master you know that.'

'No difference. History jellied and you can't drip out. You're hooked in his circuit and the current circulates.' Bigger than the first tiny Metz web so it grew in his mind another layer yet of Europlexion and walking along Troitsky Street he saw the old dimensions all shagged out and Christ on the clockwork cross with in his sly brown eyes that frantic glimpse of progress on the astralplane and from our deathbeds that vanvogtian upward surge into heaven's arms. The cult of the third day the White House open to any mother-loving son. All transdacted in the following lanes to metaphysical materials of the insurance steam shovelling society and the space race.

Heaven is money in the bank. Your cash helps our cathedral. Jesus saves his flesh negotiable anywhere.

'Colin love the world doesn't just begin anew my baby will have to have the past to build on and rebuild.'

'Breathing the old west dust and breathing out the old west dust. No. That old ethic-ethnic LSD has automated us two thousand years and now the fracture there's been a mislocation so let's jump it from the steamcross and say for ever farewell to that crazy nailedup propheteer. Look girl I don't

207

refuse to go your way or refuse to go Laundrei's way or refuse to go Cass's way or refuse to go any way. I refuse to hit the worn-out Creased or anti-creased way. For me new tracks and stuff the old ding-dong the belfrey-belt.'

Cass laughing poorly, 'No no if there's an opportunity you get in first that's nature!'

She was shaking her head running her toe in the dust as if tracing out a hieroglimpse of some secret there.

'You're mad Colin Honey it not just Christ and all that it's a bit different for you cos you're a Serb there are mountains in between but the West thing we're still on a Greek trajectory of ordering knowledge Phil told me that.'

'The Greek thing was okay but it would have got nowhere without the sufferinfusion of our nazerining friend embodying the rags to riches poorman's son outalk outsmart white-house-in-the-sky trouble-stirring miracle-working superman and then pow-wow-kersplat-but-oh-boy-on-the-third-day punchline echoed ever since by every comicstirup.'

'Master Master you can't change all that.' Trembling out a little reefer and suckling on a long light in viperbeak. 'Only through leading. You can't change history. We're what we are.'

'We're also what we're not. See Cass I can't change the churn of history but it changed itself when the sprinkler-bombs came now we live in a wornout mode and the old Glenn Miller musicrap still canting us out of a new canticle in the old worn wesciv groove.'

'Maybe you're right. Lead us only away Master we'll follow in blind belief!'

'Leading is out makes blindness and the old swingdom of heaven is just slopporific. Opium of the pupil.'

She saw him new on a fought decision. She saw him. She saw he saw himself. He saw himself new. Still lying but deeper lies? Mirror distortions embedded? Every moment its equivocation like a tile pattern she saw him new. In the omniparacusis she heard him defrock Christ. A womb-shelled thing broke and bled. She stood outside herself her scars her incompletion. Her first vision of the current time explosure.

From Cass's ears smoke poured and the tiny chambers even the metatarsals in a big big scald like the church of England burning up its bullion of belief and he craftily slipping out of the transvestory vanishing into the haze as if exorcised.

She had been conjured. Limply by one arm taking him she moved up to a nearby passing mountain and there cried solemn anger that he ploughed up every midnight corpse that ever fell to make them die again for his psychosis. Charteris laughed knowing she had never seen inside a church. She swore. The oaths in banners marched the mountainside. She owned her aggression at last. She had born him long enough his womanising his slobishness his selfhood and the godding. Now he must cut his act to play a human off-stage role.

He pushed her. 'Your act comes from the same cass pageant the cult of individuals but it's a mass life and death get it? Phases not people! Drop out that's all, Angelbird. Dig that everything else has already dropped. Play to a new music right and dance to another measure down your long within. Cass off and shack with Ruby or take me on my own road but I cant stand halfway up this mutterhorn.'

Scratching her head covering up sad for all losses she alone locatered for. 'Its Cass Colin Cass I'm afraid of you're so helpless he just a paracide to any order he might do for you you know he emanates the old iscarrot role. If the present's already past like you say Cass'll have you nailed.'

People were coming he heard and was glad to distract her.

He gestured to the band as they materilaised into the plass. 'I've the job for Cass.'

Jailgates gaped wide and the tumblebellies on the bangle-drums were all in advance with brashing autos percussed cymballically all heads on the anonymass.

So now he warmed on the ticking of another prayer wheel turning in his stream and all the faces blowing to him were with their petals and the bloom of youthair cheeking them. So now was he not crusoed a footfall further in this islanded desertion and some would carry onto his farshore. So now though his carriage had never taken him beyond the stony trees he sent his mark scudding across the printless beaches. So now he grew her elbowing arm as the force pressed at the instress of his radiance.

Hurryburlying Laundrei came on the surge with the auto-ciples but Charteris stopped them. Climbed onto a bench under a sign that told the miles to Frankfurt old cosy sign made metal from the long attic store in thought. Waved his arms caught cheers. People scuddling like leaves under his farsight the whole seas surge of them.

Told them: I was in another vision. I broke free and discarded myself my former selves my sleep chained I.

Here through me the world tumbled to a new terminator.

Here we begin a new age the postpsychotomimetic age free from anshirt shittoleths and the grey grimmages stripped off.

Here the old programming of Godspain got its long last playback in the searoots of our occulture.

Here the nails scattered from my hands and fingers.

In the square they milled and sledded letting their origins down with mood music thrombic. The body hair buttressed and limbs rebuddied. Metamorphin slipper waker-slip. What they heard they herded and sluice-juices ran underfoot. As he luted their animinds. Ages went down into oceanic undertow. Civilians poured in and the old grey and biscuit buildings titaniced down into a glacial cobblesea. Inunvation of hands, plattening feet of limbic brand. Churning flowermotion with eddying scruffles sob-streperous among the onebacked beats.

To one side apart Ruby with an own thing to peddle. Also Elsbeth sailing all in selfmassage grown apart her two stout legs foliaging flesh belonging to the fused moment under the strain of canvas her salience gybes to generationing point her wild delicacy a sapiutan as she fixes on him rattling from his orificial platform.

Now from his purgent words the mucous remembranes of the sinking swimmers distend to farcy forms and the saprophagous outpour transfluxes the time's ergot so that while it floats into her labyrinthine passages she feels the smooth buddoming trunks and timber shafts wheel and wheedle into grander growth in her skeleton the sapling stalked stuff supplanting bone nodes of branch staring under skin at hip and pelvis shin breast and elbow her obnubil features suddenly the whole unatomy its soft syruped holes its husks hairs and horned teeth beats

into greenamelled leaf!

Laundrei always more antiflowered broke his spate asked 'What's the vision on when we move to conquer?'

'The broken off gods chumble over into obscrudity – '

'Okay, very satisfactory to know 'but there's still the Berlin question.'

His old sly smile. 'Now its your blastoff down the astrabahn to the straits of power while the wind blows favourable on your high traject. All go who will and nobody constrained in any form. I stay here. Our photographs peel separate here.'

'No' – ship without figurehind and he launched into the long machineries of a vocal gripe while others also had their temperature and again mazed denizens pander to the labyrinths until finally Charteris barks again.

'It was my vision Laundrei you astracade it while it just sustains me while you image yourself into your machine-dream-role.'

'*Scheisskopf!* You haven't the face to back your prognosis!' Hirst fluttering and swatching behind with birdlife gestures of ascent.

'You take with you my second-in-commandant the Cass here as my man in your camp.'

'Wechsel is my aide-de-camp.' Peaching his plumage.

'Cass makes liaison. Cass your new commander keeps him in a mind of miracles the claws pruned and darkness at the ninth hour.'

Dark brown pantry eyes glistering up the mottled cliff of medalled white seeking lodgement. 'Meinherr glad to be of service and tote the – '

'Action man and the junkered footfill all autobreasted with all joints in my pistongrip right? Right. It's a decision then. Herr Charteris we go to escalade in the name of glory and unity. We shall meet again. Men! Men! Follow men! Action! Scramble! Form paltroons! Clap to ventricles! Astrabahn and utopia!' Cass and Wechsel astraddlediddle as the revvrevv-revving struts and pattern merges from the millrace.

'Hydrogen 12 be with you' pronounced.

Saluters.

Now espousing their autos the deutschlanded gentry marry boot to rod hand to bar knee to rod bum to seat helter to skelter in a barrackroar of infective warcalls. The autocaders also spark their plugged enzymes and batter backwards into the crass planes curling bumpers and blue monoxide wolves through the pack like feral till everyone legs or wheels like tight little humans under hair astride. But Army Burton comes to Charteris 'Hey you want your little master race girl any longer?'

'The name?'

'Your little master race girl Elsbeth?'

'She Jewish

They used to call that the master race.

No that was the Germans.

I forgot. Another world. You want her.

You want her you take her you going on with Laundrei?

Also Ruby Dymond in human shape to Angeline grasping

her hand in oldworld form moving her behind a treebole.

'Is this straight Charteris is hiving off on his own do I read the thing right?'

'Ruby he's straightening out past the world. Who knows this chemifect may all wear off in a few days and old time start up again so I stick with him and see he doesn't get himself killed in the general curfuffle.'

His furtive shrugs of pain the hurt deep under a moist pelt. 'But he tried to kill you honey – look leave him he's got nothing for you the disintegration man himself and you with me so cosy.'

'Sometimes he's kind to me maybe all I deserve.' Now from the long brackets of her inherited eyes spark the first tear.

'You all screwed up, Angey, honest I hate to see you be done down and come off with us!'

His secret words fended her. Drawing up, wiping off her wet nose on a handback, she says in bitter tone, 'Don't mix me up Ruby if he needs me I can't help it!'

'So you said about Phil and now this same mistake all over! Honey I beg I got to go the others are rolling now come on and this last time break your unlucky cycle!'

Stilly with a crumpled face, 'Ruby – Ruby – he needs me!'

'I need you, he tried to kill you!'

'Well he's desperate!'

Of a sullen the wild ox sprouted under his eyebushes, 'Oh fuck you you silly stubble bitch!' and with that he was bending his giant back among the common melée with all commotion. All were multi-backed to fusilage along dead reckoning; Army only faced the demasted master.

Looking around at the hoofers and the revvobiles with the groups starting up the Famineers and Deutchofiles and a quick brainscan. We got to orient with the action dont let grass go under our teeth eh its a lawn of asia.

Briefly they made palmhistry. High road. Low road. Scotland afore ye. Never meet again. There we all parted. Franfurt sign. Poxeaten poxibilities. Army farewell.

So the acceleration of mechanical joybox and the old foot-down thirst of essolution. Jerk of cerebral juices destiny carvorting down the long within and the crazy internal kilometrage a brown near black instressed masteracing. On the bumpers nestled the new animal plural in solidity and near life as the pinballing progress meshed from the plass. Lopped tree lopped tree lopped tree loppedtree lopptree stood ruinously neat the clibbered rectungstone cobbles the red rodentures of the town hall biting sky the buildings semisubmerged on their shoals and all else on a low primevil light as wheels bore tribe dust smoke noise away dying sullen. In the lime embedded lost lingerers sank to the fossil mouth under drab oolite.

The natives of the tableau mooched across the tattlefield or on fours dragged off the injured. Small dogs were there tearing at fingers and jugulars as life slumped back to textbook level. Two figures stood anonymously round the Frankfurt sign. Buildings burned with the cool air-burling flames of time.

Beneath this conbastion in shelfence sank the bronto-structures the rathaus and gaunt grandosaurs down under the cobblesea without windowed strata still chronsuming them-selves and on the tide big stone forests bursting green and all verdure trumpling brack out the Rhine to what was in uttered mindchaos downwards.

The saint with Angelina executing the bipedal homosap walk on the way to the banshee all yellowspeckle as of toads bellyupwoods squeeping to right themselves and chunks falling off the western wold where the alternatives feralled. The car lumbering and she mutely asking where drained from her own sacrifice.

'Where?'

'He'll swing to destruct with self-inflected Cass and all.'

'I asked you where you think we going.'

'And all the music-muckers with them to the endless ends they clave all dreaming they aren't dreaming in Kundalini-coils,' under the sediment of long custom embedded. Looking ahead at the rockwalls, tyres tweeting on curbstones.

'You don't care a bit what happens to them Col do you!'

'A new continuum has to alp itself from the screenery and potentiality is low from old corpses so mulch the old trodisues out of the worldbody.'

Her young face shrunk back to its ultimate socket. 'You hate everything!'

'Schweitz doesn't line my inscape baby we'll push east . . . Anyhow Anj I love everything that really has a shape.'

The rocking days closed over them, nights and afternoons with random weather, her womb rounding against the cracked april dayflight, the whole gestation-infestation opera yelling out on the revolutionary stage with mumps of pelting birds peeling larvae popping buds paregoric eggs in the drain downwards to emptying order-tors bared to the basalt. Until all his cogitations produced only To live with people Anj be with people love them hate their userpenting sleep, in a monosigh.

So you still breathe jesuspirations!

Get disenstrangled of this loot-in with Christ eh for gods ache its not for me that or you or anyone else ever agame that deathorglory boy with his nailed-up mystery and mixing pain with promise has all foiled up virtue against crudelty and permanan revel oution of our clockwatch west so now we break the square old charmed cycle. Be not do Anj be not do.

Amid the sprockets of his coinage he trod again the uncertain footage of his film seeing how it all fell in eternal re-currents and eddies of beening and borning with the ever-etrancing of steps slideways in tombtime to the opening price of verture where the goahead geton-or-getout of caputulist christ was turd to ambivled materialschism and every grass and brute caught for an exploit.

So as the Pleonastocene Age curtled to a closure the banshee crumbled under the chundering glearbox to grow up into deeply scarlet peony by the sacred roadslide where they finely went on foot with Anjie meandering through the twilicker her golden grey goose beside her it in its beak holding gently to her smallest twigged finger with Charteris choked in his throat's silence.

Beneath them turned a greenfused planet where foliage unscrewed itself from the earthworld and they afflected by its field down to the last gaussroot of being. The wayfarers on their way youngbuds straplings or grey elders were of that earth-world impacted and she by this soothed Angey lifted from her lost garden and said to saint in a recurrent phrase

All the known noon world loses its old staples and everything drops apart. You should show us how to keep a grip until the bomfact wears thin and fight the growing forest.

When there was no forest were mock-ups of forest. When no PCAs organised religions as mock-ups of the personal paradise. Learn it angel not too hardly that the ferrocities of white officegoers had to crackup and tuck your city inside the only building is. Even in old concretions there pattered those our starcasters who went barefoot to the real experience hold their faith.

Expurience of drugged disorient.

Disorient we want and the nonwestered sun of soma.

In the dark under piping bushes the talk was all bodies they became interchanged statement to threnody stamen to peony ransacked of all loved lute.

He had grown out of too many lifetimes but this span bridged all there was valued. For her too no longer the grey-lagging little girl but that also. Some easement in the general break.

To the evereast they talked and walked among the littling humlets with stopped steeples while to meet them avrilanched from there even from Serbia itself curled hunters forest away but a day now retidings in its roots small black ringletting pigs and its boles whisperfaced littlemen and its trunks the glowing eyes and razorbones of subsisterly glowing eyes and razorbones and its branches the quick lead thing still scunnered with eyes and bones enterbal and in the leaves scabrerattle of birdsong and in the earth beneath a whole sparce tempscape ciscumstantialing the grotted world.

She broke with elmed summer into twain and he glazed through the furry wires of his conch to see his baby girl with Anjys lip of beads touch still between them the poor wages of pain words how everstretched never pinioned truth flying feathers of lovenests sprawling at heroic dusks sumptuary in feeling midfeeling deepernal but the white always winning as light flapped and varicosed in rustickled veins it cried at night barehead in all garrots where he spoke or harped silence as the concrete towers regressed.

The girl needled her small tranjecstory by his side or sprang after the rumpattering piglets in golden time so Anjy offered again seamly thewd thighs in splicing gesture. In him inarticulate patterns fuzzed and fazed stridulant through leafmoulded enterospection daytripping beyond his old throught records fobsilled deep only sometimes distirred by menacimages someone always drowning in beanstained waters beyond shingles behind a line of noctous epijean figures where shilluettes the sherd.

Living barefate in sheughs or hams where travellers now could share salaami and bread in humbled rooms they lodged craking ramshack many citizens lined to speak many he felt he could reckonise their plane shapes crossing and recrossing between him and the recessed light all asked him What you make of christs tearching or even Are you anti-Christ

So he Friends think fuzzed in diseither-organised for mid-paths neither for nor anti what he said its Those whore not for me are agrainst me just a bit more punchy phallacy in westrun style there's a newtrality to cultivate to be more receptive look for shades patterns where this goodevil stuff cant rise he startled too many hares for Man the Drover

The shins of the flesh mere alimbic fantasy

Don't be for or against anyone only the waking thing that lies in sleep

Hold firm to dreamament

Its the pattern of percertivity

Awakes the greater sleep

Don't think we're too well made or permanent

You are more merged each than you believe

Better sensuous than sensible

All you must have within is outside among verdance Christ and the westering thing supposited the inside out

Never imagined where all the roads would lead

Here

The eternal position

You have to have been there first

Many theres

For the here no multernatives

His thought chewed deeper and deeper into the ruralities as the herding greentides lipped them

Other thought impacted two thousand years

Driver man became pedestrian. Be not do

At times he trod in every belief beneath a broken art sign or died again the thousand psychic deaths of croesus christs last autobile age

Barked the shins of the flesh under dogroses till senescence

Saw and herded many nakedassed children to become holy men and whoremongers and homebodies

Talked less wondered more thought of crafty old G only a span along the net leaning on an old rope bed picking his toes as christs millerimage hitler came and went

Never knew anger allowed himself to be laughed at by strangers

She knew they who knew did not laugh who laughed did not know

Yawned as the plumpricked autumn grilled her hearsole

Tried not to teach but learn from his disciples

Peeled off the long long sepiage of photographs

216

Watched aeroplanes in another sky
News from the statedepartmented north not reaching
Scratched himself
Taught the disciples to sit and weigh dust
All alternatives and possibilities exist through old mottled gums under a spreading square tree where some tiles still lodged but ultimately of course
Ultimately they asked listening
Poignantly shall I tell them
No way of telling anyone only through silence
Ultimately of course
They let the vast blackdrop curtain their waiting

In the hours of morning he said I will answer your ultimate question thinking that glowing eyes and razorbones burned unattended
So under the sparky starcover he let her old arms lull him but the brain still burned towards its wisdom he crept away from her guzzling sleep amid the multibrood climbed out through the stiffly hole in their thatched roof lay flat there under pulverised galaxies
Put his arm over the curved spine of roof rough and warm breathing
Gigantic beast patient
My ultimate wisdom my nonsense
Suddenly wildly flightening the hateful faces of his discarded selves when a man dreams instead of acting falling by the wayside the slow bonfire of unaccustomed words had he had a bad dream the archetypal figures or was he still lying arrowed on a hyperborean shore.
Feeling himself half-slipping from the roof he roused ultimately of course
Keeping an fuzzed open mind
That wasnt enough the forests are back
Brains just an early model half unwaked shaped for the forests
You want it both ways
Did I have it both ways
Made and destroyed lived and tomorrow maybe
Both means two more than two many ways many many ways my chief word to the world Ive been thought as well as body spirit and prick soul and stomach both

Slipping back into old astotelian ways of thought slipping off this damned roof cold

Was aristoddle also christ the proudwalker too old too damned old to think clearly back to neanderthal times

Climbed slowly down off the roof woke one of his grandaughters who went with care to blow on the embers and brew him a mug of redcurrant tea the warmth back to basics

Pinhole camera my sight of shapes all fluffed

Either too old or too young to think but who knows old angeline where was it I met her I loved her loved her in my way loved her being in many women

Thought about waking her till dawn came then she stirred bent nearly double came patted his gnarled hand and said something he had forgotten his bit I had a little speech for you

Heard too many of your speeches in my time you have to make your ultimate speech today do you know what you are going to say do you ever know

Perceived that this old place is really a great beast cantering us over the nightplane

Give me your animist patter again waking us all up in the small hours

Once they were everlasting hours

Do you know what youre going to say theyll all be under the meetree expectoring you

Meant to tell you something personal angel something about a flower or a cactus or something

Tyrannical really he still had not come to the end of words

What year was it where were they she forgot finally he went out shuffling must be ninety who knows if its still this century even

I wonder if he was jealous of christ

A doityourself christkit no nails needed

They were under the tree had his old bed there where they flies flicked about in the peeving shade he smiled his crafty old G smile and sat on the bed scratched his toes maybe he really would tell them

They waited in droves

No knowing the calendar

On this special day saint you were to speak about the ultimate Yes

Well you patterny people with hands Byzantine born to genureflect below the low hair weigh dust well let it drip an hour or two we may not have beaten time but it no longer drives us desperate before it nothing like a catastrophe to lengthen lifespan pledge my last liquors to humbug the humbuggers and the ones who never made it

If they knew the flip old thoughts I blaspheme against my own holiness

Green and tawny under the tree the patterns they mean

We learnt to sit under trees again stop looking for better trees concentrate yourself under an inferior tree

One of his grandsons sneaking away he had news of an organised state north somewhere what was his name that man dead now a white sort of gown or uniform Boreas no matter

Concentrated on his big toes the long within

We learnt to sit under trees again the longer without

In the old days

Now the empty bowl

But I can remember sitting in a car and driving all through the night

Remember the old autostrada del sole the red lights paired tinily capable ceaseless countless swarming pintabling under the hills and over the bridges viaducts mighty mountains headlines slicing nature in two not a thing ever like it never no greater thrill we were all little christs then own death or salvation right there in your steering hands.

Autocrashes full of orgone-content like copulation bayonet-practicide war nothing personal in it only all things inferfused and the exhaust-throat snarling

The sparks died into the earth finally

My capital crime nostalgia

Fault of early brain model flickering

During the long silence a small boy trotted round with fruit to eat and a disciple deferentially handed the saint an apple cut by his pocket knife the saint mumbled a segment

When they were all silent he sat up toes in the dirt

They waited

He waited

Their dull conformist minds he would have to give them holy law okay but spiced with heresy let them grit it right up their nostrils

Ultimately he said

At least they would always hold him immobile in their eyes not exactly the posture he had once aimed for but only fair he had tried genuinely tried

To hold them all in his eyes

It must embody what he had always thought must enshrine him at the same time contain the seeds of his liberation in another generation must be as old as the hills as old as the hills must gleam like headlights were holy law and heresy he started again and they listened

All possibilities and alternatives exist but ultimately

Ultimately you want it both ways

Later much later when his old bed had been devoured they propped up the branches with long poles and stuck a sign on the tree and later still they had to build a railing round the tree and later still tourists came metalboxed driving down from the north to stare and forget whatever was on their minds

Cryogenetic wings
   bourning another spring
     croaking forth on
the tundragged wrathland
   scything it allover
     and the bloodcurrencies down
stunted figures anneal in the blasts
   inner postures unrelented
     to known corporeal gestures
stubble growing on man mire cloud
   all linked by nanoseconds
     loud with the permafogs
of marching equinox
   the paradox of kernels blackly
     sprouting sour green wicks

in the small northern hour
   reptile hearts crawl slackly
     lymphatic tensions twist
necks of old lithite parrots
   chuckling through engrammatic
     viscions
           the braincage
under the screw of dreamneed
   rejects lost alltermatives
     anagrits of maters stream
in cyclic slumberth crawling
   for a far stossal round
     orrey edswill rold
be yon tigal rave

Recurrence 250-1
Reflexes 113 114
Reincarnation 31 40
Relativity applied to art 73
  applied to being
  applied to knowledge
  applied to language
  applied to man
  applied to religions
  applied to worlds
  laws of
  principle of
  of substances to planes of universe
Religion 229-304
  liturgy
  and man
  origin of Christian Church
  prayer
  a relative concept
  'schools of repetition'
Repetition exercise of 260
Rites 303 314
Roles limited repertoire of 239-40

SINGING JAIL BLUES

Something's familiar about singing in a jail
It's one of those situations you
Hit racial memories of
Singing in a jail
When freedom is compulsory sitting on a hill
You'll sometimes find you're wishing you
Could smell the can again
Singing in a jail
You sing your heart out
Or let a fart out
Everything's a cock-up
The only time you're
Free from crime you're
Sitting in the lock-up
Don't want remission or justice or bail
Down at the bottom it's just like
The top when you're
Singing in a jail

ANGELINE DISCONSOLATE

Somewhere along the unwinding road of chance
My feline lover slunk into another bed
Somewhere along the unbending read of hand
He palmed himself off on another breach
With life-lines double-crossed in semi-trance
He took maiden voyage to another beach
And I am left disconsolate

Somewhere an unsubtle effleurage of cat
In the uncertain jungledom of If
Seduced him Auto-breasted fur-lined she
Somehow all anti-flowered stole him
For his massage means more than meaning
More than buts poor purr-loined lover he
And I am left disconsolate

Where was the will involved in this affray
Somewhere along the all-winding road of chance
Where the decisions unlocked from careful chests
Somewhere   And if the minor keys of guilt
Are played no more then how is happiness
More than an organ-peeling dance
And I am left disconsolate

Always in the bad old world guilt-lines
Somewhere would trip us along the road of chance
But unlined now we spring-healed harm
Ourselves response without respons-
Ibility   The fountain only plays
A tinkering simple that effects no balm
And I am left disconsolate

LIVING: BEING: HAVING
An epic in Haiku

I

On the Rhine's chill banks
  Somebody in a raincoat
    Nobody walking

    Or a river bird
      Trying hard to memorise
        The brown nearest black

This is a tidy
  Nation even its madnesses
    Go uniformed

    We place our faith in
      Bigger and better messiahs
        Or Hydrogen 12

      Richer than God his
        Son. No wonder we nailed on
          The Cross Croesus Christ

I spat in the ditch
  It's time we got the taste of
    Nails out of our mouths

II

Every day smoulders
In the ashes of burnt-out
Possibilities

Not thinking of death
And well-combed I came across
A blank sheet of paper

The leaden birds hope
That time's pulses flow past them
And we conversely

In their plush armchair
Of blood our lusts sit waiting
For dawn or lights-out

Irrelevance
In the darkness toothache while
Digging the happenings

Bad experiences
And the deaths of old countries
Make a raree-show

III
Let's get personal
  Or is the thigh on my thigh
    Just its own meaning

    Together we dreamed
      Freedom was compulsory
        And both woke screaming

One raised fingertip
  Her red lips moving smiling
    Cells multiplying

    Stroking your slim breasts
      And slender flutes flattering
        A jumped-up penis

Tired dreams of action
  Flowers in an empty bowl
    A wooden rain falls

World and mind two or
  One? Funny how the simplest
    Question blows your mind!

HIS PROWED COURSE

Galaxy-crushing light alight on the pane
Flatters into velvet
Stands stockstill while the early motes dance
And gloom nestles deeper down a flight
Of steps. Beyond the flowering window
The scene of all disaster is awash
Would you believe a crucifixion?
The icebaus eddy on a washed-out sound
Music of the luted galaxies
All the cold vigils of the nightshift
Have robed me for my dilemma
Beyond the flowering windowpains
That input-output lends my daynight flights

THE DATA-REDUCED LOAF

Put it this way   The multidimensional stimuli
Suggest that the body lying on the eurobed
Is in some way 'mine'   The body that in some way's
'Hers' enters bearing a wooden famine bowl
Empty of all but sunlight which she sets

I go too fast   Five lines are not
By any means n photographs   The bowl
Her skirt the lines the changing light
The retina that's self-abused with sight
Shuffles the negatives into
The million-year-old data-reducer
Behind   It's a time exposure really
The changing light her legs the legs the lines
Caught in my ancient processor
Why should I trust it?
Supposing I am a chimera?

Put it this way   Perhaps a multitude
Of interconnecting cells were so arranged
About a wooden bowl
In self-interest of course
That some progression could be made
Dimensionally   The bowl the table
Its legs her legs my legs the light
Swarming between her and the deep-set panes
                              All without meaning
Until the heartbreaking isinglass
Of time seeps in to give to stimuli
Relationship and passage
                              And permanence
Did some of the fluid jelly-up
The data-reducer? Light
That holds universes spellbound
With its speed Instant light
Inexorable star-extinguishing light
Towering dark-proof light

Kindly light velvet on my knuckles
Beyond anachronism spaceshipping
Light light recordbreaking speedier
Than computer-thought
                          Light do you fall
And grovel and crawl with million year sloth
Up the sludgy both-canal between retina
And data-reducer?
Does the old optic nerve
Slow you to child's pace?
                          Should these archaic forms
Of calf and floor and leg and bowl assume
Uptodate angles and distortions

Should a new geometry inter
Their degrees inside my skull   Should
In my presbyopia
There have been a new circuitry
To sort out time's passages and sight's

Should I still be a victim of
Old neolithic close-work that
Excludes me now from possibilities?

Put it this way   Suppose that what I take
For 'me' is lying on this mattress
When what I take for 'her' arrives
Bowl in hand appears to arrive
Achieves in time and dimension
A presence verifiable
In my old time-machining eye
The greatest novelist
Of our space/time wrote his novel
Five million words about an unnamed girl
Arising one morning from her bed
Going across the room to open
Her casement window   Of course he had

The tactical sense to leave it all unfinished
But he oversimplified
Has anyone ever opened
Or finished opening

The multidimensional stimuli
But time is a multitude and to
'My' mattress what we chose to think
Is 'her'
The repetitive event of sex
        Comes in eternal recurrence

Only the old data-reducers cut
The exposures down reducing all
To unity   Put it this way
That 'she' is multitudinously among
The motes and lines and famine bowls and beds
Which punctuate that single node of time
For me and say that single node
Replicates
Endlessly to the last progressions
Of a universal web

If there were roses or daylight in the bowl
If there was someone in the middle-distance
If the faint sounds that came to 'me'
If I was there prepared to love
If we see anything but photographs
Torn from a neolithic eye
Put it this way
Time is a multitude
And 'she' far more than one

TOPHET

('Tophet: an ancient place of human sacrifice near Jerusalem;
later a place of refuse disposal.' Dict.)

> I was prepared to sacrifice
> Myself – or all else but myself.
> Too harsh. I almost sacrificed
> Myself. I would have done. One has
> To be much surer time allows
> Such liberty of gesture or
> That the gesture is not just
> In essence someone else's. I
> Saved myself to do some further good
> I say some further good. The tide of faith
> Dawdled. What did I do unto myself?
> Acidhead mind and flesh corrode. Too harsh.
> I am the refuse tip of all I was.

Boot of Revelations

Letting their origins down
      with mooed music
The cattle milled and sledded
      in the clapped out square
Boddihair buttressed
      limbs rebuddied
Metamorphic sleep-awake-asleep
      perception flickers

As he disintegrates
      himself
          into their programmed
Brainclumps with unbuckled words
Bending the ticked time-factory
Each circadian partment stuffed
      with old writs

As words begin disimigrate
      upripe postures fold
          into a sea of herdivores
under the diss o' loot ness
      words began

What they heard they herded
    churned through mass orifices
      fossils mouth-vented

EIGHTY

Under the scoured thatch
Locked beams bar our disorder
Once maybe I had religion
   Suffering had a future

Now I need only a shawl
I'm a crab's claw
A broken wing blunted instrument
   Won't work or play

His veins are dried string
Not even knotted
His thoughts keep kicking
   Every day further to the well

This place will never be home
Problems keep their old address
Now I'm just an old householder
   And the house holds me.

TWENTY

The days burn like a hairdryer   Rattle
Out loud as Friday's money
Suddenly see problems like opening twots
   Needing my thrust

Events make tyres strike concrete
Slicing me forward every direction
Negotiable   Nights are jackpots
   Giving back and front

Style does it all style
The city's open to the nomad
Everywhere's home and clear eyes
   Never questioned

Friends wink like traffic lights
I can do more than yesterday
Motorcameleon-like
   I'm change itself

DEATH OF A PHILOSOPHER

Oh, no, he went well at last – more his old self,
And yet as if *sure* at last. . . . Perhaps the Way smoothes
For the Gooduns. . . . Cryptic as ever his last words were –
Surprised – 'So
          Soon
          Sooth
          Soothes. . . .'

CHARTERIS

He was a self-imagined man
Old when still young
But there's always
Time and everywhere
Recurrently eternally
A hive of selves

He left in the air
Skeleton structures
Of thought
And thoughtlessness

To some of us
They are unfinished
Palaces to some
Slums of nothingness

An ambiguity
Haunted him haunts
All men clarity
Has animal traits

The bombs were only
In his head
On his memorial tree
A joker wrote
KEEP VIOLENCE IN THE MIND
WHERE IT BELONGS

THE SHAPE OF THINGS TO COME by H. G. WELLS

THE SHAPE OF THINGS TO COME
by H. G. Wells is one of the great classics of science fiction. First published in 1933 it was described by Wells as 'A Short History of the Future', and spans the period from A.D. 1929 to the end of the year 2105. It is the chronicle of world events, a memorable catalogue of prediction involving war, technical revolution and the cultural changes which await mankind in the years to come . . .

0 552 09532 X – 75p   T208

THE SHAPE OF FURTHER THINGS
by BRIAN ALDISS

THE SHAPE OF FURTHER THINGS
by Brian Aldiss is a profoundly original and thought-provoking book by one of the leading writers of science fiction. It is a critical appraisal of the way science fiction has evolved and the part it plays in society today. But more than that, it is an intelligent and highly credible glimpse into a future in which science fiction will rapidly become science fact . . .

0 552 09533 8 – 35p   T209

EARTH ABIDES by GEORGE R. STEWART – *a Corgi S.F. Collector's Library Selection*

The Corgi S.F. Collector's Library is a series that brings, in uniform edition, many of the Greats of S.F. – standard classics, contemporary prizewinners, and controversial fiction, fantasy, and fact . . .

EARTH ABIDES is one of the few S.F. novels to break the barriers of S.F. readership and reach a huge and universal audience. Winner of the International Fantasy Award and First Choice of the Science Fiction Book Club, it tells of the death of civilisation and of the brave new race that emerges – stronger, self-reliant, primitive . . . It is the story of Isherwood Williams and a small handful like him, who rise from the ashes of a destroyed world and begin again . . .

0 552 09414 5 – 35p   T56

NEW WRITINGS IN SF. 21 Edited by John Carnell

NEW WRITINGS IN SF brings to lovers of science fiction strange, exciting stories – stories written especially for the series by international authors. This edition features stories by Keith Roberts, Douglas R. Mason, James White, Sydney J. Bounds, Colin Kapp, H. A. Hargreaves and Michael G. Coney, and is the last edition to be edited by the late John Carnell.

0 552 09313 0 – 35p   T85

DRAGONFLIGHT by ANNE McCAFFREY – *a Corgi S.F. Collector's Library Selection*

The Corgi S.F. Collector's Library is a series that brings in uniform edition, many of the Greats of S.F. - standard classics, contemporary prizewinners, and controversial fiction, fantasy and fact . . .

DRAGONFLIGHT is Anne McCaffrey's novel which won both the Hugo and Nebula Awards. Set in a medieval world of the future, it tells of Holds, and Castles, and Keeps, and of a great flight of dragons, led by a golden queen and ridden by men sworn to the defence of their fantastic and incredible planet . . .

0 552 09236 3 – 35p   T82

FANTASTIC VOYAGE by ISAAC ASIMOV – *a Corgi S.F. Collector's Library Selection*

The Corgi S.F. Collector's Library is a series that brings, in uniform edition, many of the Greats of S.F. - standard classics, contemporary prizewinners, and controversial fiction, fantasy and fact . . .

FANTASTIC VOYAGE is the novel based on the 20th Century-Fox Motion Picture of a journey into a new dimension. Four men and one woman, reduced to microscopic size, are injected into the carotid artery of a dying man. Their mission - to fight their way into the cranium and destroy a blood clot. At stake - a man's life on which depends the fate of the entire world . . .

0 552 09237 1 – 35p   T83

A SELECTED LIST OF SCIENCE FICTION
FOR YOUR READING PLEASURE

☐ 09184 7	SATAN'S WORLD	Paul Anderson	35p
☐ 09080 8	STAR TREK 1	James Blish	25p
☐ 09081 6	STAR TREK 2	James Blish	25p
☐ 09082 4	STAR TREK 3	James Blish	25p
☐ 09445 5	STAR TREK 4	James Blish	30p
☐ 09446 3	STAR TREK 5	James Blish	30p
☐ 09447 1	STAR TREK 6	James Blish	30p
☐ 09229 0	STAR TREK 7	James Blish	30p
☐ 09476 5	STAR TREK 9	James Blish	30p
☐ 08276 7	DANDELION WINE	Ray Bradbury	30p
☐ 08275 9	MACHINERIES OF JOY	Ray Bradbury	30p
☐ 08274 0	THE SILVER LOCUSTS	Ray Bradbury	30p
☐ 08273 2	SOMETHING WICKED THIS WAY COMES	Ray Bradbury	30p
☐ 65372 1	TIMELESS STORIES FOR TODAY AND TOMORROW	Ray Bradbury	30p
☐ 67297 1	THE WONDERFUL ICE CREAM SUIT AND OTHER PLAYS	Ray Bradbury	40p
☐ 08879 X	NEW WRITINGS IN S.F. – 20	ed. John Carnell	25p
☐ 09313 0	NEW WRITINGS IN S.F. – 21	ed. John Carnell	35p
☐ 09492 7	NEW WRITINGS IN S.F. – 22	ed. Kenneth Bulmer	35p

CORGI S.F. COLLECTOR'S LIBRARY

☐ 09237 1	FANTASTIC VOYAGE	Isaac Asimov	35p
☐ 09333 5	THE GOLDEN APPLES OF THE SUN	Ray Bradbury	35p
☐ 09413 7	REPORT ON PLANET THREE	Arthur C. Clarke	35p
☐ 09473 0	THE CITY AND THE STARS	Arthur C. Clarke	35p
☐ 09236 3	DRAGONFLIGHT	Anne McCaffrey	35p
☐ 09474 9	A CANTICLE FOR LEIBOWITZ	Walter M. Miller Jr.	35p
☐ 09414 5	EARTH ABIDES	George R. Stewart	35p
☐ 09239 8	MORE THAN HUMAN	Theodore Sturgeon	35p
☐ 09532 X	THE SHAPE OF THINGS TO COME	H. G. Wells	75p

All these books are available at your bookshop or newsagent; or can be ordered direct from the publisher. Just tick the titles you want and fill in the form below.

CORGI BOOKS, Cash Sales Department, P.O. Box 11, Falmouth, Cornwall.

Please send cheque or postal order, no currency, and allow 10p per book to cover the cost of postage and packing (plus 5p each for additional copies).

NAME (Block letters) ....

ADDRESS ....

(NOV. 74) ....

While every effort is made to keep prices low, it is sometimes necessary to increase prices at short notice. Corgi Books reserve the right to show new retail prices on covers which may differ from those previously advertised in the text or elsewhere.